VOICE ON THE WIND

VOICE ON THE WIND

THE OUTCAST ROYAL™ SERIES BOOK 02

AARON D. SCHNEIDER

MICHAEL ANDERLE

THE VOICE ON THE WIND TEAM

Thanks to our Beta Team:

Kelly O'Donnell, John Ashmore, Rachel Beckford

Thanks to our JIT Team:

Zacc Pelter
Dorothy Lloyd
Diane L. Smith
Dave Hicks
Jackey Hankard-Brodie
Jeff Goode
Paul Westman

If we've missed anyone, please let us know!

Editor
SkyHunter Editing Team

We are dirt, we are alone
You know we're far from sober!
We are fake, we are afraid
You know it's far from over
~ *"Ugly," The Exies*

And on the pedestal, these words appear:
My name is Ozymandias, King of Kings;
Look on my Works…
~ *"Ozymandias," Percy Bysshe Shelley*

Masks
She had blue skin,
And so did he.
He kept it hid
And so did she.
They searched for blue
Their whole life through,
Then passed right by—
And never knew.
~ *Everything on It, Shel Silverstein*

This book is dedicated to my second daughter and quite possibly the sharpest wit I know. You came into this world demanding to be heard, to be seen, and to be known and praise God, I've been part of all three from the very beginning. Lightning and sass in a pint-sized bottle doesn't begin to touch it, but I don't know anyone who's quicker to care about things that matter or to speak up for what's right. Poppa Bear was thinking of you in this one and hopes you find it worthy of a creature so fearfully and wonderfully made.

Although it was only mid-autumn, winter seized Lorlu's Girdle with frosty fingers and left many to look grimly toward lean and hungry times, none more so than those who dwelt beneath the boughs of the Wooden Cord.

Lorlu's Girdle—or simply the Girdle to anyone familiar with the area—was a sparse region filled with those folk hardy enough to dwell without king or prince and their subsequent protection. The lands were no stranger to violence and predators, both man and beast.

All this applied doubly to the strangling woods called the Wooden Cord that stretched like a constricting snake across the Girdle. Those who journeyed across this stretch of land that separated the rest of the East from the Norling Steppes were largely obliged to fend for themselves. Only walled hamlets and fortified trading posts offered anything remotely resembling succor or aid, and these were few and far between with dismally limited resources.

An odd pair of travelers astride a single dappled gray mare approached one of these fortified trading posts.

They cantered up the path and noted the half-dozen horses

corralled in a pen too small for so many beasts before they drew up alongside the structure of thick timber and roughly hewn stone. The first to dismount was a towering woman in armor, whose action the mare greeted with a grateful chuff. She held the horse's reins in one hand and used the other to assist the second passenger from the saddle, a young dwarf just growing into his dark beard.

"Let's be quick," she said, her voice slightly muffled behind the mail skirt that hung around the edges of her helm.

"I hope they have what we need." Her companion grunted as he took the reins from her. "I don't think anyone got any sleep last night on account of his screams."

She nodded and busied herself in careful scrutiny of their surroundings while the Wain Dwarf used one of the beast charms of his people to give instructions to the mare.

The forest had been cut away from the trading post enough that those who launched arrows or other projectiles from the windows or balconies would have fifty to seventy-five yards of open ground in which to fire at their foe. Beyond this killzone, the woods of the Girdle held many open avenues, not nearly so narrow and tight as one might find in the pined regions of the Reach, much less the green hell of the Scadian jungles. There was little reason for anyone in the trading post to be taken by surprise if they set a watch, but a quick study of the structure seemed to suggest that no watch had been set. Not even an inquisitive eye glanced at them from any of the shuttered windows.

If it hadn't been for the horses and the thin curl of smoke rising from the stone chimney, she might have thought it abandoned.

"Come on," she said to the dwarf as she moved to ascend the plank steps to the heavy timber door. "Let's do this."

He scuttled to catch up and reached the last step as her fist thumped on the door. After the sound of rough voices and some jostling, a slat fitted into the door slid open. Bloodshot eyes glowered from the darkness within and met the armored women's gaze.

"What do you want?"

The visitor's eyes, like copper taken fresh from the forge, flashed within the orbits of her helm.

"Is this still a trading post?" she asked and her tone made it clear she was losing interest.

Hushed voices neither she nor the dwarf could make out spoke quickly, but they did catch glimpses of faces appearing behind the shudders. The owner of the eyes at the door was about to say something when a stronger, clearer voice forestalled her.

"You'd best open the door, me thinkz."

The warrior woman drew back at the words spoken in a thick northern accent.

"Brekah?" she asked in a low tone, almost to herself.

"Who's Brekah?" The dwarf at her side looked both curious and concerned.

"How does she know you?" the one at the door asked and turned his head so those without had a clear view of one ragged ear. If she were to guess, the man had been indentured in Narlish and had torn the servants' bar out a few years earlier.

As surreptitiously as she could, she slid her hand to the head of the ax at her belt.

"Open the door before she kicks it in," Brekah instructed sharply. "It would be better open as friends than broken as enemies, me thinkz."

There were quite a few profane and crude mumbles in response to the instruction but despite these, the door swung open and the familiar voice called out in welcome.

"Welcome, Ax-Wed, my old friend. It has been some time since we are seeing each other, me thinkz."

The dwarf peered into the smoky dimness of the trading post and then at the woman beside him.

"You didn't mention anything about friends in the Girdle," he said softly.

"Because I don't have any," she answered quietly before she strode inside.

The front room of the trading post was fairly typical with a wide space filled with tables where supplies and tools had been laid out. In the center of this display area stood Brekah with five hard-eyed men at his back. Beyond the front room was a seating area at the hearth with a ladder up to the loft, as well as a walled-off corner to create a smaller room whose door stood slightly ajar.

"You are looking for something particular, me thinkz," the gaunt-faced mercenary said with one of his skeletal grins. "How can we be helping?"

She let her gaze rove the room and noted a few askance tables and numerous dark stains on both the floor and furniture before she met Brekah's eye.

"Since when were you a trader?" she asked, one hand still on the ax at her belt.

He laughed warmly and when the others joined in behind him, they sounded like hyenas giggling over a carcass.

"Not trader as such but working with merchants," he explained with a sweep of his hand. "Guards watching post while merchant away getting more supplies. But we can still be helping you, me thinkz."

The mercenary detached himself from the leering group behind him and moved forward to place both his hands on a table where sacks of feed were laid out.

"What you needing?"

The young dwarf's emerald-eyed gaze darted from Ax-Wed to Brekah. He sensed the tension growing in the smoky air like the first tremors of a storm, cleared his throat roughly, and drew the mercenary's eye toward him.

"I need a few things for a sick friend," he said and ignored the leering stares of the men behind the man. "Garlic—preferably fresh—mashafic honey, and cloves. Do you have these?"

Brekah scratched his stubbled chin and gestured to one of the men behind him.

"Srecko, take the young master to the back room," he instructed. "There are some stores there he could use, me thinkz."

Srecko, the youngest of the group with barely more than a dusting of whiskers on his pimpled chin, opened his mouth to protest but at a sharp look from the mercenary, he shuffled toward the room in the corner of the structure.

The dwarf looked at his companion, who nodded while she kept Brekah and the rest of his men in her field of vision.

"Quickly, Durra," she said under her breath.

The young dwarf nodded and hurried to follow. He didn't bother to hide the fact that he gave the company a wide berth.

Both younglings stepped into the back room and left the former comrades to stand opposite each other, their gazes locked and expressions flat.

"How long have you been holed up here?" Ax-Wed asked, her gaze unflinching.

"The winter," Brekah replied, his voice much colder.

She nodded and broke the stare for a quick survey of the goods spread on the tables.

"I'm surprised you left this much intact," she said. "Or are these what you took from those who've come since the thaw?"

He shook his head while the men behind him exchanged nervous glances that rapidly degenerated to snarling glares.

"We were hired by post-keeper to guard all three of his posts for the winter," he insisted and ignored the growing irritation of those behind him. "We did so and even lost two men while fighting off Bone-men and brigands. That is earning our keep, me thinkz."

She looked at the stains on the floor.

"But when payday came," she said evenly, "he refused to pay what he promised."

Brekah shook his head and his mouth twisted in disapproval.

"Says he gives silver wage for each man but not the dead." He sighed heavily. "Some not taking this so well, me thinkz."

Ax-Wed studied the men behind her old comrade in arms and wondered which of them had lost his temper and killed the post-keeper. As her gaze swept over them, all met her scrutiny with defiance and bared badly-kept teeth. The last mercenary she looked at—the one with the torn ear who must have manned the door—had curled his mouth into an ugly smirk and settled one hand on the dirk handle at his belt.

"What are we waiting for, Brekah?" the doorman demanded and slid his blade free slowly. "If she knows all this, there's only one thing left to do."

Brekah gave Ax-Wed a knowing look before he turned to the men behind him.

"You are, of course, meaning let them have what they need and letting them go?" he asked innocently. "Would be wrong to even charge them, me thinkz."

The response from the four men was a chorus of growled curses.

"I knew you were soft," the challenger snapped and tugged a hatchet from his belt as he pointed with his dirk. "You didn't have the stomach to kill that worm of a miser and now you don't have the stomach to kill a nosey woman and her pet runt."

Her old comrade squared his shoulders and moved one hand to the sword at his belt.

"If you were knowing this, you would have tried to kill me much sooner, me thinkz," the tall northerner replied before he took one measured step back. "But if Dejan Backstabber is so brave, let him fight Ax-Wed."

Dejan's compatriots voiced their support for this idea, either with encouragement for the man or slurs against the warrior woman. She now had her namesake in hand and seemed to be waiting, her face inscrutable behind her helm and aventail. The mercenary slid his gaze insolently from head to toe over the towering, armored figure and his lips peeled into a hungry smile.

"I'm gonna break you and then I'm gonna take you," he threatened deep in his throat as he began to stalk forward around the table between them. "And before I'm done, you'll be beggin—"

The movement was so swift and so simple that he never saw it coming. Ax-Wed lunged one foot forward while she thrust to meet him with the horn of her ax-blade. The hard point slid home and burst his left eye. With a scream, the mercenary turned brigand staggered back and dropped both hatchet and dirk to paw at his marred socket.

"Dirty whore!"

"Cheater!"

"Snake!"

The condemnation flew so fast that she barely had time to laugh at the childishness of the angry declarations before Brekah's voice cut through the whining cries.

"You boys best help him, me thinkz."

Like hounds loosed from their kennel, the other three sprang toward her as they yanked weapons from their belts. The boldest of the three vaulted onto a table and swung a repurposed sickle in a downward arc for an impaling swing, while his compatriots veered to either side to encircle her.

Ax-Wed leaned back to let the strike pass an inch from the front of her helm before she swept the man's legs out from under him with an ax stroke. The wretch's shins parted with a wet snap before the grinning edge of Thulian sylver and he tumbled back with a wail.

The warrior woman whirled to face the brigand on her left, blocked a heavy chop of his maul with the haft of her ax, and drove him back a step. The stout man set his feet and tried to shove in return, but rather than match him muscle for muscle, she slid to the right past the table and swiveled to deliver a powerful elbow to his jaw.

She tried to come about with a quick stroke across the back of his neck, but the other attacker was coming in fast and low. A sharp pivot brought her ax into a low warding stance and the Thulian caught the flail swing before it could shatter her knee. The force of the blow trembled up her arm and she gave ground before another looped swing toward her hip and a third toward her head.

In the back of her mind, she knew she would run into a table or the wall eventually but the determined assault and the crowded confines of the room left her few options. Another wild swipe made her shuffle back again. The man with the maul was recovering and wiped the blood from his jaw that now hung at an odd angle. She was about to be assailed on multiple sides and that was a distinct change in her odds she couldn't allow.

An opportunity presented itself when she ducked another blow and her attacker leaned his weight over his toes. With no room for a proper swing, she thrust the ax past the forward foot and immediately yanked back. The unbalanced flail-wielder toppled with a surprised shout and before he could even position one hand to push himself up, the grinning ax parted his face from crown to teeth.

It took only a sharp tug for the weapon to come free with a moist pop and Ax-Wed turned a blazing glare upon the man with the maul. The sight of both the ruin of his compatriot's shuddering corpse and the towering woman with her bloodied ax in hand was too much. With a snarled oath he threw his top-heavy weapon clumsily at her and darted to the door.

His hand was on the latch when Brekah sprang forward and

stabbed his red sword with sufficient force that a tongue of metal burst from the man's chest. His legs buckled as he clawed at the length of steel jutting from his breast but his adversary put one foot on his back and freed his blade as he shoved the dying man hard enough to crack his head upon the stout door.

Ax-Wed swept the room for further threats but it seemed Brekah's sword had won its battle-sweat in dispatching Dejan and the man on the table before he'd focused on the runner.

"I need better friends, me thinkz." He sighed as the two of them stood for a moment to survey the human wreckage. "You keep killing them."

Not quite ready to lower her guard, the warrior woman nodded to the corpse on the table and Dejan's still form as she held her ax in a low guard.

"Those two don't go on my tally," she replied flatly.

He looked at the two bodies and shrugged.

"I am finishing up," the tall mercenary said as he stepped closer to Dejan to clean his blade on the man's ragged cloak. "Both were better off this way, me thinkz."

Ax-Wed couldn't help smiling behind her metal veil.

"Agreed." She sighed and her muscles had barely begun to relax before a young dwarf voice drew her attention to the door.

"Uh...excuse me," Durra said as he shuffled forward and winced. A jagged falchion was pressed to his neck hard enough to draw blood.

Srecko, the youth holding the rough blade, looked around the room in bewilderment.

"What's going on?" he cried and his voice cracked. "What happened?"

Ax-Wed took a step forward, a lioness's snarl in her throat.

"Let him go," she commanded. "Or you die like the rest."

His eyes widened at the force of her words but something hard and dangerous glinted in his eyes as he crouched behind

Durra. The jagged edge of the cleaver-like blade dug a little deeper and the dwarf hissed in pain.

"Throw that ax down or I carve the runt's head off," the youth threatened venomously.

She responded with a low growl and took another step but to her surprise, her advance was checked by Brekah. His sword was held down and off to one side but his feet were set and his gaunt face was grim.

"All are needing to calm down, me thinkz," he said in a low, firm tone. "Srecko is letting go of dwarf and we is all leaving here as friends."

"Friends!" the cleaver-wielding youth shrieked loudly enough to make his poor hostage wince from something other than the blade at his throat. "They killed our crew—our family!"

"One moment, please," the mercenary said and raised a hand placatingly at Ax-Wed, who obliged with a stiff nod but focused her gaze on Durra.

"Srecko," the mercenary said gently and gestured with a hand across the bloodied display floor. "These were not your family. They were not even your friends, me thinkz."

His eyes wide with hurt and confusion, the boy looked around frantically before his expression hardened into a suspicious glare.

"You are only saying that because you turned traitor," he retorted accusingly. "You want me to let the dwarf go so you can kill me and take all the shares for yourself."

Brekah shook his head slowly and locked his pale gaze with the young mercenary.

"No, me is telling you to let go of the dwarf because we are friends," he said slowly as he took a step forward. "Which is something you are needing right now, me thinkz."

Srecko bared his teeth as his eyes made another futile, frenzied search around the room for support.

"You are not my friend!" he shrieked and lifted the falchion to jab it accusingly toward the older man. "You're a liar and a traitor and a—"

With the blade now moved from his neck, Durra seized the gesticulating arm by the wrist and with an extraordinary heave, threw his erstwhile adversary over his shoulder and onto the floor. The youth landed with a heavy grunt combined with a cry of pain when Durra tore the falchion out of his hand with a sharp twist.

"Don't hurt him," Brekah shouted as the boy fumbled at his belt for a knife.

The dwarf kicked down and the young man's head bounced off the floor. Srecko's whole body seemed to lose coordination and his head lolled drunkenly from side to side. Ax-Wed and Brekah rushed forward but Durra shuffled clear of the stunned human at his feet, the falchion already flung behind him.

The mercenary sank onto one knee and cradled the lad's head in one large hand.

"Easy…easy now," he murmured in a soothing voice.

Ax-Wed's shadow fell across the two of them but she held her ax in one hand while she wiped the blood from its edge with a torn scrap of cloth with the other. For a second, she considered the boy's features and noted the way his youth-softened face already had the sharp cheekbones that made the rest of his face seem sunken.

"Yours," she stated before she stepped to Durra, who'd retrieved a scarf from his satchel.

"Not such a bad boy, me thinkz." Brekah grunted and wiped a little blood trickling from the boy's nose. "Only needs some teaching."

She bowed her head without comment and checked Durra's neck. Satisfied that it was only a surface cut, she looked knowingly at the backroom. The dwarf nodded and patted his satchel. When she gestured at the door with her chin, he headed out to see to the mare.

The boy made a lurching attempt to rise, his eyes still unfocused, but Brekah's hand kept him firmly upon the floor.

"Does he know?" she asked as she moved to a table and inspected sacks of oats and barley for feed.

The mercenary shook his head as Srecko stopped trying to force himself into a seated position and shook his head drunkenly.

"Where's everyone, boss?" the lad asked with a wince as he raised a hand to his head.

"Shhhh, quiet now." Brekah calmed him softly before he turned to look at her as she threw a bag of feed over her shoulder. "A favor for an old friend, maybe? Be easier to explain if you aren't here, me thinkz."

Ax-Wed shrugged and headed to the door, mildly curious as to how her old comrade, the exceptional liar that he was, would weave this tale of their latest misadventure.

"We're for Carnyxia, then Aruhkahm before we make for the Caged Sea," she said and paused in the doorway. "What will the story be by the time we reach Bykairlious?"

He gave her a wink and smiled at his son.

"By the time you reach the Marsh Jewel, your name will be legend, me thinkz."

Again, she smiled behind her metal veil and stepped through the door.

CHAPTER ONE

The caravan of Vahrem Kal'Stru had barely cleared the Girdle and been upon the Norling Steppes for a day when they saw Carnyxia's bonfire-capped perimeter tower glinting in the cold night. It wasn't until the next dusk when the sail-like banners could be seen by the naked eye in the dying daylight.

The caravan leader and Ax-Wed sat astride two horses outside the circled perimeter of the nesting caravan and watched the wind-swollen expanses flex and ripple in the late afternoon sun.

"How do they make them?" she asked, a hint of marvel in her voice.

"Stitched beast hides," he answered in a hushed tone and allowed himself to be swept into the momentary intimacy of shared wonder. "It was once said they were made from the tanned skins of land leviathans, but it has been a long time since any of their kind walked the earth."

She smirked slightly at that and Vahrem had to stifle a sigh as the moment shattered. The question of why she smirked burned at the back of his throat even though he knew why. It was always the same answer—old memories. And like it was always the same answer, it seemed it was always the case that this strange woman's memories emerged in those moments when he felt they were beginning to share something.

Sometimes, the recollections were sad or painful and caused her to look away with something that could be a tear in her simmering copper eyes. At other times, they were like this moment—a kind of grim, not quite mocking inside joke she seemed to tell herself. It was maddening how much he could see played out in her expressions and yet how little he understood.

Still, he didn't dare say anything for fear the helm and aventail of mail would return and she would become as brooding and remote as the bloodthirsty idols of his childhood.

Vahrem forced a smile and appreciated the fact that she'd started taking her helm off when they spoke. He didn't dare to flatter himself that familiarity had begun building into something more during the last month or so of travel, but he still liked to see her face.

"The road-wise sell-sword who has never traveled to Carnyxia?" He chuckled with a wink when she spared him a glance. "I would have thought the feuds of the *Vitzerka* clans would have been a regular source of coin for you."

"I heard the savages paid in livestock and slaves." She shrugged. "Having no interest in either, it never seemed worth the trek."

"You weren't entirely misinformed." He nodded. "They usually keep their precious metals and coins for a very particular use."

Now it was Ax-Wed's turn to raise her eyebrow at him and he responded with an enigmatic smile.

As the sun sank lower, a chill wind stirred from somewhere in the far north and swept its biting path across the Steppes.

The merchant folded his arms across his broad chest and she didn't seem to notice except for a slight narrowing of her eyes. After a moment, she raised an arm and pointed to the city. Her blue-streaked hair snapped behind her and drew his gaze. She seemed like something out of a myth, one of the heroic statues of storied Bykairlious come to life.

"There are markings on the banners," she said and her brow furrowed as she squinted toward the horizon. "A coat of arms or totems?'

"Of a sort." He followed her gaze. "Each one is a declaration of the deeds of the great Vitzerka clan to whom the banner belongs. It is a matter of honor that when autumn comes and they gather for the Thunder-Crush that they have added some sigils and marks to their banner in honor of the great deeds their chieftain performed during the raiding season."

Ax-Wed had nodded with the explanation until two particular words caught her attention and she turned from her horizon-gazing to look at him.

"Thunder-Crush?" A small smile tugged at the corner of her mouth not touched by scars.

Vahrem's smile widened and his white teeth flashed in his dark beard.

"Oh, I won't spoil it," he teased. "We may have missed the first few days but it only means that by tomorrow, the grandest contests will have begun."

She seemed about to press him but saw something in the twinkle of his eye that dissuaded her and she settled for a slow shake of her head.

"I suppose tomorrow isn't too far away." She sighed and sniffed the air as the wind had died down. "It smells like dinner is cooking. We'd best get back."

The caravan master—who had more than simply a healthy appetite—struggled to hide his disappointment at having to settle for something as mundane as food.

"I do suppose dinner would be nice," he said and failed to hide a tone of resignation before he brightened with an idea. "You'll do me the honor of sharing a fire with us tonight, yes?"

He saw the internal struggle behind the woman's flashing eyes and cursed himself internally. Was he being too obvious, too forward, and too insistent? Not enough of any of those? What was he hoping for? How was he to know?

"I'm sorry but Zoria…" Ax-Wed said and her voice trailed off.

"Is more than welcome to come as well," he declared and regretted the outburst even more as something hard flashed behind the woman's eyes. "I'm sorry I interrupted. Please forgive me, but you were saying…."

His gaze found the front of his saddle and settled there, waiting for her rebuke yet fearing the continuation of her silence

"Thank you, but she's enjoyed spending time with some of the other children," Ax-Wed replied, her expression a blank mask. "One of the Teitel girls offered to comb and braid her hair this evening, I believe, and since I can barely keep the food out of the feral creature's hair, I won't let that opportunity pass."

"I'm willing to bet that is Sybil, the second eldest," the caravan master said as they both began to wheel their mounts. "She's feisty and as smart as a whip but still a sweet girl, although she can be as sharp-tongued as her mother when she wants to be."

The merchant looked up from his saddle to see his companion smiling but this time, he didn't have to sit and wonder as to its cause.

"That's good," the Thulian commented as they returned to camp. "Sybil will need to hold her own with that girl. Zoria is not for the faint of heart."

As they rode back, Vahrem nodded but decided it was wise to say nothing more.

He would never have expressed his thoughts on the matter out loud, but Ax-Wed's assessment was a gross understatement. In the last month of traveling together, the troubled girl had managed to break or at least attempt to break every rule, spoken or unspoken, in the caravan, and many of them were repeat offenses in tandem. She stole, she fought, she lied, she sought affection and attention in some of the lewdest ways possible, and seemed generally incapable of maintaining any semblance of respectful, decent, or even functional behavior.

Despite this, when not in the grasp of whatever dark mood took her at a moment's notice, Zoria could be a sweet, clever, and thoughtful youth on the cusp of womanhood. At a turn, she could go from being little better than a feral dog, ready to snap at anything within reach, to the most gentle and respectful of creatures, all cream, honey, and tender words. Sometimes, this kind of behavior could last for days but in the end, something—perhaps some mental malady born of her wicked upbringing—would cause the dam to burst and Ax-Wed was left scrambling.

It had weighed heavy on Vahrem's mind when the problem first arose but now, he felt a quiet sense of pride and thankfulness in his heart on behalf of his people.

More than once, he had expected the outcry in the caravan to rise to the point that he would have to address the issue but it seemed that once the child's woeful tale was known, every mother had decided they were a watchful aunt for the girl. The warrior woman never made an issue with the others seeing to discipline in her absence and as such, there was never a time when Zoria was unwatched or, for that matter, unloved. Unfortunately, this didn't seem to dissuade her unsavory behavior but it put both Vahrem and Ax-Wed's minds at ease to know the girl could never do too much damage under such thoughtful care.

"Give my regards to Iyshan, Numi, and Durra," his companion said as she turned her horse to the Teitel's wagon.

"And pass my warm regards to the Teitels and good sister Zoria," he called after her and tried to tell himself he didn't feel a pain kick in his chest with the parting thrum of her horse's hooves.

CHAPTER TWO

"Svarah stirs the heavens," the old woman declared, her voice croaking and hoarse.

Dragahn Shieldshiver, Wind-Spoken of Perukh, stirred from contemplating the fire at the sound of the crone's declaration. With a grunt and a thrust of his chin, he directed one of his retainers to tend to the ancient creature. A brawny man with a bristling mustache rose, shuffled closer to her with a waterskin, and held it to her wrinkled lips. Another with an elaborately woven topknot offered honey-glazed berries to be gummed moments later.

The warlord rose slowly to his feet and held one massive hand out. Another retainer—this one with filed teeth and eyes stained completely black—stepped forward clutching a huge sword whose graven hide scabbard bore the trophy bones of fifteen chieftains upon thongs of tanned manhide. The tokens clicked against each other softly as the hilt was extended to him. He settled the blade before him and the scabbard point pressed into the fur that carpeted the interior of the lavvu. The wind outside beat upon the elkhide walls of the tent as though the gods were impatient for the wise woman's answer.

Despite his impatience, he waited and his deep gray eyes glinted beneath his scar-laced brows.

The last of the berries were finally consumed and another greedy swallow of water slurped before the old woman looked at the waiting warlord. A toothless smile spread across her sunbaked and wind-worn face as she stretched her limbs and scratched herself.

He knew the woman was stalling, which only suggested good for him, but his face refused to show that he knew this fact. The men around him, battle-hardened and blood-sworn, were not so gracious and begun to mutter under their breath and ease their hands surreptitiously to their weapons. The crone met each of their gazes in turn and despite their scarred muscles and well-honed weapons, not one of them held her stare for more than a few heartbeats.

All except Dragahn, upon whose mauled face even the wise woman could not look without a spine-chilled shiver.

"The Winds awaken and it is said the shades scattered by it whisper of the Dragon-Slayer riding out." The old woman wheezed as though the words were heavy on her sagging chest. "She will speak to one from a foreign land fleeing a god-haunted prince. But when Svarah is revealed, as ever, two scaled queens shall fall at her champion's feet."

His tattooed lips twitched into a slow smile.

"Where will I find Svarah Vjetgo?" he asked in a voice that sounded as though two mountains tried to grind each other to dust.

Her gaze seemed to slide into the space between spaces as she recalled the dreams that had gripped her during the last two days. For a moment, her gaze searched around her and lost focus and her mouth worked as though something far harder than berries lay between her jaws. Finally, with a shiver, her eyes refocused on the world before her and she looked at the warlord.

"The south," she said hollowly as though the answer had

drained her even further. "She will come upon one coming out from the lands below the Girdle."

"Sandlurkers!" scoffed the retainer with the topknot and the pejorative for southerners blurted from his lips before he could stop himself. "How could the gods choose one of them?"

Despite the interruption, Dragahn's gaze never left the woman who squatted before him but one hand swung and the man dropped as though poleaxed. The retainers conspicuously refused to look down, while the old woman regarded the crumpled warrior with a kind of dread fascination.

"Please," the warlord said with the barest of nods. "Continue."

The hag's eyes shone as her tongue worked across her brown lips but in the next moment, her breath caught in her throat. Her features twisted in pain but she mastered the sensation before she spoke again.

"The champion will come from the south but this will not be their home." The wise woman grunted. "The meeting of these Wind-Spoken will be nothing like what has been seen in these lands before or ever will be again."

Her words spoken, the wise woman lapsed into silence and turned her gaze to the fire. It was running low and although she knew it would soon do her no good, she tossed some kindling onto it to awaken new flames.

Although her skin shined with the oily sweat of exertion, her flesh shivered.

"Is that all?" Dragahn asked, his tone unchanged from the beginning of the conversation.

"That is enough," the old woman replied as she reached for another handful of bundled hay. She stopped suddenly and uttered a cry as she clapped both hands to her stomach. "My time grows short."

He nodded and lifted the sword in his hands before him, turned its blade perpendicular to his body, and waited for the black-eyed fiend to draw the betokened scabbard off with reverent slowness. The blade was as savage and magnificent as one would imagine and its gleaming edge flashed in the firelight with naked hunger.

"Thank you," the warlord said with a slight bow as the wise woman uttered another cry and rocked. "You have set me upon my destiny."

"There are worse things," she croaked and smiled weakly in the split second before the sword swept through her neck to part shriveled flesh and age-weakened bone with ease.

The corpse slumped forward and blood pumped out to hiss on the flame-warmed stones that ringed the fire, while the grinning head landed on the furs with a soft thud. A thick, coppery smell filled the tent, but the warlord barely noticed it as he stretched through the smoke and retrieved the head by its stringy hair. After a cursory examination, he handed it to the retainer with the bushy mustache.

"See to it that she is honored in cedar oils and pitch," he instructed as he handed the weapon to his sword-bearer to wipe clean and sheath in its scabbard. "She will join the honored upon Kollung."

"What of Belug?" the brawny man asked and nodded to the man still flat on the tent floor.

"Try to rouse him but be quick about it," he said before he turned to depart the lavvu. "If he doesn't rise before we ride out, take his beast so it may be butchered when we make camp."

The burly man nodded and cradled the head in his hands like a fragile treasure as the warlord swept from the tent in two strides. The black-eyed retainer hurried to keep up with his master's steps and his perforated lips drew back from his mutilated teeth in a hideous grin.

Outside the tent, the night winds swept across the Steppes with a harrowing fury and drove stinging flurries into the men's faces. The cold expanse of the area stretched around them, except for a series of dark shapes that rose from the horizon like small hills.

"So we are headed south, then?" the sword-bearer asked and almost had to shout over the howling gale.

"No," the warlord said in his tectonic voice. "The Wind-Spoken of Svarah and I shall meet when it is our time. Until then, we head east to Hoarlin."

The man's steps faltered as he stared at his war leader.

"The Frozen City?"

Dragahn nodded as he trudged toward one of the dark shapes that resolved itself into a huge, shaggy beast who turned dull eyes to regard the humans. Its iron-banded tusks scraped the hard ground as it bowed its knees at the coming of its master. Nearby, worrying at the sparse grass with their trunks, were two similar beasts, markedly smaller than the warlord's mount but each one capable of flattening a small house through their muscular bulk alone.

He grasped a length of chain that dangled from the kneeling beast's harness and with a heaving leap, pulled himself onto the saddle that rested on the creature's humped shoulders. The sword-bearer shouldered his burden as he clambered aboard as well. With practiced alacrity, he took his place on a small platform of gut-lashed bones where quivers of javelins rattled together in the wind.

"Up, Kollung," Dragahn ordered and with a huff like bellows, the beast rose and its height afforded a better view of the plain where hundreds of small dark masses sat patiently in the wind.

"Sound the call, Tadzi," he instructed as he hauled on the chain in his hands to turn Kollung's heavy head westward.

Tadzi the sword-bearer tugged a spiraled horn from his belt, drew a breath that stretched his scar-crossed chest, and blew a long, skirling note.

As one, the lumps across the plains shifted and hundreds of hulking brutes stirred to life. Their tread was erratic at first with a rumble like the earth grumbling under their weight but soon, the instincts of the beasts and their owners' brutal tutelage won through and their feet rose and fell like rhythmic thunder.

The army of Dragahn Shieldshiver was on the move and it seemed the whole world trembled at their passing.

CHAPTER THREE

Carnyxia could not have been more different than Jehadim.

The latter city, although tall and proud, was bound in its quarters behind its towering walls. In the former, however, in place of looming stone walls and gates of bronze-girded timber, the immense banners stretched over lines of sharpened logs that ran from the heart of the city like rays from the sun.

A sprawl of various tents, stalls, and timber-framed structures spread in, around, and between the lanes created by the free-standing wooden walls. Beasts Ax-Wed had never seen nor had words to describe moved amongst throngs of people who seemed only like ants in the distance. She could not imagine how such fortifications could be defensible and as they approached, she said as much to her riding companion.

"Those palisades seem more like channels for traffic than actual protection," she said to Iyshan as they trotted along the caravan line on Vahrem's fine dappled mares. "That can't provide much protection for the city."

"Because they are channels and Carnyxia isn't like most cities," the manservant said in his raw, gravel-throated voice.

"Carnyxia is like an overgrown trading post and serves as a gathering place for the tribes during certain times of the year."

The warrior woman frowned as she spurred her horse to gallop toward the head of the caravan, thankful that although she was a mediocre rider at best, Vahrem's exceptionally well-trained animal was quick and responsive.

"So what happens when an enemy force comes to seize it?" she asked, knowing that her companion would spur his mount to match her speed.

"Well, if they come during the times when only one of the lesser tribes is lingering about, nothing much," he explained and moved alongside her with such smooth ease that she felt a little embarrassed to be beside him. "The beast-riders will simply mount their pet monsters and ride away. If an enemy comes during a time like Thunder-Crush…"

He pointed to the wide plain west of Carnyxia. What looked like dozens or perhaps even hundreds of wiry-haired hillocks shuffled across the expanse, tended here and there by a scattering of men and women who scurried like mice about their feet.

She drew back on the reins and brought her horse to a sharp stop, which the mare protested with an irritated whinny. Iyshan wheeled to a much gentler stop and eased his mount beside hers.

"What are those?" Ax-Wed asked, unperturbed by how her amazement stole into her voice. "They look as big as houses."

"Mammoths," he stated and a smile pulled his drooping mustache upward. "A favorite of the Vitzerka, as far as the heathen go, but hardly the strangest thing they keep."

She wasn't sure she could manage anything stranger.

I thought the world had no more surprises and now, I find men keeping hairy hills.

"If you think that's impressive, wait until you get to see the Thunder-Crush." He chucked and guided his horse to their original trajectory. "There isn't anything quite like it."

The warrior woman felt a twinge of irritation that yet again, she was told about the wonders of this "Thunder-Crush" but no explanation was given. Last night with the Teitels, even the children had been strangely tightlipped about it and stated that it was impactful but offered no explanation. When Zoria had asked her friend Sybil what exactly it was the answer was the same—"I don't want to spoil it. Wait until tomorrow."

She fought the urge to let suspicion establish a foothold, especially given how much Vahrem and his people had sacrificed for her.

"Well," she muttered as she squinted toward the front of the caravan. "At least we're almost there."

The caravan settled on the outer perimeter comprised of a band of camps and temporary structures at the end of the timber walls that radiated from the heart of Carnyxia. There had been a slight delay when Ax-Wed and Iyshan had rode ahead and found three Scadishite merchants instructing their porters to pitch their tents in the location Vahrem had designated.

She stood grim and imposing behind the manservant as he discoursed with the merchants in Scadishi and told them the place they'd chosen was one of honor granted them by the chieftain of the tribe under whose immense banner they now stood. The merchants—all brothers, if she had to guess—alternated between arguing with each other and with Iyshan for almost five minutes. Finally, the one who appeared to be the eldest struck the youngest, a youth not yet twenty, across the face and all three of them set upon one another with fists, feet, and teeth.

The warrior woman moved to separate them roughly but her companion stopped her with the comment that it would be better to simply do what they needed to do and let the brothers resolve their differences. She'd complied and gone with him to the porters to issue instructions to have them gather the tents and wares for delivery to an adjoining lot.

By the time the three brothers had finished their little brawl, straightened torn robes, and pressed sashes to bloody noses, they realized they had to hurry after the porters who had already departed with their things.

After this, Iyshan had whistled the all-clear and the caravan had set about the business of making camp. Ax-Wed, knowing she would merely be in the way of the carefully orchestrated procedure, turned her attention to locating Zoria and was quickly directed to the Teitels. When she rode to the family's rising tent, she was surprised to find Vahrem there with Zoria and Sybil. The merchant was not dressed in his typical plain tunic and breeches but had wrapped himself in a striking robe of crimson trimmed in gold thread. A snow-white turban crowned his head, with a thumb-sized garnet set in the center like a crystalline drop of blood over his brow.

It was the first time she had seen the caravan master dress in a manner befitting his station, but she couldn't deny that he wore it well.

"Are you ready to go?" he called as she strode forward, leading the mare with one hand on the reins.

"Where?" she asked, partly distracted as she tried to keep herself and the horse clear of those busy unloading wagons, pitching tents, and lighting fires.

"To the Thunder-Crush!" Zoria almost shrieked as she bounced on the balls of her feet. "Vahrem is taking us with him when he meets a business partner. Isn't that wonderful?"

"Master Kal'Stru," Ax-Wed said in a hard, flat voice.

Zoria ceased bouncing and sensed that she'd transgressed but was uncertain of exactly how. She darted a glance to Vahrem and Sybil, but both found something else to look at.

"What?" she asked and the first snarl of defiance curled one corner of her mouth.

"He is Master Kal'Stru to you," the warrior woman said as she came to stand over the girl with one armored fist resting against the other. "He is master of this caravan and you will give him the respect he is due."

Zoria blinked and the blood seemed to drain from her face at first as she looked guiltily at the merchant. In the next moment, a flush suffused her cheeks and she turned a defiant stare upon her guardian.

"He doesn't care what I call him," the girl all but snarled.

"I care," she replied in a voice that made it clear she felt the argument was over. With a final long stare at the girl, she turned to Vahrem, who looked incredibly uncomfortable.

"Are you sure you want both of us to be present for your meeting? It may be distracting."

The girl made a noise in the back of her throat that drew another sharp look from the warrior woman.

My mother would have already had me peeled like an onion for such impertinence, Ax-Wed thought, but the memory of her mother's curse settling upon her shoulders reminded her of what a bad example that would be to follow.

"Not at all," the merchant said with an uneasy look at the woman and her ward. "It is a rowdy but spectacular event and I wouldn't have you miss it."

She couldn't deny that despite Zoria's embarrassing behavior, she wanted to see it and even wanted to see it with the girl.

Perhaps, if luck smiles on me, it will give us something to enjoy and not fight over.

"Do you wish me to change before the meeting?" she asked Vahrem with a sweeping gesture at the battered armor she wore. "I don't have anything formal but I have a few things that haven't seen battle."

"Not unless you wish to," he replied and seemed eager to move past the spat between her and the girl. "If it is convenient, we should probably depart immediately so we don't miss anything. Emerik will not complain if we are late but you may miss the first match."

"Match?" Ax-Wed frowned. "Is This some type of competition?"

He bestowed the same twinkling smile on her and despite her irritation, she couldn't deny that she felt something stir at the sight.

Remember the Ashen Road, she warned herself and almost forced herself to look away. *Remember the road you are on!*

She fortified her heart with shafts of ice that crept into her look and although it killed part of her a little more, she held his gaze until he could see the frigid edge there.

"So are we going?" Zoria asked and drew both adults away from their strained stares.

The caravan master turned away and smiled warmly at the girl.

"Well," he said and struggled to clear his throat. "If you can promise me to be on your best behavior, we can be off presently—assuming that is fine with your...eh, that is...as long as good sister Ax-Wed is willing and ready."

Zoria nodded vigorously and turned a pitiable face to her guardian, the contrived expression not quite successful enough to hide the glint of anger in the corner of her eye.

Morah take me now. She resisted the urge to roll her eyes and instead, simply nodded.

"Very well. Let us go, then. We wouldn't want to miss the first match."

CHAPTER FOUR

The heart of Carnyxia was not some grand palace or fair plaza but rather a massive amphitheater carved into the very bones of the earth.

Following an earthen ramp from the sea of stalls and other mercantile constructions, Vahrem, Ax-Wed, and Zoria moved with the thousands who swarmed into the craggy stadium. The entire upper half of the "seating" was rough stone, sometimes hewn into long piles which served as benches and at others, bare boulders on which spectators gathered and jabbered and chatted excitedly as they squinted at the floor below.

The merchant led the way and they bustled down switchback steps cut into the stone until they reached the next level of spectators. This tier included an odd mixture of actual stone benches and pavilioned alcoves where entrepreneurial souls prepared food and drink for the crowds. From these caves, the smells of searing flesh, baking breads, and various pungent alcohols all wafted strategically to tempt those above to venture down for a bite.

Zoria sniffed and looked longingly at some hanks of meat on bone skewers, but her guardian shook her helmed head. The girl rolled her eyes in response and although Ax-Wed couldn't hear it over the crowd around them, she could tell the girl had made the infuriating sound of disgust in the back of her throat. It took more will that the Thulian would like to admit to not cuff her across the back of the head, gauntlet mitt and all.

If the coins have to last us until Bykairlious, we can't waste them on frivolous things. How can someone who used to live on the streets not understand that?

She tried to put the thought out of her mind as they followed Vahrem down another set of stone stairs to the final level.

Much of the lowest quarter of the stony descent to the bottom of the bowl-like formation had been worked by pick and chisel to form seating for the barbaric royalty of the Vitzerka. Chieftains and their retainers lounged on pelt-draped couches cut from the living stone while their wives and concubines moved about and proffered food and drink when not caught up in their gossip and observations.

Over their heads were pyramidal pavilions of stitched hides with the looping, interconnected symbols of their clan emblazoned upon each side. A walkway of daubed wattle supported by lashed timbers driven into the stone slope swept around the amphitheater to mark the edge of the lowest tier. Below that, the stone fell away much more sharply and soon became a sheer drop to the floor below.

Vahrem followed this walkway until they reached a pavilion whose symbol resembled nothing so much as a multispoked wheel with jagged runes between each spoke.

"Vahlin!" cried a bright voice within and before he could step beneath the hide shelter, a lanky figure rushed out and wrapped him in a fierce hug.

"Emerik!" He returned the hug vigorously, to the point that Ax-Wed feared the stout merchant might damage the far thinner man. "It is good to see you, my friend."

The two separated after a moment, shared a fond smile as

they surveyed each other, and still with an arm around one another, turned to Ax-Wed and Zoria. At a glance, Emerik seemed everything the caravan master was not, being exceedingly tall and lanky, with pale, freckled skin and wispy red hair that barely managed to cover his head and cheeks. The only thing that seemed to bind the two men was the beaming smiles they wore with their arms around each other.

"It is my pleasure to introduce to both of you my good friend, Emerik Burning-Beard, Chieftain of the Lecall," Vahrem announced and squeezed his friend's shoulders jovially before he swept an arm before him. "Emerik, this is Lady Ax-Wed and her ward young Zoria, recent additions to our caravan but fast friends, as well as those uninitiated into the spectacle of the Thunder-Crush."

"We appreciate your hospitality, Chief Burning-Beard," Ax-Wed said as she bowed her head and gave Zoria a sharp look when she did not do likewise. "We both do."

Her ward began to roll her eyes again but thankfully, the gesture was partially concealed when she conceded and bowed her head to Emerik.

"Oh, yes," the girl said with obvious distraction. "Thanks."

The warrior woman had to fight the sudden urge to throttle her ward in public.

"You are most welcome," Emerik said expansively and stepped away from his friend's side to take their hands in his to brush his lips quickly over the knuckles. "Come under my tent and honor me with your presence. Whatever I have is yours to enjoy."

Still holding their hands, he practically dragged them under the awning and settled them on a stone couch blanketed by thick furs. Their seat positioned them to the left of a throne-like mound of pelts which was undoubtedly where their host would sit, while a smaller seat than either the couch or throne stood on the right. As they were settled, Emerik turned to the woman lurking—and, Ax-Wed noted, glaring—in the back and called for drink and food. She was so preoccupied with the sharp, pale eyes of the woman that it took Zoria two attempts to elbow her hard enough to draw her attention.

"Look at that fat sack," the girl whispered and pointed surreptitiously.

Given Zoria's background and her abominable behavior in the caravan, the warrior woman was genuinely afraid of what her eyes might see with such an inducement to look. When she did, her eyes widened with surprise rather than embarrassment. A literal leather sack rested open at the foot of the furry throne and its metallic contents glinted in the shade. At a glance, she noted no less than five different kinds of silver money and two different types of gold denominations on the top of the metal coinage.

"He said to enjoy whatever was his," her ward said with a waggle of her eyebrows that inspired dread.

"Try not to get us killed before we even know what a Thunder-Crush is," she said quickly when she saw the woman approaching with food and drink. "And don't embarrass Vahrem."

She looked up and nodded a greeting to the blonde-haired woman who looked less than pleased to be serving food to them. Without preamble, the attendant thrust a large drinking horn of mead into one hand and a wood tray into the other. On this, raw strips of meat lay next to a small bowl of what looked like a dark jelly.

"Thank you," Ax-Wed told her stiffly, but the woman had already turned away. Bangles clinked on her wrists and beads of amber clicked in her braided hair. The warrior woman's gaze followed her to where she stopped behind Emerik's throne with one hand resting conspicuously on the furs.

Does that pasty cat honestly think I would seduce her husband?

The thought made her suddenly look at the food with suspicion although to be honest, that was only partly to do with who had served it. The uncooked flensings of flesh didn't seem particularly appetizing and she didn't have the faintest clue how they could be served with a thick jelly the color of ripe mulberries that smelled like sweet wine.

"Morah, come quickly," she whispered, thankful that her helm and aventail gave her an excuse to not eat.

"It was only a joke," Zoria huffed irritably. "You don't have to be so mean."

Ax-Wed shook her head and looked to where the girl sat with her arms folded and her face composed in such a way to be the utter picture of youthful indignation.

"No, I didn't say that about you—" Ax-Wed began but her explanation was cut off when Emerik sat next to her and gave an exultant cry.

"Ah, I see you've never had phol!" He stretched a hand to the tray. "Here, let me show you."

The chieftain selected a strip of meat with long, callous, thickened fingers and deftly rolled it tightly before he plunged it into the bowl. He gave the submerged meat a quick swirl, drew it out dripping dark jelly, and popped it into his mouth. It seemed that he barely chewed it twice before he gulped it in one swallow and turned to them with a brilliant smile.

"See. It's as easy as that."

"It truly is quite good," Vahrem said as he settled into his seat next to Emerik with his tray and horn. "Although I was skeptical the first time I tried it."

"Skeptical?" The chieftain rumbled with sudden laughter and Ax-Wed noticed how rosy his cheeks and nose were. "I think it took you years to finally stop that Shepherd nonsense long enough to enjoy what was put in front of you."

She cut a quizzical glance from one man to the other, who held out a hand that was soon filled with a brimming drinking horn. As far as she knew, the merchant—together with those in his caravan—was still very much a follower of the peculiar cult and she had never known him to be so great a liar as to hide the fact, especially to one he called a friend.

Vahrem saw the look as he took a mouthful of phol, shook his head, and raised a beseeching hand as he hastened to wash the food down with a swig from his horn.

"What he means is that I let go of holding to a...a different creed of my faith," he explained. "When I first met him, I was new to the faith and its teachings and thus easily swayed by less than sound doctrines. I am both the wiser and the happier for it now."

Ax-Wed nodded, understanding at least in part, but the chieftain uttered another loud blast of laughter after he'd drained half his horn in one long draw.

"Well, you southerners, be you sheeple or those father-botherers of Myrnatt, can keep all that nonsense." He chortled as one hand pawed traces of mead from his beard. "I say to the Bonelands with all of it."

He didn't seem to notice or care how the caravan master winced more at the slur of "sheeple" than the volume of the alcohol-thickened declaration.

"You mean you people don't have any gods?" Zoria interjected around a mouthful of the jelly-dipped flesh. Her guardian looked down, startled when she realized that in her distraction, the girl had managed to eat the lion's share of phol. Even while she waited for the answer, her jelly-stained fingers groped for another strip.

"Here." The warrior woman handed her the tray and her ward took it eagerly before Emerik waded in with his explanation after another swallow.

"Oh, my people are as superstitious as the next." He chuckled but there was an edge to his voice that chilled the words as they left his mouth. "We have all manner of demons, spirits, and yes, even what might be called gods, with all types of rituals for dealing with and appeasing them."

"But you don't believe in them?" she asked mildly after she took an experimental sip of the mead beneath her metal veil.

It was not as though she hadn't heard of those who didn't believe in the gods before, but to hear the opinion from a chieftain of a savage people surprised her. Most often, it was men filled with their own scholarly significance who would wax on about how the gods, of whatever ilk, were nothing more than elevated heroes of old or even archetypal symbols from history given fabricated personalities. Even in demon-haunted Xhult with its many temples and blood sacrifices, there was an understanding that they were observing empowering traditions and appeasing rituals, not actual veneration or worship. Only Morah, Blackwinged Plucker of Heartstrings, approached such a place, and then it was only a nebulous dread which compelled them to see their damned souls carried away in her talons in death rather than gobbled up by the horrors they bartered with in life.

Her own opinions had not become any less convoluted since she'd left her city and given her most recent experiences beneath Jehadim, they were more muddled, if anything.

"Do I believe there is magic? Yes, of course. I've seen our wise-ones do it and some southron magicians as well." Emerik flapped a hand as though dismissing some as yet unasked question. "And are there things—creatures—that can use magic in ways men cannot yet understand? Certainly, but that is a far way from anything I would worship."

The last word came out like a slur and although she couldn't quite explain it, she decided she disliked the loquacious chieftain intensely.

"Besides, I—"

Any further comment he might have made was halted when the throb of drums rose like thunder. Ax-Wed and Zoria turned to look into the arena but so far, nothing seemed to have stirred besides some loose debris from the crowd tossed by the wind.

"Ah!" their host shouted as he flung his arms up. His friend ducked the drinking horn but could not escape the spray of mead. "About time! Vahrem, come hold my mead."

"I believe I already am," the merchant muttered as he wiped alcohol from his eyes. Despite his frown, he took the horn being shoved at him.

Emerik lurched hard to one side and almost toppled from his chair as he groped at the foot of his throne. His hand came up with a fistful of coins from the sack, which he promptly began shoving into Zoria and Ax-Wed's hands. When he ran out, he snatched up more and bundled them into another fistful to push them into Vahrem's waiting hand.

The warrior woman shared a stunned look with her ward as the rumble of the drums grew to a rabid tempo that could be felt in their chests.

"Are you ready?" the chieftain asked brightly and retrieved a handful for himself. "Remember to wait for the right time to throw."

"Throw?" Zoria cried her face and her face began to fold into a crestfallen pout.

Emerik was already on his feet and moved to the edge of the wooden walkway, but Vahrem saw the confusion on both their faces and paused to speak to them rather than follow his friend.

"It is tradition." He shouted to be heard over the pounding drums. "To display confidence in your champion, you shower the arena behind them with coins, jewels, or other trinkets."

Some type of gladiatorial games then. Ax-Wed was glad the quizzical glance she gave him was hidden behind her helm. *I would never have expected that he would have an interest in blood sports.*

"So we don't get to keep this?" the girl asked and stared forlornly at the collection of coins in her hand, which was probably more wealth than she'd ever held before.

"It would be very ungracious to not use it as your host intended," the caravan master explained, his voice as gentle as could be managed at a shout. "But hurry—we'll miss his entrance."

Following the merchant, the warrior woman and a sulking Zoria moved to where Emerik rocked at the very edge of the bound logs. Beneath their feet was the faintest quivering and she thought she heard the rattling of heavy chains. The screech of metal upon stone was followed by a final resounding crash before the drums ceased and an incredible hush fell across the amphitheater.

"Behold!" Emerik roared at the top of his lungs as he teetered over the arena floor. "Jakash, get of Marud, champion of the Lecall!"

A sound like a blast from a titan's trump, ringing and terrible, issued from beneath their feet. Her body tensed at the huge and primeval sound, while Zoria jumped and started to duck behind her caregiver. In the echoes of that terrible cry, the thousands of spectators within the arena raised a raucous cheer and it felt as though the earth trembled beneath them. When she looked at the flushed and screaming faces, she saw all their eyes were fixed directly below where she stood. She followed their gazes and looked at what now entered below her.

At first, it seemed like a hill of dark, silver fur slid from under the walkway. A moment later, the creature raised its huge head and a serpentine snout curled level with their platform although its shaggy feet thudded into the stone floor of the arena. Another roar sounded from the massive monster's chest, and the screams of the crowd rose even louder. The creature—Jakash, she guessed —tossed its head so the sun flashed on curved tusks almost twice as long as Ax-Wed was tall.

"So that's a mammoth," she called as she looked at Vahrem, who grinned at her as he raised his fistful of coins in a salute.

"When do we throw these?" she asked and nodded to her fist full of mammon.

"Now!" the caravan master shouted as he cast his handful of

silver and gold into the widening space behind the plodding behemoth. She followed suit and even Zoria, her attention captivated by the huge beast, threw the coins without a second thought.

The warrior woman caught flashes of metal in her peripheral vision and saw that several of the women who'd stood under Emerik's awning had stepped forward. They threw their smaller collections of coins or coaxed small children garbed in animal hide garments to do the same. Before their host threw the final handful, each coin shining and golden in the sun, the impressions of Jakash's massive footprints were covered in gleaming coins.

As the last one fell, the chieftain took a whistle from his belt and blew a long note which cut through the rowdy noises of the crowd. In answer, Jakash stopped, reared on his back legs, and uttered a third earth-shaking bellow.

This time, the triumphant cry was answered by a challenge of equal volume and might. Every eye in the amphitheater, once raptly focused on the living titan, turned and saw the source of this new roar. The huge brown mammoth—almost as large as Jakash but without the fleck of silver marking his coat—emerged from under the walkway as the portcullis set into the stone began to descend into place to seal it again.

Not quite the gladiators I'd expected. Ax-Wed shook her head as coins showered in the challenging mammoth's wake.

The crowd lulled long enough for her to hear a hoarse woman's voice announce the challenger.

"Witness him!" cried an exceptionally stout woman from a walkway section opposite theirs. "Narund, get of Khaba, champion of the Bulgan!"

The crowd resumed its yammering as the opposing chieftainess spun something on a leather thong that emitted a series of chirps. Narund responded with another belligerent roar.

Jakash tossed his grizzled head, swung dull eyes toward the newcomer, and loosed a low rumble that the warrior woman could have sworn she felt in her chest. Narund stamped his feet in response and swung his tusks from side to side. The twin lances of ivory glinted and seemed almost eager. The elder of the two swept his wooly trunk across the earth and cast dirt toward the rival bull mammoth before he turned his face away, a veteran dismissing some upstart yapping at his heels.

This repudiation had the expected effect. With a single furious trumpet, Narund set his huge bulk in motion, not to be outdone or dismissed. At first, they seemed to execute lumbering and almost comical charges toward one another. As momentum built and each footfall struck the stone hard enough to leave cratered cracks, the incredible power and speed brought to bear became clear. By the time they were strides away from each other, the two mammoths moved as fast as one of Vahrem's mares at a gallop and neither showed any intention to slow.

When the two met skull to skull and tusk to tusk, it was with an incredible thud of tons of meat and bone colliding at impossible speeds and Ax-Wed's body responded with a visceral shiver. It was frightening and yet exhilarating, her mind both primal and rational in a matched response that recognized the incredible spectacle she witnessed.

And this was only the beginning.

Despite both striking with a force that could have splintered the gates of Jehadim, neither Jakash nor Narund seemed even slightly staggered by the impact. Their tusks locked and they drove against each other with chest-trembling grunts and puffs. Heavy steps struck the earth and flurried showers of fractured stone as each creature fought for purchase and leverage. Narund bellowed, fresh and vigorous, while Jakash huffed along, as steady as blacksmith bellows without any sign of flagging.

From the stands, every voice cried encouragement for their chosen competitor and curses, oaths, and encouragements joined these in the tongues of the Vitzerka along with a smattering of others far more exotic.

"Come on, Jakash!" a small but savage voice shrieked at Ax-Wed's shoulder. When she saw Zoria, her eyes bright and her face almost as flushed as Emeriks', she was swept along with the swirling maelstrom of communal exultation.

"Push, you ol' beast," she hollered and one arm swooped around the girl's shoulders on instinct. "Knock him flat!"

To her pleased surprise, her ward did not try to slip away but rather wound her arm around her waist as she joined her enthusiastic exhortation.

"Yes! Knock him on his ass!" she howled and together, they laughed and screamed in wordless communion.

"Take him now, you old bastard," Emerik bellowed, while beside him, Vahrem beat a heavy fist against his breast and raised his thunderous voice.

"Crush him, Jakash!"

With a sudden cunning glint in his weary eyes, Jakash threw his head up and out to drag the entangled ivory spears upward. Narund blasted an angry protest but the older mammoth was already in motion and surged forward with one massive shoulder. The crowd winced with a collective gasp as the old bull's weight butted the side of the challenger's head with a heavy thunk. For the first time, Narund staggered and his tree-thick legs wobbled as his huge, hairy feet slid over a patina of crushed rock.

Jakash pressed his advantage mercilessly and drove forward while he twisted his tusks higher to force his adversary further off-balance. The younger mammoth felt victory slipping away from him and freed his tusks with a vicious yank. It was no good, however, as the forceful exit only allowed the old bull to drive his weight that much deeper under his opponent.

The end, although perceived in a heartbeat, seemed to come in a series of stretched, trembling moments.

Slabs of muscle thicker than a man bunched in the aggressor's shoulders and haunches as he gathered himself for a final, unstoppable heave. Narund, his forelegs already almost off the ground, fought to bear his bulk down and crush his attacker. The elder bull's tusks swept under his rival's huge chest and braced in preparation to move tons of belligerent muscle, fat, and fur.

In an instant, those quivering stacks of sinew sprang and Jakash threw his body forward and his head up. The younger mammoth's feet flailed and his trunk whipped as he rose, spun helplessly with his feet in the air, and plummeted with the force of a falling mountain. This final impact was different than the initial collision, but Ax-Wed paused in her raw-throated cheering to feel it in her chest and bones.

Narund, beaten and panting, lay on his side. Jakash tossed his head and pitched a final splash of crushed pebbles before he strutted about the amphitheater and unleashed repeated blasts of his booming trumpet-like victory calls.

Ax-Wed and Zoria joined the crowd in exhorting each step of the victory lap with screams, whistles, and wild applause.

The warrior woman paused for a moment when she realized Vahrem was smiling at her. He winked and raised his voice to shout over the crowd.

"That, good lady, is Thunder-Crush!"

CHAPTER FIVE

Hoarlin was not the northernmost habitation in the Norling Steppes and despite its name, the climate in the western region was far milder being closer to the volcanically warmed waters of the Sulphurous Sea. When Dragahn's army approached the city, an unseasonably warm turn made the warriors shed their cloaks as the flanks of their mounts lathered and sweated.

When the Wind-Spoken warlord crested the hill, he had to raise a hand to his brand-knotted brow as the glittering city shined with spires that seemed like nothing so much as spikes of ice. About those crystalline spires rose the walls, which sparkled and gleamed like the glassy assembly of some glacial mason in the ancient fables of the frost giants who some claimed dwelt near the poles of the world.

"It is said that only bad omens and worse fortunes come from this city," Tadzi grumbled as Kollung's rolling gait plodded below. "That within its walls are all the shades of the long-dead Storm-Callers, and none see those blood-hungry shades and live to tell the tale."

His leader chuckled, shrugged his massive shoulders out of his cloak, and left his pierced and inked skin to glisten in the sun.

He stretched one arm until it gave a deep pop and did the same with the other until he received the same result, still laughing softly.

"It's true!" the sword-bearer insisted and his black eyes narrowed as his sharpened teeth champed in irritation. "Do you doubt the stories?"

"I do," Dragahn confirmed. "If nothing else because I never trust those that end with no one lived to tell the tale. It seems a contradiction, doesn't it?"

The man's face scrunched in confusion but he had little time for reflection as the warlord hauled on the chains in his fist.

"Hold, Kollung."

They were close enough that despite the glare of the shimmering walls, both men could see the deep azure of the Frozen City's central gate. Wide enough that two mammoths could enter abreast, the massive portal stood mighty but ruined, a powerful blow having shattered the central portion of the gate. Even the warlord marveled at the force it would have taken to strike with such efficacy.

Other than the soft moan of the wind and the rumbling tread of his army over the plain, no sound rose to his ear. He decided that a city of ghosts was likely to be a quiet place, although he wondered if it would stay that way once he and his retainers broke its serenity by passing through those broken gates.

"Give the signal to make camp," he instructed and his gaze swept past the gate to the cloud-stabbing structure beyond.

Tadzi did as he was ordered, drew his horn, and blew three short trills before he turned to look at the city in trepidation.

"Are you certain it is in there?" he asked and ran his tongue across the points of his teeth.

"No," Dragahn said. "But if it is there, I would not face the chosen of Svarah without it. Our people will never accept me otherwise."

The sword-bearer nodded but continued to watch the city

as though it were a slumbering beast. As a child, he'd heard of the great and terrible deeds worked by the Storm-Callers and how, even in their fall, their fury and vengeance were unmatched.

Hoarlin, once a fortress city from which they held dominion over the entire Steppes and the sea to the west, would not be surrendered to lesser hands. To prevent this, it was encased in hungry ice that would not thaw and from its frigid heart, the Frozen City sent fell winds that plagued the Norling Steppes and turned a harsh land into an unlivable one.

It wasn't until the first Vitzerka sent their heroes to break the curse within that the effects on the Steppes had been relieved and the land began to heal. But all things had a cost, and that was the reason they were there now, standing before a city that had haunted the minds and dreams of his people for generations. When he looked at the looming figure of Dragahn Shieldshiver, Tadzi felt bolstered again and he slid his hand along the sword he bore honorably for his master.

The Frozen City was a dread legend, but what he'd seen the warlord do on the battlefield or in their adventures together was also the stuff of legends, equal to any tale of the wise-ones. His spine trembled treacherously at the sight of the city but he knew from experience that nothing stood in the way of the Wind-Spoken of Perukh.

At least not for long.

The next morning, after a night of specter-haunted dreams that drove hardened warriors to wake shivering and weeping, Dragahn gathered his retainers to him. The fire burned low but the interior of the tent was suffocatingly warm and within a moment of stepping inside, each man had beads of sweat forming at his brow. Even the warlord's flesh gleamed in the frail light with a sheen of sweat, but as with most mortal discomforts, he barely seemed to notice.

"We will go into the Frozen City," he declared after a long moment while his retainers stood in silence before him. "Perukh speaks to me and tells me that within is that which I shall bear against the Beast-Slayer."

The men looked nervously at each other for a moment but none spoke. One look at Belug, the man with the topknot, and his misaligned jawline reminded them to keep their misgivings to themselves. They were retainers, not hetmans, chieftains, or leaders. Each of them was a living weapon bound to his will, not fit to give counsel to a Wind-Spoken.

"What do we seek?" Tadzi asked and his fingers moved nervously along the token-hung scabbard.

"It will seal the circle between Perukh and Svarah," the warlord replied and his tectonic voice hinted at boredom. "And ensure that the prophecies that came at the Wyrm-Spine Mountains are true."

"A weapon then." The sword-bearer hissed a breath and grinned eagerly. "A god-forged weapon to fell another Wind-Spoken."

"Or a totem," said the brawny man with a wooden chest tucked under one meaty arm. "That which draws the eyes of all eyes in the heavens or under the earth."

Belug remained silent, although whether because he had nothing to say or the blow his master had dealt him made speech difficult, it wasn't clear. Dragahn's gaze lingered on the chest under the man's arm before it shifted to stare outward.

He was prone to doing this and it seemed as though he watched some distant vista even if all mortal eyes could see was a campfire or tent wall. Some, not least of all his retainers, whispered outside of his presence that he heard Perukh's words upon the wind but as he rarely spoke of such things, none could know for sure.

The men waited in silence, comfortable beyond embarrassment with such stillness, until Dragahn's attention returned to them.

"Volu." The warlord grunted as though he had only now recalled the name. "You have something for me."

The powerfully built retainer presented the chest to his master and drew the lid up.

"She is prepared as you instructed," he said with a twitch of a proud smile beneath his mustache. "She will make a fine addition to the honored."

"No," he said as he inspected the chest's contents. "I have found a better use for her."

Dragahn turned to Belug and settled a heavy hand upon his shoulder. He didn't seem to notice or care how the man flinched when his hand rose toward him.

"Prepare her as a Witness and mount her upon Kollung's yoke," the master instructed. "Then we shall enter Hoarlin and claim what the gods have prepared for us."

As the noon sun rose to shine with painful brightness over Hoarlin, a procession of three mammoths harnessed for war entered the city. The riders shielded their eyes against the piercing glare as they urged the beasts through the breach in the gate that dwarfed even their mounts.

Upon Kollung's humped shoulders, Dragahn squinted at the glittering streets with a frown before he drew a small blade from his belt. He sliced a thin line across his meaty forearm, dabbed a thumb in the welling blood, and turned to the Witness that now rose to eye level next to him. With words whispered to his people on the winds centuries before, he drew the red thumb across pitch-sealed lips and stared expectantly into the glazed eyes.

"Which way to my destiny, wise one?" the warlord rumbled as

Volu and Belug drew up on either side of him on their mammoths. Both retainers were grim-faced and stony-eyed, but the mounted lancers looked with open dread at the deathly quiet streets of the Frozen City. As a cold wind kicked up around them, the warriors looked with equally frightened gazes at their war leader.

The cold wind, full of strange syllables, whirled about the Witness and with a wheeze that smelled of cedar, the wise woman's lips quivered. Jaw muscles, no longer anchored by a neck to a body, worked with strange, alien actions and the pitch-plastered tongue shuddered with sluggish, flaccid movements within the toothless mouth. After a ghastly few seconds of this crude animation, a thin, wheezing voice rose to answer.

"Ssseek-k-k…ss-cent-t-tral…sssp-p-pire," the Witness instructed as the congealed blood cracked with the tortured movements of the lips.

Dragahn turned his gaze toward the glassy spikes that thrust into the belly of the sky and nodded. It was easy enough to see that the largest of them stood at the very heart of the city.

"Thank you, wise one." He grunted as he snapped the chains in his fist. Kollung responded with a low huff but obeyed. Without a word, the retainers bade their beasts follow and the streets filled with the crunch and groan of ice beneath heavy steps.

The Witness trembled again, its brittle voice almost lost amidst the tread of the mammoths.

"Fffear-r-r…rrred-d-d…mmmouth-th-thsss," it warned.

The warlord's brow furrowed and his gaze shifted to the severed head again before he returned his focus to the dead city.

In answer to his suspicious glare, a chorus of melodic laughter cut through the air like a sharp gale.

CHAPTER SIX

The battling mammoths had been only the beginning and as the contests continued into the evening, Ax-Wed saw all manner of strange adversaries in battle.

Huge creatures that loped on clawed knuckles, wooly brutes with spike-mounted snouts, and others that resembled stags but were so large that their antlers were like thickets of stabbing points were only a few.

Each time a portcullis rose at the start of a match, she wondered what new bestial marvel would emerge to engage another in combat. Some struggles were frantic, bloody affairs while others were more methodical and ponderous, but to one especially who had never seen these beasts before, it was intensely fascinating. Add the bellowing crowd to each barbaric spectacle and more than a few sips of mead, and the entire process was like nothing she'd experienced.

Along with all of this came a fascination with the significance and motivation behind the perpetual struggles that played out before her.

"You see, immediately before the teeth of winter close in, many of these creatures are in rut," Emerik explained as they watched two challengers swipe tusked heads at one another. The beasts seemed to be some chimeric mixture of boar and draft horse with knobbly, long-toothed skulls that rivaled the hippopotami she'd seen in her travels along the southern border of the Wallow. The chieftain had told her they were called *Borbenja* and when properly trained, could be used much like hunting hounds or even war dogs.

Her mind was distracted for a moment when she imagined a pack of the knobbly creatures facing her on the battlefield while they squealed battle cries and firelight glinted off their tusks. The sun had long since set but great stone braziers had been lit to fill the amphitheater with light.

"So the beasts think they are fighting for females?" she asked and did her best to pay attention as the sound of boney heads cracking together rose alongside the cheers of the crowd.

"Well, they don't only think they are." Emerik chuckled, drained his horn, and turned in his seat to bellow to the women behind him. "Anja! More mead. Our guests are thirsty."

The warrior woman winced a little at the lie but remained silent. The only one who seemed to be invested in drink was the chieftain and at this point, she was uncertain how the man was even conscious. A glance at the furtive ways in which the chieftain's wife prepared a flagon to bring to her husband seemed proof enough that he had received less and less mead since the sun went down.

Anja caught her gaze upon her and the woman's eyes flashed and nostrils flared in a challenge. Ax-Wed turned to the arena with the slightest shake of her head.

Is it because I'm not there with the other women? Or is it truly because she thinks I have designs on her husband?

"What do you mean they don't only think?" she asked but after a moment, she realized Emerik was too busy holding his drinking horn out while he muttered half-formed curses to bother with an answer.

"He means that to have your beast compete in the Thunder-Crush, a chieftain has to wager something," Vahrem explained, his voice heavy and his brow furrowed. "This often means they wager fertile females, so Jakash's harem has added a few more cows with his victory."

"Not merely a few!" the chieftain protested as he swung and almost splashed his friend with his sloshing horn again. "A full dozen of fat ladies ready for the old stud's rapacious attention."

Before the caravan master could respond, he lurched away from the sweeping drinking horn again as Emerik twisted to shout toward the gaggle of women.

"Do you hear that, Anja? Your good husband grows his herds by twelve—*twelve*!—mammoths in one night."

The woman's pale face reddened and her whole body stiffened but she gave no answer other than her cold stare.

"I'm sure she appreciates it," Vahrem said quickly. "But it has been an eventful night and we are all growing tired, I think."

His friend muttered something in his barbaric tongue before he turned to watch one of the swine-horses flatten his rival with a tremendous headbutt.

Ax-Wed looked at the merchant over the chieftain's sulkily hunched shoulders and caught him forcing his face into something resembling a smile. His cheerfulness seemed to be wearing thin as the night continued, especially with each time that Emerik drained his horn and demanded more. Despite the initial introduction stating deep affection and regard, it seemed their friendship was strained.

Is it only for their business dealings or for the memory of something they once shared?

"What's that?" Zoria cried at her side in a voice grown hoarse with shouting. "It's beautiful!"

The warrior woman swung her gaze to the amphitheater floor where a truly peculiar monster strutted and bobbed its head. With long powerful legs that ended in hooked talons, the creature was taller than a man and from the tip of its toothy snout to its plumed tail, almost twice that length.

It seemed an odd amalgam of reptile and avian, with closely packed scales and a lizard-like head for the former and mottled, viridian feathers and a sharp, upright stance for the latter. Eyes as cold as a snake and as piercing as a bird of prey swept a disdainful gaze around the arena with each twitch and sweep of its head.

"What a treat," Vahrem called after he'd waited for a long and awkward moment for Emerik to answer. "It is a rare thing to see one *Strajkubo*, let alone two. Most have been migrating to the west as things have become colder and colder over the years."

"I can't imagine that this will be much of a fight," the girl said, her gaze still fixed on the strutting animal. "It's so beautiful and dainty. Why would it want to fight?"

Ax-Wed saw the lethal curve of the *Strajkubo*'s talons and the razored rows of teeth in its jaws and decided dainty was not the word she would have used to describe it. Impressive or even striking, certainly, but there was no doubt that unlike all the other creatures thus far, this one was a true predator. She could almost see in the movements of the creature that the violence of the encounter would be in an entirely different order.

"Perhaps it is best that we retire for the evening?" Vahrem suggested as if he'd read her thoughts. She nodded slightly over Emerik's shoulders, though the drunken chieftain seemed utterly disinterested in them for the moment.

A series of chirping whistles, barely heard over the crowd, issued from the strange creature as it sniffed the air. Another portcullis rose and the *Strajkubo* froze for a moment before it threw its head back to utter a shrill, hissed screech.

In answer, a defiant trill was punctuated by the popping sound of jaws champed forcefully as a second *Strajkubo* with rippling sapphire plumage emerged.

"Emerik," Vahrem said and placed a broad hand on the lanky man's thin arm. "I think we will return to camp. Thank y—"

"What's he doing?" Zoria shouted as she stood, her tone sharp and concerned.

Ax-Wed shifted her gaze to followed the girl's pointing finger to a section of the walkway a few strides from where they sat. A boy, less than ten summers old if he was a day, had clambered over the edge of the logs and now lowered himself to the sharp slope beneath that led to the arena floor.

The two predators had begun to circle each other and their feathers rippled as they bared tooth and talon. The green-feathered *Strajkubo* raked the air with a slashing kick and the Thulian had a sickening vision of what those powerful claws would do a child foolish enough to get close.

"Someone needs to stop him!" Zoria cried and rushed to where the boy dangled before her guardian could stop her.

"Zoria!" she shouted and bolted to her feet. Her half-drunk mead horn and platter of forgotten food scattered. Some of the alcohol splashed across Emerik and woke him from his stupor to curse and roar in protest, but she was too focused on the girl to pay him any mind. Out of the corner of her eye, she saw Vahrem surge to his feet, but the chieftain's startled flailing held him at bay for the moment.

"Zoria!" she bellowed loudly enough to draw the attention of several groups of spectators around them, but it was no use.

The boy disappeared over the edge and began his scrambling descent into the arena. Zoria, as nimble as a cat, vaulted over the side after him.

She muttered a stream of curses as she rushed after the girl, then dove to the edge of the platform, hoping to snag her, but her hand groped through empty air. Her ward had already dropped far out of her reach and now traversed the steep incline after the boy. He was already close to the point where the slope became a sheer drop to the floor below.

"What can I do?" Vahrem asked, slightly out of breath as he rushed up behind her. His dark eyes were wide and flashed fiercely.

"Find some rope or something," she told him brusquely as she spun and began to lower herself over the edge of the platform. "And pray to your Shepherd that I don't kill that girl when I catch up to her."

He nodded and the hint of a fierce smile tugged at the corners of his mouth and caught her by surprise.

Maybe there's something sterner to this man than I thought.

"I'll find some. Go," he told her and she looked away from him to hurry down the stony incline.

Despite how easy the youngsters had made it look, she was still dressed in armor with her weapons belted about her hips. With this added weight, it required every ounce of focus and control simply to stop her sliding scramble from turning into a crashing roll. The stone underfoot was mostly smooth and what points of traction she could find with her feet were treacherously loose and threatened to send her tumbling as they came free and joined her descent.

Ax-Wed's heart twisted in on itself as she spared a single glance to watch the young boy and then Zoria disappear over the lip of the slope. It was almost half a dozen feet or more to the arena floor and the landing would be made on unforgiving rock.

And that's before we even get to the monsters down there. She pushed the thought aside and focused all her attention on her descent.

Her main concern was to slow her speed down the slope or she was liable to sail into the open air and make a very hard landing when her armored bulk crashed onto the arena floor. Through a combination of leaning back and canting her feet wide in a series of choppy, almost crab-like steps, she managed to arrest enough of her momentum so that when she reached the lip at the bottom of the slope, she was able to stop with legs dangling in the open air before she went over.

Perched on the thin, rocky rim, the warrior woman saw that two struggles had broken out in the arena below. In the center, the *Strajkubo* had engaged each other. They feinted snaps of their jaws and swipes of their talons as they tested each other. Directly below her, Zoria grappled with the boy who snarled with animal intensity as he scratched, bit, and gouged.

The Thulian spared a moment to look at the platform, from which several faces, all unfamiliar, stared curiously at her. There was no sign of Vahrem or the rope yet.

"Morah's beak," she swore as she swung and began to lower herself cautiously to the arena floor. She managed to dismount from the rim without too much difficulty and rose to her full height before she stalked toward the two youngsters. At the same time, she darted watchful glances at the dueling predators that thus far, seemed to not have noticed them.

"Gerroff!" The boy snarled as he twisted in Zoria's grip and alternated between heaping abuse upon her and trying to escape. He was a tough little scrapper, dirty and scarred in the way of most urchins. One hand raked at her face with grubby nails while the other fought to pry her encircling arms from around his waist.

"It isn't safe!" the girl snapped in response with equal zeal and managed to retain her hold mostly by the fact that she was considerably older and bigger than the emaciated boy. His nails scraped across her face and left a quartet of red welts and she cursed volubly. In retaliation, her arms still locked about his waist, she butted her head against his body with such force that it knocked the wind out of the emaciated lad and he gasped and gaped like a landed fish.

Seeing her opportunity, Ax-Wed stepped forward, clamped an armored hand on both children's shoulders, and dragged them bodily away from the battling creatures and toward the edge of the arena.

"That's enough," she declared in a voice so stern that it shocked both of them as much as the cold grasp on their shoulders had. "Come on."

The boy looked up with a mixture of confusion and desperate fear before he craned his neck to clamp his teeth on the metal-shod fingers, which predictably, had little effect.

Zoria still clung to his waist but looked up in surprise. Suddenly, her expression became a twisted battle between relief and indignation.

"I'm only trying to keep him safe!" she shouted and winced when she remembered their proximity to the *Strajkubos*.

"Let's get to the edge and hope Vahrem brings that rope quickly," the Thulian responded sharply as she dragged them toward the rough stone wall. "And you stop that. You'll hurt yourself before you bother me."

To punctuate the remark, she flexed her fingers slightly to scrape the boy's clamped teeth. He released his bite with a pained grunt and reared back to provide her first good look at his face. His skin was pale and almost gray, while his stringy hair and blazing eyes were both as black as pitch. Along with some assorted scars from what was clearly a dangerous early life, a ring of bone was driven through the bridge of his nose and what looked like a fang pierced the lobe of each ear.

He bared his teeth at her and before she could think to stop him, threw his head back and uttered a tremendous screech that easily passed for a cry that might come from a *Strajkubo*.

An uneasy silence, both from the crowd and the embattled creatures, drew her gaze upward as her heart sank.

Both bloodied predators stood with tufts of feathers scattered about their feet and stared at the trio. Thin, venomous hisses issued through their fangs. With unsettling coordination, they both pivoted and began to stalk forward. Talons clicked on the stone in the breathless silence.

Ax-Wed drove the boy to the ground, piled Zoria on top of him, and drew her ax from her belt.

"Keep him down," she said, her voice as cold and hard as the grin of her blade.

For all her pugnacious youth, Zoria couldn't find it within her to argue as she watched the monsters advancing toward them.

With instinctual ease, the blue *Strajkubo* swept right as the green swept left in an attempt to flank their quarry from both sides. She watched them with a wary eye and adjusted her footing with a series of even, shuffling steps, her ax held before her. Her mind raced but her breathing remained steady and her grasp sure as she studied every subtle shift of sinew as the two, only seconds before locked in a mortal struggle, sought to outmaneuver her. She knew she had to be careful as adjusting her orbit too far would provide an opening for them to rush after Zoria and the boy and force her into a fatal race that would leave her exposed and most likely dead.

The green stepped a little wider and the muscles bunched along its hindquarters. In a snap judgment, Ax-Wed rushed forward with a shout and swept her ax in a diagonal cut. The beast, taken aback by the preemptive charge, sprang back with a warning snap of its jaws while its partner rushed in toward her exposed flank.

She had anticipated this attempt to take advantage of a perceived weakness and turned the momentum of her dodged swing to bring the butt of the haft around for an upward thrust. The cap of fine steel, backed by stout wood and driven by her entire body weight, thrust up under the charging creature's jaws. The blue *Strajkubo*'s head twisted upward on its serpentine neck but momentum drove it forward blindly and she had to leap clear or be trampled underfoot.

The warrior woman narrowly avoided the rushing saurian

but took a haphazard stroke across her helm from its feathered tail as it fought to turn itself. She grunted as stars burst over her eyes and she fought to stay on her feet and bring her weapon to bear, certain she was about to be pounced on as an angry screech rose in front of her. At best, she could hope to spit one of the creatures on the horn of her ax before both beasts tore her apart.

Her vision cleared and she realized that the wrathful scream was not meant for her. The two *Strajkubos* collided, the counter-attacking blue having blocked the green's charge. Talons gouged through brilliant feathers to streak them with blood as irate hisses issued from between clamped jaws.

Seeing an opportunity amidst the thrashing limbs and discordant cries, Ax-Wed ducked the blue's sweeping tail to deliver a hewing strike across a knee. Scale, muscle, and tendon parted beneath the sharp smile of Thulian sylver but she pulled the swing before the blade could bind between joints of bone. The creature's leg buckled and it wailed a cry. She hacked into its exposed back and the blade sank between the vertebrae before she tore it free in a spray of blood and chipped bone. A third cudgeled blow at the back of the neck pitched the blue limply forward onto the green's head and they both rolled across the arena floor.

A renewed cry rose from the crowds in the stands and despite her good sense that responded with a surge of irritation, she felt the urge for a theatrical flourish with her weapon.

Whatever exhilaration she had at crippling one of her foes and the crowd's approval, it all evaporated when the green *Strajkubo* pounced. The creature was taller and heavier than her, even in full armor, and given the momentum of its prodigious leap, the Thulian decided to roll with the attack rather than resist it. The haft of her ax caught the talons that arced to puncture her chest cavity but she simply fell back and let the driving force roll over her. For an instant, she felt she'd succeeded and forced the predator to sail over her, but its jaws drove downward on her head.

She exploded in a storm of horrifying sensations. Her vision darkened with the shadows of gnashing teeth and a lolling tongue, her ears were stung by the sound of metal tortured by something sharp, and her head felt as though it were being crushed and torn off at the same time. Every breath seemed to fill her mouth and nose with the stench of festering meat.

Her back hit the stone as she was carried into her backward roll. The weight of the creature passed over her head and something snapped beneath her chin. After a sharp, ripping sensation across her face, she was suddenly free of the horror that threatened to tear her skull off.

Ax-Wed rolled to one side on instinct and the evening air washed across her face as blood streamed from her gouged chin and lower lip to her throat.

Claws grated on the stones when the green fought to retake its feet while it shook its head violently from side to side. Her helm, fang-gouged and buckled, appeared to be stuck and the creature whipped its head frantically to try to dislodge it. The mailed veil and snapped chinstrap waved with each sharp action.

The warrior woman drew a steadying breath as the green *Strayjkubo* finally dislodged the helm, but not without the cost of a few teeth. Woman and beast locked gazes and both understood what came next.

She twisted her head to one side and then the other and was rewarded by two dull pops, while the feathered monster bared what fangs it had left and flexed its talons.

"Come on then," she challenged and a leonine sound tore free from within her chest. "Morah's waiting!"

Thulian and saurian rushed toward each other, their weapons brandished and eager for blood.

The creature leapt forward with its talons splayed, but she was prepared and she jerked to avoid the attack while she attempted a passing stroke at its side. The smiling ax split more than feathers, and the feathered reptile was forced away. It lunged its head viciously, the monstrous teeth ready, but discovered too late that this was exactly what she had counted on. With split second timing and precision, she pounded the spiked bill at the back of her ax into her adversary's skull.

Thunderous applause from the crowd was like a storm, everywhere around her and yet as distant as the heavens above.

The *Strayjkubo's* body spasmed violently and almost wrenched the weapon from her hand when it pitched onto its side. One final shuddering breath rattled its chest before it sagged to the stones. With one foot braced at the back of its neck, Ax-Wed tugged her weapon free and turned to study the other predator.

Blood-spattered plumage twitched with each ragged breath and its tail gave a feeble twitch. One foreclaw scraped at the stone, perhaps a feeble attempt to drag itself to shelter, but its other limbs couldn't manage even that as they twitched and shivered. Froth rose to its lips and the eyes seemed far less cold and lethal as it watched her.

She stepped forward and its claw ceased worrying at the stone. Its breathing, while still pained, slowed to even gasps.

It knows what's coming, she thought and that somehow made her ax feel heavier in her hands. She wasn't sure when, but the amphitheater had grown quiet again. The warrior woman couldn't bring herself to look up and bear the weight of all the faces waiting and watching for her to finish what she'd started.

"Morah comes," she whispered and hoped the invocation would lighten her leaden limbs. Instead, memories of a fiend's haughty words only bowed her shoulders further. She wished she could have closed her eyes to do the deed but she feared her stroke would go astray and another blow would be required. Without the option of respite, she let her gaze drink the creature in—perhaps one of the last of its kind, broken and bloodied at her hand, and waiting to be put out of its misery.

"Zoria was right." She sighed and hefted the ax. "You truly are beautiful."

The fallen monster watched her patiently and its flat stare neither condemned nor absolved her as it waited. All around her, the silence of the crowd thickened until it seemed the tension would suffocate her.

With a firm and decisive motion, the ax fell and bit through flesh and bone. From the tumult that arose in response, she might have thought she'd split the heaven's wide open.

Her teeth gritted, she ignored the shrieks of adulation all around her, tugged her ax free, and turned to where Zoria straddled the boy who had started the entire mess. As she began to trudge toward them, the sounds of coins and other trinkets falling in a ringing rain upon the arena floor joined the praise of the howling crowd.

"Svarah… Vjetgo… Svarah Vjetgo." The words began to emerge from the general babble of the crowd and cracked voices gathered together until it began to devour all other calls. "Svarah Vjetgo! Svarah Vjetgo! Svarah Vjetgo !"

The two words rolled off Ax-Wed like water off a duck's back as she stopped before Zoria and the boy. Both youths stared at her, their expressions a mixture of dread and wonder. She thrust her bloodied ax into her belt, drew Zoria to her feet, and took hold of the bone-pierced lad by his collar.

"You'd better have something very good to say for yourself," she told him belligerently, although she wasn't certain he could hear her over the raucous crowd. "I'll deal with you once we're out of here."

He looked into her face and to her surprise, tears beaded at the corners of his hard, dark eyes. Taken aback, her firm grasp on his collar slackened and not exactly sure what she would say, she sank stiffly into a crouch to meet his glittering gaze.

"Steady now," she said as gently as she could while shouting to be heard above the din. "I know what you saw might scare you but—"

"You killed me." He sobbed and stared at her face with a watery glare.

"No, you don't understand," she said, shook her head, and winced when she realized the gash that began under her chin might be deeper than she'd thought. "That's what I am trying to tell you. I don't plan to hurt you, boy."

"No, you don't understand," he cried and beat a fist against her armored shoulder as his head lowered. "You killed me! It's all over now. I'm dead."

CHAPTER SEVEN

"From the look of him, I'd say he's an acolyte of one of the Bone-men cults," Vahrem explained as he brought a bowl of warm water and fresh linens.

They'd cleaned the wound that ran from below her chin to her lower lip, but *Mehk* Numi had insisted that the portion under the chin needed stitching. Ax-Wed wasn't looking forward to the process but at this point, she knew better than to argue with the venerable dwarfess.

"Bone-men? Those dead-buggering murderers?" Numi scrunched her nose up as though she smelled something foul. "I shudder to think what deviants like them would want with a sweet boy like that."

The merchant nodded as he deposited the bowl and linen before he stepped to the open tent door. Outside the entrance, a sizable fire blazed to keep the night chill at bay. Zoria sat with the rescued boy, one arm around his shoulders, while Iyshan strummed on a small harp and hummed a soft tune. The pierced child had been like one of the battle-stricken since his declaration on the arena floor. He could be lead around and his body moved as though each step was a burden, but he neither spoke nor seemed compelled to do anything for himself. His gaze had remained fixed on the ground as though raising it was more than he could manage.

"Sweet or not, the boy is probably dangerous." Vahrem sighed and stared through the aperture. "Each one of those pieces of bone in his body comes from confirmed kills."

Ax-Wed frowned and tried to crane her neck to get a better look at Zoria, but Numi's strong fingers seized her face in a gentle but inescapable grasp.

"Hold still now," the matriarch muttered as she inspected the wound, her threaded needle in one hand.

"But we don't know that he is one of the Bone-men," the warrior woman said out one side of her mouth. "Not for certain."

"Perhaps, but I suppose that means we don't know that you are Thulian," the caravan master said with a weary smile and continued to stare out the open tent. "But we know that if you aren't Thulian and he isn't Bone-men, you both went to considerable trouble to look like one."

"Fine. That is a fair point." She tried to nod but was rewarded by Numi's needle stabbing into the side of her wound.

"Hezkel two-backing!" she swore.

"Well, that's what you get for flapping yer trap while someone's trying to stitch you up," the old dwarf chided with a sharp cluck of her tongue. "Now hold still and shut up. I'll be done quickly enough."

Her teeth gritted audibly between her clenched jaws and she submitted herself to the needlework. If the truth be told, as someone who'd been patched together half a dozen times by battlefield surgeons and backstreet barbers, she knew good stitching and she could confirm that she was in the hands of an expert. No movement—and thus no pain—was wasted as she wove needle and thread masterfully.

"More important than if the boy is dangerous is who might come looking for him," the matriarch said, her squinted eyes almost lost in a nest of wrinkles. "If the Bone-men do have a claim on him, we could expect a visit from them very soon now."

Vahrem nodded and turned to face the tent interior, his broad shoulders now a little hunched.

"I know." The caravan master almost groaned as he came to inspect Numi's work, his arms folded. "Which is why I asked Emerik to have some of his sentries patrol around our camp."

"I'm sure that cost you," the old dwarf muttered as she bound a knot into place. "But do you think that will keep those monsters away? And exactly when are those beast-riders supposed to arrive?"

He paced to the tent door again and swept his gaze across the camp.

"They should be here soon," he responded reassuringly but with the slightest growl in the back of his throat. "And I don't know if it will dissuade the Bone-men, but it may even the odds somewhat as the only true warrior among us is wounded."

His gaze rested heavily on Ax-Wed and her cheeks reddened a little at the compliment, even though she knew it wasn't quite true. Several of the men in the caravan had training and she knew for a fact that Iyshan had once served as a soldier and was a damn fine one if she was any judge.

"This scratch won't slow me," she promised as she tried to look at him before Numi tightened her fingers in warning. "Assuming Numi gives me my head back."

"What use would I have for the foolish thing?" The old dwarfess snorted. "But if you don't stop talking, I'm liable to return it to you with your lips sewn shut as well."

The Thulian raised an eyebrow and leveled a fearsome glare at her, but the dwarf was too busy with her stitching to pay any mind. The warrior woman looked at Vahrem, who gave her a knowing smile and stalked to the tent door as he shook his head.

He stood silhouetted in the portal by the firelight and her gaze traced the outline of his frame through the fine robes he wore. True, he certainly was not the towering and chiseled specimen who had filled her childish dreams as a young woman growing up in Xhulth, but she'd begun to wonder if fantasies grown from men of marble and painted canvas could compare to creatures of flesh and blood. Men of stone, or even those seeking to be such, left a heart and a bed cold in her experience.

Could those heavy hands hold me close enough to melt the ice? Would they even want to?

"Well, that's done," Numi announced and pulled Ax-Wed from her musings. "It's not bad work if I do say so myself."

The Thulian made to rise but the elderly dwarf thrust a hand out to push her down again. Not wanting to snap her arm, she allowed the attempt without protest.

"Not so fast, lass." Numi grunted and seemed to rifle inside her garments. "We're not quite done yet."

"What now?" she grumbled but couldn't sustain her irritation as the dwarf matron wrestled about inside her clothes. "What are you doing?'

"Hush now," the old dwarf snapped with a huff before her hand finally emerged with a small bronze locket. "When you get as old as me, the difference between a wrinkle and a pocket is slight at best."

Ax-Wed wasn't sure whether she wanted to understand what the latter statement meant so instead, she waited and watched as the dwarfess popped the catch on the locket. Within it, the tiny bowl was filled with a dark green substance upon which rested the faintest glimmer of an oily sheen. Numi swiped a gnarled fingertip across it and collected a thin coat on one digit before she snapped the locket shut.

"What is that?" the patient asked as her Thulian-educated senses pricked at the faintest hint of magic.

"A balm that goes with a little charm I know to keep things clean," Numi explained as she moved toward the wound with her finger raised. "Now, hold still and no talking."

She spoke in a soft, guttural tongue unknown to the Thulian and the faintest embers of magic within the balm brightened like a rallying candlewick. The warmth of the charm spread with the salve across her wound. It was simple and relatively weak magic, nothing compared to the sorcery Ax-Wed, an admitted novice among her people in such matters, could bring to bear.

Yet it felt pure and untouched by the insidious corruptive influences that seemed woven into the fabric of the magic she knew.

"There." The matriarch sighed and stepped away. She seemed, impossibly, to have aged a little more with the effort. "Give it a moment to dry and tomorrow, you can wash it off."

"Thank you." She rose gratefully to her feet as Numi set about cleaning her hands with the linen. A combination of the evening's earlier events and then being stuck in one place as the old dwarfess worked had left her bones stiff and her muscles aching.

She stretched to her full height and her head almost brushed the tent ceiling. Her back popped several times and triggered relieved tingles to radiate down her legs.

"I don't remember it being so much work to sit still," she said as she moved to stand beside Vahrem.

The caravan master grunted but gave no answer as his gaze swept the edge of the camp repeatedly. One arm remained across his chest while his other was raised to run a hand over the point of his beard. His deep brown eyes shined beneath knitted brows in the firelight and without moving a muscle, he seemed to tremble with frustration.

"Emerik's men aren't here," Ax-Wed observed.

He nodded and his jaw worked in irritation.

"He was drunk," she said and tried to tread carefully as she began to talk to the merchant about a man he claimed was a very good friend. "Very drunk. Maybe he doesn't remember or didn't understand…"

She let the statement hang for a moment. He continued to tug his beard before he turned to look at her, his eyes smoldering. Before that burning gaze, she suddenly felt a desperate yearning for her mail-veiled helm as a shield and covering. She felt for a moment like he would see to the very heart of her and knew he wouldn't like what he saw there.

"Emerik uses his love for mead as a shield against consequence," he told her bluntly and anger flashed in the windows of his soul. "He'll swear to Anja that he made promises to me only because he was in the horn and then give in to her wrath for the same reason. I keep thinking he will remember the man he was before he became chieftain but each year, it seems hope dies a little more."

By the heat of his words, Ax-Wed realized it was pain and not wrath that stoked the fire. Somehow, that made it easier to bear his glare, even though she would rather he looked elsewhere.

"It is hard when friends change," she said and felt foolish as the words left her lips but uncertain what else she could say. "They change and forget what once mattered."

"Maybe." Vahrem tore his gaze away from her to scowl across the camp. "But I'm not sure it is the change that bothers me so much as what he's changed into. A drunk can't be trusted and a double-minded friend even less so."

The Thulian turned with him to the tent opening but instead of studying the camp, her gaze settled on Zoria and the boy. He had begun to nod and when the girl drew his head into her lap, he didn't argue, although he still stared blankly at the fire.

In the firelight, Ax-Wed realized how Zoria, still so small and childish in frame, seemed more like a woman in her face and bearing. It was an ongoing source of wonder that at some moments, the girl felt like a child to be tended to and reprimanded and at other times, seemed like a sister who only needed her support. For the warrior woman, who had been neither mother nor sister, it was an incredibly uncomfortable situation. Still, she felt that it somehow fit like a key to a lock.

She raised her gaze from the girl and realized that Iyshan had set his harp down for the moment. He continued to hum softly as he tended the fire and kept the youths company, the rest of the camp already having settled in for the night. At the edge of the camp, the figures of the first watch stood sentinel over their sleeping friends and family.

"Let's hope the Bone-men don't come then," she said and feeling more than a little foolish, added, "although I'm not sure exactly who or what they are."

Vahrem spared her a curious glance followed by a conciliatory half-smile.

"Forgive me. I forget that you've never been this far north," he said heavily as he turned to watch the camp. "And that you've never had the pleasure of being around the White Cult of Perukh and its deranged followers."

The caravan master's hand left his beard and both arms settled across his chest as he drew a deep breath.

"The White Cult of Perukh is a collection of Vitzerka of various tribes who have dedicated themselves to Perukh the Striker, a god of not death but killing. They serve him only and are dedicated to killing, preferably with violence and against a worthy opponent. As long as they can claim a piece of bone from the victim, they are not overly selective as each kill is a totem they believe elevates them before Perukh. That is where they get their name from—each claimed kill is commemorated by driving a bone through their flesh. The decoration doesn't necessarily have to be from the victim as long as it is approved by a skull-keeper—what passes for a priest among them."

Vahrem nodded to the boy at the fire, whose eyes had finally closed as his breath rose and fell in a steady rhythm.

"It is part warrior fraternity, part religious heresy, so I am surprised he has already been inducted," the merchant said and the lines about his eyes seemed to deepen as he spoke. "But if he earned those bones, perhaps a group of Bone-men took him in as a promising acolyte."

Ax-Wed's gaze rose from the boy to Zoria and a strange, almost perverse thought squirmed through her mind.

Perhaps that's what drew her to him—the smell of death reaching out to Zoria...and to me.

"If they wear these tokens openly, how do the Bone-men mingle with other tribes?" she asked as she fought to shake the invasive thought from her mind. "I can't imagine that any sane person would want such zealots lurking anywhere near them."

He chuckled and while it might have been at her expense, she was glad to hear him laugh, even if only for a moment.

"I'm not sure I'd ever accuse a people who tame mammoths of being sane," he replied. "The truth is that as long as the Bone-men keep their weapons turned toward the enemies of the tribe most of the time, most are quite happy to tolerate their presence."

"Even though they know the fanatics might one day turn on them?" she asked. "That they must turn on them if they are to be faithful to their god?"

Vahrem opened his mouth to answer, but the words faltered in his throat as a sharp whistle rose from the edge of the camp, followed quickly by another. The warrior woman moved her hand to the head of her weapon before he turned to her, his face grave. One whistle meant someone was coming. Two meant they didn't appear friendly.

"We have company and it's not Emerik's riders," he said and squinted into the murky darkness before he called over his shoulder. "Numi, get some of your dwarves to stand guard at my tent. I'll go to meet our visitors."

Without bothering to wait for a reply, he strode out of the tent with the warrior woman following.

As he swept past the fire, Iyshan moved to fall in beside him but the merchant shook his head and pointed to Zoria and the boy.

"Get them into my tent," he instructed. "Numi will station some dwarves to stand guard. You keep watch over them until they arrive."

The manservant patted his new saber at his hip as he nodded and stooped to take the slumbering boy from Zoria's lap.

"W-what's'appening?" the girl slurred and struggled into some semblance of wakefulness.

The boy didn't stir.

"Follow Iyshan," Ax-Wed instructed and hauled her ward to her unsteady feet with one arm. "He'll show you where you can sleep next to the boy."

"Boy?" Zoria muttered and swung her head heavily from side to side before she yawned and saw Iyshan carrying the limp form into Vahrem's tent. "Oh, the boy."

"Go," the Thulian urged her as gently as she could and mercifully, the girl made no protest and merely lurched after them.

Vahrem had already continued to the edge of camp and the warrior woman hurried to catch up, eating up the ground between them with her long strides. As she rushed past, she saw faces peeking out from the tents and covered wagons of the camp as bleary eyes squinted into the dark. Up ahead, four sentries had formed a line opposite a far larger group of figures.

She slowed to a determined walk and fell in beside the merchant, her hand still upon grinning Thulian sylver.

"Whisper of the Serpent and he is in the grass," he muttered as they approached what had begun to feel like a battle line. "Shepherd have mercy."

"What?" she asked as the group opposite the sentries resolved into several armed men.

"This is not good," the caravan master rumbled in his chest as the first angry challenge roared through the night air.

"Stand aside or I'll add you to my totems, little man!"

CHAPTER EIGHT

They wore the forms of women—or at least something like a woman. In truth, none of the retainers or Durzag had ever seen such beautiful creatures, but the sight of their cruel, red lips threatened to chill the blood.

"Such strong, hairy, virile brutes," one of them purred as it swayed lasciviously down the street, its hips swinging with a stirring rhythm. "And their beasts are quite impressive too."

The laughter that rose at the jest was like bells chiming in chorus, but Dragahn's retainers groaned at the sound and even their warlord felt a shiver run down his spine. The others swaggered with flaunting gestures and tantalizing movements and their pale flesh shined with the reflected light of the ice around them. Long, delicate fingers tugged and flounced the gossamer gowns that flowed around their bodies and drew lingering gazes.

"Have you come to be with me?" another moaned and traced the outline of her body with dagger-sharp fingers. "To warm me in your burly arms until we cry your names to the heavens?"

Belug, his hands trembling, nudged his mammoth toward the speaker, his eyes wide with terror but his skin flushed with longing. Behind him, his lancer could barely keep his knees from knocking as he leaned forward hungrily.

"Have me now!" cried a third and arched her back. "Take me with your crushing hands and bruising kisses. Show me your ruthless lust that I may burn in your fire."

Volu's skin was the color of milk but he licked his lips as he turned his mount toward the creatures.

"I need you," the first panted and now crawled across the ice in a shivering, slithering rush. "I need you like I have never needed anything! Come to me!"

With a clank of chains, Kollung started forward and the warlord leaned forward in the saddle.

"Yes, yesss…come." All three beckoned with a sibilant hiss. "Come to usss."

Kollung's pace quickened with the invitation as his master stood in the stirrups, his heavy sinews taut and marred face stretched into a wild grin.

"Come, come to—"

The mammoth's trot had increased to a thundering run and rune-carved tusks were leveled as the rush became a charge. The red mouths twisted into feral snarls to reveal row upon row of hook-like fangs, but it was too late. Kollung fell upon them like an avalanche. The one on the ground was pulped by his tread, another took a tusk through its chest, and the last sought to jerk aside but was hurled against an ice-framed building with one toss of the beast's head.

The impaled one squirmed and clawed at engraved ivory while the veil fell away. Every mortal eye could see the shriveled hags with skin like a bruise, red mouths like a nest of barbs, and garments of tattered hide that still bore the faces of their victims.

Before Kollung cast the wretch off with a shake of his head, the fiend threw its head back and uttered a keening howl. It seemed the call was taken up by some fiend in every street across the city, a terrible baying of infernal hounds set loose.

"Demons—a nest of them," Dragahn bellowed and wheeled his mount to face his stupefied retainers. "To the central spire! Move, damn you!"

In the end, it was instinct that spared his men from being left stunned and vulnerable on that icy street. Over a decade of following him into battle had beaten a dogged determination into them to do as he said and go wherever he bade them. With mouths still slack and eyes not yet unglazed, they stirred their mammoths to follow the lead beast's crushing tread as they raced through the streets to the very heart of Hoarlin.

The wailed hunting cries along with the sharp cracks of ice under their beasts' tread eventually dragged the men from their stupor. Each one, retainer and lancer, swore bitterly and took a weapon in hand, eager to answer their disgrace with blood.

But for all the tumult, only flashes of dark forms and darting shadows pursued them as they proceeded down the street.

"Dey're ev'ryw'ere!" Belug snarled around his mangled jaw and his topknot whipped wildly as he swept his gaze from side to side. "We're zurroun'ed!"

"Good!" Volu growled with battle ire as he urged his mammoth toward scurrying sounds from an icy alley. "It means less time wasted hunting them."

"Stay together!" Dragahn roared. "If they separate us, we are dead."

Volu cursed viciously but corrected his trajectory to run at Kollung's flank again.

For a time, it was like a nightmare where every second spent rushing down the broad, frost-encased street seemed to position them farther from the spire. Hoarlin appeared to stretch forever and each building looked the same under a shell of ice. The only thing that changed for some time was the growing sounds of the fiends that scuttled and howled out of sight. Before the illusion of the eternal thoroughfare broke, the air trembled with the cacophony of the creatures that lurked around every corner with bright crimson smiles.

"We should turn back," Belug's lancer wailed and clutched a javelin with both hands as though it were a lifeline. "This is madness."

The topknotted retainer's spine went rigid and he gave his mount his head as he spun in the saddle. He rose in the stirrups, caught the man on the platform by the throat, and drew him nose to nose.

"Wunt teh go back?" he rumbled as muscles knotted across his back and shoulder. "Go!"

He hurled the lancer from the mammoth's back and the man screamed as he landed heavily upon the ice. They thundered on while fiends swarmed out from their hiding places like rats scenting carrion. The lancer struggled to his feet, still clutching the javelin for support, but one arm now hung limply at his side and the bone of the upper arm pushed against the skin above the elbow. The doomed man had time only for a final terrified shriek before the red mouths descended on him in a hissing, sucking flood.

"Well done," Volu shouted jauntily as they continued their headlong race down the street.

"Shhut'p!" Beleg retorted and sent the brawny mustached retainer into a fit of laughter.

Dragahn seemed ignorant of the episode and merely urged Kollung forward until, like a cork bursting from a bottle, they rushed out of the thoroughfare into a wide plaza. At the heart of that freezing plain was the central spire, a tower of ivory bound in a pristine prison of ice. A squat wall surrounded its base and one section jutted forward into what must have been a courtyard at the entrance to the towering edifice that reached heavenward with strength and arrogance that seemed to resonate within the very architecture.

"How is this possible?" Volu exclaimed as he craned his neck to try to comprehend the enormity of the structure. "What kinds of gods built such a thing?"

"Not gods. Men," Dragahn said and lashed at Kollung with the chains. "Men greater than any who walk the world now."

"Storm-Callers," Tadzi whispered in reverence. "The god-tamers who once ruled every land whose rivers feed the Caged Sea."

"I thought they were stories," the other retainer admitted as they crunched across the plaza, conscious of the gathering malicious presence of the swarming creatures as they lurked around the plaza. "Tales for children around midwinter fires."

The sounds of the gathering fiends rose to a fever pitch when they reached the ice-barred gates of the spire courtyard. When they looked over their shoulders, the retainers saw that a ripple of bruised bodies with hungry red mouths had begun to spread across the plaza like a stain. Still, their leader's eyes were fixed only on the gates.

"Forward, Kollung!" he commanded and lashed mercilessly with the chains in his fist. "Forward!"

Weary from the rush through the city and uncertain of the strange scents offending his trunk, the mighty mammoth found the might and will to drive forward in the pain and certainty of his master's will. He trumpeted an angry bellow from deep within his cavernous chest and hurtled the last half-dozen strides to power through the frozen gate in a shower of raking ice shards and piercing splinters of wood.

Momentum carried Dragahn's mount into the courtyard. He cracked frigid stones beneath his massive feet until, too late to stop, one foot made impact with a pool that seemed like a sheet of black glass. The layer of ice quivered and with a tremendous crack, gave way. Still fighting to slow his bulky inertia, Kollung pitched tusks-first into the dark waters below.

Dragahn and Tadzi sprang free of the plunging mammoth in time to clutch at a dais of stone that rose from the frozen pool.

Kicking and scrambling, they managed to haul themselves to level ground while beneath them, the mammoth thrashed in the cripplingly cold waters. His dark eyes rolled in sudden terror as he fought to climb out of the pool, but it was deep and everything around him was ice that gave way when his bulk tried to gain purchase.

The dire situation became even worse when Belug and Volu rushed into the courtyard with their beasts, who found the pool exactly as Kollung had. Like their warlord and his sword-bearer, the two retainers leapt clear with practiced ease but their beasts plunged into the waters atop the flailing Kollung. Volu's lancer was not so lucky and struck the side of the dais before he tumbled into the water in stunned silence. He was instantly lost and forgotten amidst the chaos.

As the three mammoths fought the impossible depths and each other, the pool became a churning, roiling soup of pulverized ice, wailing beasts, and dark, frothing waters. Trunks cast about like the hands of the ocean-doomed while their tusks gouged the ice and each other. Slowly and painfully, the three great beasts succumbed to the unnatural cold and the suffocating waters that eventually settled. Chunks of ice bobbed in the black pool that gave no hint as to the titans it had swallowed.

Four men stood upon the dais and their breath plumed in front of their faces as their gazes rose slowly from the grave of their trusted beasts to the walls of the courtyard. Hisses and snarls could be heard as claws bit and scratched over ice. The first grinning faces appeared and lank hair dangled over eyes that shined with ghastly hunger. A heartbeat later, the walls teemed with stooped, emaciated shapes and some even crawled on all fours like beasts.

"Come to usss." The hissed invitation issued from hundreds of shriveled, thrusting throats.

Belug, Tadzi, and Volu turned to their warlord, pale-faced and wide-eyed, but as before, Dragahn's gaze was fixed beyond their petty concerns. He looked at the middle of the dais on which they stood and saw the altar of rough-hewn stones positioned beneath an immense disk of black stone. The altar and the sable circle appeared to be the only things in all of Hoarlin untouched by the unrelenting ice, and when he stepped closer to lay a hand upon the stones, he found them as warm to the touch as willing flesh.

The red-mouthed horrors began to creep from the walls and into the courtyard while he inspected the altar. The warlord tilted his head to one side as though listening to something only he could hear as the fiends gathered at the edge of the water. A fell wind stirred and raced with a whistle over the teeth of the courtyard battlements, and the retainers shivered.

"Tadzi, attend me," he commanded without bothering to turn. "The rest of you, see we are not disturbed."

"Rest of you?" Volu muttered and looked at Belug, who only shrugged as he tightened his grasp on a narrow-headed ax in one hand and a long-bladed knife in the other.

The brawny retainer's mustache twitched into a smile and he flexed his fingers around the haft of a short stabbing spear to shake off the stiffening cold.

"Remember that time at the Terlioch River?" he asked and half-turned to note that some of the creatures were gathering for a jump. "When the Hujali had us pinned against those rocks at the waterfall?"

Belug nodded and what passed for a smile pulled at the mismatched corners of his mouth.

"A gewd day." He grunted and raised the ax in salute

"A good day," Volu agreed and brandished his spear as the first of the fiends sprang at the dais, its body arced into the leap. The red mouth stretched to reveal a grotesque nest of fangs, but it only tasted an iron spearhead.

Behind the embattled men, Dragahn whispered and muttered as his gaze darted from the altar to the black disk that loomed overhead. His sword-bearer stepped to his side and struggled to keep his attention on the warlord and not the descending horde of demons.

"Tadzi," he said and his gaze settled on the altar with a weighty stare. "Blade."

Fighting to not dishonor the venerable sword with his trembling hands, he extended it to his master. The warlord's massive hand closed around the hilt and drew the brutal piece of steel with a deliberation at odds with the frantic movements of mortal struggle around him.

The sword-bearer studied his leader and for the first time in their many years of bloodshed and wandering, saw hesitancy and doubt. His sharpened teeth clacked together as he rocked with almost physical pain. Dragahn Shieldshiver uncertain drove a spike of fear through the retainer's soul deeper than any demon could.

What in all this world could have shaken the certainty of such a leader, a man he'd followed through the jaws of death more times than he could count? What could fate ask that he would not give, now at the utmost end of need?

Volu screamed and Belug snarled as they struck repeatedly but the tide continued to rise, ready to drag them down.

"Please," Tadzi cried. "Not after everything. You can't lose heart now."

Dragahn turned to his sword-bearer and the world seemed ready to crumble. Tears, heavy and glittering like the ice around them, raced down the warlord's scarred cheeks.

"You never doubted did you, little brother?" he whispered and the words passed his lips like a funerary invocation. Tadzi, his black eyes stinging with tears, stared at him in confusion in the moment before his master seized him around the neck, raised his squirming body, and pounded it upon the altar. Bones snapped in his back as his body folded around the rough-hewn stones, and breathing suddenly became a burden. He looked at his warlord and tried to stretch his hand beseechingly toward him, but his limbs would not answer his calls.

The blade's tip drove into his heart and his eyes rolled upward toward the sable circle that yawned above like a black sun. As his last breath slipped between his chiseled teeth, he thought it looked like the Void had opened to swallow him.

Horrors clung to Volu with their ravening maws but he laughed like a man drunk at a feast before he threw himself into the pool and dragged his killers with him. Belug was already sprawled on the dais and his fingers strained toward the knife he'd dropped as he was submerged by half a dozen fiends who buried their faces in his flesh. With a sob, he snatched the blade up and thrust it in the skull of the monster slurping at his chest before he turned the edge on his own throat with a curse.

Dragahn, Wind-Spoken of Perukh, drew a heavy breath and tightened his hands around the hilt of his sword. The hardest part was over. Whatever came—destiny, doom, or both—he would face it knowing he'd already killed the last part of himself that could die.

Somewhere within him, syllables separated from mental cocoons driven into the darkened fabric of his mind.

Speak my words, said the whisper that had known him since he was a child. *Speak my words and take the key.*

In defiance of the hungry eyes turned toward him, he let the syllables rise out of him like a swarm of razor-winged flies, buzzing and jagged, until their droning became an incantation from his tearing, splitting lips. They spewed upward, wet and trembling as they raced toward the black disk, drawn like insects to nocturnal brilliance, and gathered thickly on the black stone until they formed a glistening coat of blood and unlight.

With a final shiver, Dragahn fell silent and the stream through his shredded lips ceased as he slumped against the sword driven through the heart of his brother. Strands of blood and rent flesh from his ruined mouth dangled, but all he could see were Tadzi's empty eyes looking through him.

"I am almost there." He coughed and spattered red droplets on the slack features before he straightened and dragged the sword from the stilled breast.

The warlord stood surrounded by a ring of gleaming eyes and gaping mouths. The fiends darted nervous looks at the disk but when they focused on the ragged figure again, hunger began to beat back their fear.

"Oursss now." They sighed through hooked fangs.

The warlord managed to curl one corner of his mouth in disgust and with an exultant cry, thrust the blade upward.

The tip, dipped in Tadzi's blood, met the sorcery-encrusted circle overhead with a sound like the mountains splintering. The black disk crumbled like a curtain of ash and tumbled like corrupted snow, but before each flake could land upon the dais, a sudden gust drove them back to the upthrust sword. Where they met steel, darkness bloomed until the sword, from blade to pommel, was jet-black but still more of the ashen motes came.

Pain seared his hand as though the hilt had grown a dozen thorns and he stared as the veins on his hands and arms blackened beneath the skin. The darkness spread through him and it was like the thorns had worked into his blood vessels to pour ice venom everywhere they could not carve through.

By force of will alone, Dragahn kept his feet, although his upraised arms lowered and the black sword's blade touched the icy surface of the dais.

Whisps of gray steam rose and in the blink of an eye, the ice was gone.

"Imposssible," the horrors whined and drew his heavy glare and a suspicion of a smile.

"You should run," he whispered and felt as though his limbs were lead when he raised the sword before him. The fiends hesitated for only a moment, then in a flurry of clawing hands and spindly limbs, they fought to be the first to escape the dais. In the end, they merely presented a tantalizing if tangled target for him.

The warlord descended upon them like a thunderbolt and in seconds, the black blade had reduced them all to smoldering husks while their ichor rose as an acrid smoke from the blade. The horde gathered around the pool took one look at the fate of their companions and as one, decided there was a darkness at work beyond their petty cravings. Screeching and scrambling, they fled the courtyard and the plaza beyond.

Dragahn Shieldshiver stood amongst the blackened remains. He was still so incredibly weary but knew there was more to do —so much more.

He turned to the altar and held the black sword before his eyes. Despite the blood in his mouth and throat, all he could taste was ash when he whispered blasphemous words.

A gory smile spread across his face as Tadzi's body began to smoke and sizzle and finally rise.

CHAPTER NINE

"What seems to be the problem here?" Vahrem asked, his voice steady and even.

Ax-Wed was a little surprised that he had not unleashed the booming voice he used when he wished to stir men and cow bullies. It was a voice fit for the battlefield and although she would never admit it to him, she often enjoyed hearing him use it.

But one look at the assembly before them informed her of the caravan master's wisdom.

In the dimness at the edge of the camp, it was hard to see them all clearly but no less than a dozen men, perhaps more, stood opposite the sentries. Each was well-armed, although proper armor seemed in short supply as she saw an abundance of pale flesh bared on their bodies despite the chill in the air. A glance at this scarred flesh and the osseous decorations driven through it seemed proof positive that they were the Bone-men. If what Vahrem had explained about their practices was correct, each man was a seasoned killer with a dozen or more kills to their name.

His eyes narrowed, the merchant planted his feet firmly despite what he faced.

"Move out of the way," demanded a lithe man whose lower lip was studded with what appeared to be finger bones. "We have business with one in your camp."

The man took a small step forward but Vahrem did not budge. He seemed rooted to the earth but when he spoke, his tone was warm and almost friendly.

"Who is it? Perhaps I could bring them out to you?"

"They are trying to delay us," one of the Bone-men snarled to reveal sharpened teeth beneath a nose that resembled a waterfall of bone disks from bridge to nostril. "He wishes to keep us from her."

Her. Ax-Wed froze and although it was hard to tell in the dark, she thought she saw her companion's implacable expression flicker for an instant.

"So it is a woman you seek?" he asked. "Well, I doubt very much if we have any woman who would interest men such as you, but let me have her name and I will be able to at least tell you if you are in the right place."

Some of the group looked ready to draw weapons and rush forward, but the one with the bristling lower lip held a hand up and they settled reluctantly.

"We know she is here," the fanatic said and his eyes and teeth glittered in the distant firelight. "She passed through the Lecall gate and all know you trade feeds and pet horses with the Lecall. There is no doubt that Svarah Vjetgo is in your camp."

Her stomach knotted painfully.

Only two females— humans, at least—had passed through the Lecall gate beneath Emerick's pavilion. As best she could tell, only one of them had been called Svarah Vjetgo. She knew they were looking for her and the fact that they hadn't recognized the silhouette with the sentries behind Vahrem was probably a benefit of the dim light, but that could not be relied upon to keep her hidden for long.

"I don't know anyone by that name," the caravan master said with a shrug. "Does she perhaps go by another name? I'd hate to go looking and start on the wrong track."

"Move," the lithe man snarled and a sword licked out from his belt. "We're moving in to look for her and if you or any of yours get in my way, they'll join my collection of trophies. Now stand aside!"

Several things happened at once.

The Bone-men immediately pressed forward led by the spokesman with the drawn sword, who put his free hand out to either grab or shove Vahrem. At the same time, Ax-Wed stepped around the caravan master and drew her weapon in one smooth motion. The man with finger bones in his lip had only the blink of an eye in which to register her presence and turn before the haft of her ax caught him under his outstretched arm and shoved him back against his fellows. She didn't drive after him which was just as well as his blade flashed in return and a step farther would have seen her face opened.

Despite this, she didn't hesitate as she positioned herself implacably before them with her ax held at the ready.

"Are you looking for me?" She growled deep in her throat. "I'm flattered."

For a moment that was almost comical if not for the promise of death and dismemberment that hung in the air, the Bone-men squinted into the dark to determine if she was indeed Svarah Vjetgo, whatever that meant. When the squints became wide-eyed glares, however, something even more absurd happened. A ripple of whispers all repeating the strange title she had first heard in the Thunder-Crush arena swept around them and to a man, all of them dropped to one knee and bowed their heads.

Confused, the Thulian glanced at Vahrem, but the merchant looked as surprised as she felt.

"Svarah Vjetgo," the spokesman intoned reverently as his head remained bowed in deference. "You must come with us."

She looked past the grin of her ax and refused to lower the weapon despite the sudden outpouring of honor from the fanatics.

"Why?" she asked, her tone almost as sharp as the Thulian sylver in front of her. "I don't know you."

Several confused looks were exchanged among the Bone-men and a sudden burst of whispered and grunted instructions and exhortations from the kneeling men in their own tongue. As best she could tell, the words were all directed at the man with the drawn sword, who nodded several times as he listened before he issued a sharp command that silenced the others.

"You are the Svarah Vjetgo," the lithe man said as if that was an answer in and of itself. "It is only right and proper that we bring you to a conclave of the followers of Perukh as quickly as possible so the Perukh Vjetgo may present himself."

Her narrowed gaze swept the congregation of kneeling murderers, certain there was some trick being played. What were they on about and why did everyone keep calling her by that name?

"Vjetgo... Vjetgo?" Vahrem muttered behind Ax-Wed. "Wind talk? No wind—"

"Wind-Spoken," one of the Bone-men offered helpfully.

"Thank you," the merchant said distractedly before he raised his voice to address them. "So you believe she is the Wind-Spoken of Svarah? Svarah the goddess?"

"It has been witnessed," the leader said and several of his companions nodded vigorously. "The chosen of Svarah, Dragon-Slayer and Guardian Goddess, has always appeared before the people with the striking down of two beasts. It is as in the days of legend when Svarah saved the children of mortals by felling two hell wyrms that came to devour them."

Ax-Wed stared at the man as though he were still talking an incomprehensible foreign language.

"What?" she asked and her mind reeled.

Vahrem cleared his throat and she could somehow hear the edge of a smile on his lips

"It seems," the merchant began as he stepped forward to stand at her shoulder, "that they believe your heroic defense of our young friends in the arena today is proof that you are the chosen of a dragon-smiting goddess."

Her weapon still held before her, she swiveled first one way then the other to stare in bemusement at the Bone-men and the caravan master in turn.

"What—no!" she protested. "There were no dragons, only those *Strajkubo* creatures. Those are not dragons."

Vahrem shrugged.

"In ancient days, it is said," the lithe man began and recounted the details as though prepared for this argument, "that the Scaled Kings of Fire and Wind, jealous of the gods as they fashioned mortal men, made the scaled creatures like the *Strajkubo* to be akin to their offspring. In these degenerate days soon to be brought to a merciful end, a *Strajkubo* is as close to a true dragon as any could hope to see."

Incredulity stole over the warrior woman and her guard lowered incrementally as she looked at the assembly of bowed men. In a strange, demented way, she could see how the myth they described could be made to fit what happened in the amphitheater, but that they would take it as proof positive of her being divinely chosen seemed nothing short of madness. Besides, when she'd once acted the privateer along the Scadish coast, their ship was almost destroyed by something much closer to a dragon than the feathered creatures she fought in the arena.

One look at the bone-adorned men, however, told her that she was unlikely to convince any of them that they were wrong.

"Where is this conclave?" Ax-Wed asked, hoping that with

more information she could find her bearings or at least have more time to think. "And why do I need to be there?"

"The conclave lies at the heart of the Steppes known only to true Bone-men who have made the pilgrimage to where Perukh struck the earth," the spokesman explained. "And as I said, you will wait there for Perukh Vjetgo, the Wind-Spoken of Perukh."

Ax-Wed held her weapon at arm's length with the haft resting on her thighs.

"Yes, you said I must wait for him, but why?" she pressed, afraid she was about to be told she was destined—or doomed—according to their mad faith to wed one of their choicest madmen.

"Once Perukh Vjetgo arrives, you shall join the Eternal Dance as it has been ever before," the leader explained and Ax-Wed had to fight the urge to groan. "If you survive, your body will be broken as an offering of thanks to the gods and if he is victorious, it finally begins."

She stared at him in silence, surprised by the turn of events. All she could think was that the Eternal Dance was not the nuptial event she had first imagined it to be.

"What begins?" Vahrem asked, a note of uneasiness in his tone if not his expression.

The spokesman for the Bone-men raised his head for the first time since she had revealed herself. His eyes flashed with a feverish light and she suppressed a shudder.

"The End," he breathed and the word came from his lips like the name of his beloved.

"End of what?" She suspected that she knew the answer but her dread fascination with the creatures before her turned rapidly into disgust. Even with their heads bowed, she could see the gathered men wore wistful, longing expressions. A few of them even seemed to tremble with what she could only assume was anticipation.

"Everything," the leader said, his face rapturous, and tears began to well in his eyes. "That has ever been Perukh's promise to us and all of existence. Some day, he—the Striker and the Ender—would strike this rotting reality and bring an end to it."

"Do you mean to end it and bring about a better, newer world?" Vahrem asked cautiously and his gaze searched the bowed faces. He was rewarded with a chorus of what must have been curses and sudden scowls from the men.

"That is Zhibogian heresy," the spokesman pronounced frostily. "True worshippers of Perukh understand and know that there is nothing after the End. Once the Striker has led us in that final scouring, he will grant us all the gift of the annihilation and turn the last blow upon himself. Then there will be only pure and unending oblivion, a return to the truth of what once was before the offense of the gods."

Vahrem and Ax-Wed shared a horrified glance at the apocalyptic confession and with a quick look over their shoulders, both noted that Iyshan walked quietly from the camp with several of the men and dwarves with him, all armed for violence. She gave Vahrem a level look and the merchant responded with a slight nod as he surreptitiously shifted back half a step .

"And what if I don't want to go with you?" she asked and her fingers tightened fractionally around the haft held at her thighs.

With a ripple like a snake coiling for a strike, the reverence radiating from those gathered changed. Hands strayed to hilts and hafts as bone-festooned flesh grew taut over clenching, gathering sinew.

"You will be treated with all honor and lavished with the very best that can be had among our people," the lithe man said as he rose slowly to his feet, his sword still in hand. "Your safety and strength are precious to us for without vigor, you cannot join the Eternal Dance and thus bring about the End."

With no word or flourish, Iyshan and his reinforcements assembled along the flanks of the original four sentries. The Thulian noted the change although she didn't look directly at them and decided that she liked this arrangement far better. The men and dwarves of the caravan numbered at least as many as the Bone-men now if not more, and while she didn't doubt that the fanatics were ferocious fighters, a lack of armor and shields meant that ferocity could only count for so much against the doughty resistance that would be presented.

"That wasn't what I asked," she said and the grim smile that spread across her face tugged at the stitches in her chin. "But I think I have my answer and now, you have mine."

She raised her ax before her and her voice became a leonine snarl.

"Leave here now and you might live to see your mad god's fever dream come true."

A smirk made the finger bones in the spokesman's face wriggle before he moved, ready to bat the weapon out of her hand with the flat of his sword. Her sylver-smiled weapon moved as well but for a far more permanent disarmament.

The ax swept down and both the attacking sword and grasping arm fell after a single blow. The mortally wounded Bone-man uttered a short, sharp cry, but she couldn't decide if it was pain or ecstasy that drove the words as he collapsed to one knee.

"Svet'nisto…" He groaned as the blood spurted from his wound. "Glorious."

A moment later, he collapsed and everything happened very quickly.

It seemed that half the group was eager to follow their compatriot into oblivion, while the other half seemed content for that great day to find them. As a result, several Bone-men rose and sought to draw weapons but their fleeing friends complicated things when bodies collided and limbs entangled.

In that moment of confusion and hesitation, Ax-Wed spearheaded the attack on the disorganized zealots. In the space of a few seconds, almost a third of the foe were dead and most of the rest were running, although she and Iyshan each had time to duel a ferocious foe before it was finally over.

The warrior woman's opponent was a hulking brute with two stone-headed maces that he wielded like willow wands. More than once, his blows rang against her armor but thankfully, the battle-tested plates and mail held together and gave her time to execute a feint that put the warrior off-balance.

Exposed as he was and with nothing to protect him, she almost pitied him as her grinning blade parted flesh and bone from the yoke of his shoulder to his breastbone. The pity vanished, though, when she saw the dull smile creep across the Bone-man's face as he fell.

"Zealots," she muttered, shook her head, and turned in time to see Iyshan parry a wide swing from a snarling adversary with a spear.

The manservant darted back, as nimble as a dancer, when the longer weapon thrust toward him with a stabbing point. Vahrem, having snatched a blade from the dead, lunged at the spear wielder's side with a ferocious strike through the ribs. The Bone-man tried to twist to face his attacker as blood welled in his mouth, but the caravan master drove his weight forward and pitched him onto the earth. With a heavy, red cough, he rolled onto his side with the hilt of the stabbing sword jutting from his ribs. He shuddered once and lay still.

All this had taken place in a handful of heartbeats, but Ax-Wed drew in slow, weighty breaths and after a moment, steadied herself by leaning on her weapon.

Vahrem surveyed the scene quickly and was pleased to see that no one from the caravan lay among the fallen. A few had sustained superficial wounds in the Bone-men's death throes but by and large, nothing of much concern except perhaps a sizable tear in his fine robes.

"Iyshan, take a handful and do a sweep through the camp," he instructed as he looked out into the dark. "We can't have any more surprises tonight."

The man saluted with his saber and set off as he called the names of those to follow him.

"The rest of you, gather this mess and bury them in a ditch." He sighed. "The last thing we need is the children to come out tomorrow and stumble over corpses."

With stout nods but also a few deep sighs, the men went to work.

"Well, I suppose that's what I get for dressing to impress," the merchant muttered as he moved toward Ax-Wed and scowled at the damaged garment. "I suppose that is why we can't have nice things."

She smiled but it was an effort as the events of the day weighed heavily on her.

"I suppose so," she said and leaned a little more heavily on her ax. "But I imagine a torn robe will be the least of our worries."

He nodded and stood next to her as they surveyed the broken bodies upon the ground.

"You go and get some rest," he said. "Tomorrow morning, you and I will have a very uncomfortable conversation with a very hungover Emerik."

CHAPTER TEN

Suffice it to say that Vahrem's prediction was, if anything, an understatement.

Emerik lay limp and listless on the fur-mounded bench in his tent and Ax-Wed wondered if some of the Bone-men in a ditch between their camps might have more life. Certainly, they'd be more useful and perhaps most painfully, Vahrem was aware of that fact.

"Emerik!" the merchant said sharply and a trace of heat slid into his tone. "Are you even listening?"

Perhaps the third time's the charm, she thought as she resigned herself to the fact that he would have to explain the situation yet again to the insensate man.

The chieftain groaned and lolled his head to one side and then another as though the weight of it was too much for him to bear. Bloodshot eyes rolled in sunken sockets until they finally came to rest upon Anja, who stood to one side and looked as sour and disapproving as she had the night before.

"Anja… Anja, my love," he croaked and made a pitiful pawing motion toward her with one hand. "Fetch me… Ugh, my head… Fetch me something to drink, would you?"

Her every movement stiff and jerky, the woman stepped aside to comply and a strange expression of one part guilt and one part disgust wormed across her face. She had only taken a few steps when Vahrem, with an angry snort, raised a hand and turned to the chieftain's wife.

"Hold on, Anja," he said with an irate look at Emerik. "I'll fetch him something to drink. While I do that, maybe you can convince him that we have something serious to discuss."

"If he ever listened to me, he wouldn't be in this condition," she replied in as flat and cold a voice as her eyes promised. "But there's mead in Bisera's tent since I at least have made sure he won't bring it into ours."

The caravan master appeared ready to say something but he swallowed the words that must have been hard and sharp given how difficult it seemed to be to keep them to himself. He decided instead to draw a long breath through his nose and nod before he left the tent.

Ax-Wed, perhaps a little slower on the uptake due to the fitful sleep she'd had, suddenly realized that he had left her alone—or as good as—with Anja. As she raised her coppery gaze to the chieftain's wife, she realized she might have preferred to be in the arena with a score of killer lizard-birds than stuck in the tent with the glaring woman.

Emerik seemed to have slipped into unconsciousness again, so nothing except his steady breathing interrupted the silence as blue eyes did their best to bore a hole through the Thulian. Still without her helm, she felt naked but returned the glare with a flat stare, determined to not let the chieftain's wife see how she squirmed internally at the hostile attention.

This must be part of Mother's curse. She groaned mentally. *That woman always knew exactly what would make me miserable and by all the gods, this might be the worst. And where in all the hells is Vahrem? How long does it take to get a drunk the hair of the dog that bit him?*

The tension stretched to a trembling point where she wasn't

certain if she would cry out with relief or scream when Vahrem returned. With a sound like a sniff, Anja's mouth curled into an ugly smile to match the cutting laugh that followed.

"You're scared of me," she declared and her eyes flashed. "Aren't you?"

You'd still be wondering what happened when pieces of you hit the floor. Ax-Wed seethed internally. *But she's not entirely wrong.*

"I'm ill-suited for diplomacy," she admitted but refused to break eye contact. "I prefer steel and blood to smiles and lies."

The woman laughed and every note of the sound seemed a weapon.

"How poetic if utterly redundant." The chieftain's wife nodded mockingly at her. "With one look at you, I can tell you'd be better suited to playing some Storm-Caller war-princess on a sweltering southern battlefield than being a wife and a mother."

The warrior woman wasn't sure what a Storm-Caller was but allowed herself a challenging smirk as she folded her arms. Her armor shifted as her sinews rolled and flexed.

"Fair enough," she said with the hint of a growl in her throat. "But who said anything about playing?"

Anja bared her teeth in what was only a smile by technical definition and raised her chin in defiance.

"And you ride to battle on the back of an ax-tooth as well, I'm sure," she responded in a way that suggested she was not amused at the attempt at humor. "Honesty, I don't know what Vahlin was thinking bringing you to us."

I'm beginning to wonder that myself. Ax-Wed settled for a sullen silence rather than dishonor her employer and...friend?

"Seriously, how old are you?" the woman asked and wrapped the sharp question in a giggle. "Can you even bear children?"

The Thulian's eyes narrowed at the question.

Is this a Vitzerka oddity or did I miss something? She was uncertain how to respond but the question pricked a part of her she'd almost forgotten was there.

The chieftain's wife seemed to take her silence as some kind of admission and she nodded as she took a bold step forward.

"He may be a drunken lout who won't care," Anja stated softly with a nod at Emerik and she dropped the thinning pretense of good humor. "But I'll be crow food before I let some battle whore and her scarred, riddled womb anywhere near my Javor."

"Scarred riddled what?" Ax-Wed recoiled and tried to process the declaration.

"You heard me, sword slut." The woman thrust her chin forward in challenge.

Before she could reply, Vahrem swept into the tent and water sloshed in two buckets he carried, one in each hand.

"Apologies." He grunted as set the buckets on the floor with a splash. "I decided that as thirsty as Emerik was, I couldn't get only one."

The chieftain's wife managed a shrill squeak but that was the only warning offered before the merchant picked a bucket up and pitched its contents on Emerik's recumbent form.

Ax-Wed wasn't sure if a lightning bolt from the skies would have brought the man to his feet so fast. Spluttering, shivering, snarling, and swearing in at least three different tongues that she could identify, the chieftain bounded upright and looked ready for murder. His gaze settled on the caravan master, who was already bending to lift the second bucket, and with a wordless scream, he threw himself forward like a man possessed.

She considered intervening but the merchant's meaty hand delivered a tremendous slap to Emerik's wet cheek and the man's long legs tangled. Vahrem took one step back to allow the chieftain to land on all fours, careful to not spill the contents of the bucket he held. His friend looked up, utterly horrified, and a welt with the distinct shape of the caravan master's thick fingers was visible across the slack face. It took an exercise of exceptional will for the Thulian to not burst out laughing as the second bucket was emptied on his head.

Emerik, still on his knees, launched a jabbing punch at his tormentor's groin but like the charge, the merchant seemed ready for this. He swiveled his hips and the clumsy blow glanced off his thick thigh, and the chieftain received another ringing slap for his trouble before Vahrem's hand snared the front of his sodden tunic.

"Vahlin," Anja shrieked. "That's enough."

Vahrem's slab shoulder quivered for a second as he hoisted the man bodily off the wet furs and shoved him onto the soggy bench.

"Now," he warned in a hard tone. "That is enough."

The chieftain wobbled on the bench and with a quivering cry, Anja rushed forward and wrapped her arms around him. Ax-Wed had to stifle a chuckle again, although she wasn't sure anyone would have noticed amidst the drama playing out before her.

This might even have been worth the time spent being glared at. She chortled inwardly as the woman turned her piercing gaze upon Vahrem.

"He's your friend—since before you were even men!" she practically wailed and tears welled in her eyes. "He loves you like a brother, Vahlin!"

"And I him," the merchant said, folded his arms over his chest, and set his feet wide and resolute. "And if I'd fallen into such dishonor, it would be a brother's duty to give me similar treatment if not worse."

"One morning with bloodshot eyes is hardly worthy of dishonor, oh righteous sheep!" Anja shrilled. "Or have you forgotten those nights in Aruhkham?"

"I've forgotten nothing," he snapped, his stance as unmoving as the one he'd assumed the night before with the Bone-men. "But as the Shepherd leads this sheep, I'm a child no more and so I put away childish things. Especially when lives are at stake."

Ax-Wed suddenly felt as though she were intruding on a private matter, akin to witnessing a squabble between siblings where any response or even none at all might provoke a thorny response.

"What are you talking about?" Emerik groaned and traced his long fingers gingerly over his purpling cheek. "Whose life is at stake?"

"Last night, a horde of Bone-men came looking for Svarah Vjetgo," Vahrem said and his dark eyes bored into the hungover chieftain. "Not only were none of your men there like you promised, but I didn't know that those fanatics would come on a holy mission to abduct Ax-Wed."

The other man straightened and blinked like a sun-struck owl as Anja's expression hardened into a jagged snarl.

"If only they'd succeeded," she snipped at the Thulian, who returned the hateful remark with a pitying shake of her head.

"I'm not done with you," the merchant promised Emerik with a scowl before he turned to address his wife. "Anja, what is going on? Since we arrived, you've glared daggers at my friend and acted as though I've brought a viper into your tent. Please, explain so we can get back to what matters."

Ax-Wed winced at the last word as Anja rose from where she held her husband. Left suddenly unsupported, he almost fell off the bench but she strode forward until her flaring nostrils were close enough to be tickled by the merchant's beard.

"What matters? What matters?" she screeched into a face that might have been made of stone. "If I were a man I would strike you dead where you stand."

It wouldn't stop me if I were that mad. Ax-Wed felt only a little guilty for the petty quip.

"I am asking you to explain." Vahrem ground each word between his teeth. "What are you angry about?"

She might have cheered in support if she didn't feel a keen desire to remain invisible.

Anja uttered a strangled cry, her fingers curled into claws, and it seemed she might forget her gender-enforced handicap.

Instead, she took a quick step back and spun on her heel as though the sight of him was more than she could tolerate in her fury.

"What am I angry about?" she parrotted in a faux basso voice as she stared at the back of the tent with her arms crossed. "Why would any mother care that the man bringing the bride of her eldest son trots in with some scarred trollop with dye in her hair and blades between her thighs!"

"Bride?" both Ax-Wed and Vahrem shouted in unison and looked at each other.

Is this the answer, then? She felt a pain in her chest before the frost could numb her against it. *Is this the reason he seemed so quick to adopt me into the caravan? Was it all manipulation to make me a bargaining chip with a business partner?*

"I-I have no idea what she is talking about," Vahrem said and raised his hands in a placatory gesture. His unassailable stance dissolved as confusion knit his brows and hobbled his tongue. "I would never, ever—she must be… I don't know where she…"

The caravan master's voice trailed off before his gaze drifted to Emerik.

"Emerik." He growled in disgust and his arms folded again.

Anja's gaze darted to her husband and her cheeks reddened. She looked at Ax-Wed in a panicked flutter before she turned to Emerik again. The chieftain sat with a bruised face and bulging eyes and his mouth opened and closed like a landed fish.

"Emerik!" The woman shrieked loudly enough that the others in the tent all recoiled.

The chieftain of the Lecall looked helplessly from Vahrem to Anja like a naughty child caught between two scolding parents. It might have been more humorous if it weren't so pitiful to see a man reduced to such a state.

"I-I… I can explain," he began but she pounced on him and her delicate hands flailed at her husband.

"Explain! Explain! You can explain!" she shrieked.

"A-Anja," he cried and raised his hands sluggishly to shield his face. "P-please—ow! Just listen—ow!"

One grasping hand had caught the man by the hair and began to yank so ferociously it seemed she had every intention to pull his head off.

"You lying, whoring, drunken, son of—"

The torrent of vilification spewed at a speed to match her stinging slaps, and it was Vahrem's turn to look to Ax-Wed as though they'd stumbled into a painfully personal matter in which both were unwelcome. With a quick nod at the tent door that she mirrored, both made their way to the portal and out into the cool morning air.

The sounds of Anja's fury followed them as they moved into the lane that led out from the gathering of tents around the chieftain's domicile to the Lecall tent at large. They strode past armed guards who made variably convincing attempts to pretend to not notice the sounds emerging from their leader's tent. In silence, they walked until they reached a wide path that wound between and around the scattered dwellings of more prosperous tribe members before it continued to the more common shelters and the places where the tribe's beasts were kept.

Finally, they stopped and looked up the slight rise they'd descended at the large central tent from which they could still hear the faint sounds of Anja venting her wrath.

"It makes me glad I'll never marry," Ax-Wed said at last with a dry chuckle. She turned to the merchant and realized that her words had a strange effect upon him.

His expression was dour and almost angry, but a pained look was in his eyes as though she'd said something which had cut him to the quick.

"It makes me glad I'll never get married to either of those two," he said heavily and in a blink, the wounded look was gone. "I can't imagine what kind of nightmare life is like for either of them."

"I can't imagine what kind of nightmare it would be like to have that woman as my husband's mother," she said and gave him a pointed look. "Something I would never have considered a possibility up to this point, yet here we are."

He groaned by way of explanation and ground the ball of his thumb between his eyes and up across his forehead to massage a growing headache.

"I can not even begin to explain how utterly abhorrent Emerik's behavior has become," he said and squeezed his eyes shut as he focused through the pain. "But I hope it goes without saying that I would never, ever try to trick you or anyone else into joining the caravan simply to marry them off to a business associate."

"I thought you two were friends," she said with one eyebrow raised. "The very best of friends."

"Perhaps that was more wishful thinking than truth," Vahrem sighed as he opened his eyes and she noticed how very tired he looked. "I apologize that I misled you in that regard."

"You're forgiven." Ax-Wed shrugged. "But we still have the matter of me being the subject of some fanatic's prophecy and the potential for every Bone-man on the Steppes coming to whisk me away to my destiny."

"That's true." The caravan master nodded and threw a mournful look toward Emerik's tent before he turned to the path that stretched before them. "I still think the Lecall can help but if I know those two, it will be a few hours before he's groveled and lied enough to cool Anja's temper."

"They make quite a pair." She chuckled as she remembered the chieftain's damp, welted face. "And in the meantime?"

Vahrem seemed lost in thought for a moment but then he straightened and motioned toward the stretch of path that would lead them out of the Lecall camp.

"In the meantime, we should get back to camp." He sounded like he was trying to coordinate things mentally as he spoke. "I'll try to have our business dealings accelerated and even then, it might be wise to send you, Zoria, and the boy ahead with Numi and her folk. She mentioned in passing last night when we returned from the arena that she has done brisk business and most of their stock is already spoken for."

"So I'm supposed to run away to Aruhkham?" she asked as she stepped onto the path with him. "Run and leave you to face the zealots alone."

He shook his head as they stepped around a small gaggle of Lecall women carrying baskets of washing. They all stared at Ax-Wed as she passed and more than once, "Svarah Vjetgo," could be heard between muffled whispers.

"I don't plan to be quiet about your departure if that were even possible," he said with a nod to the passing women. "If you aren't here, the Bone-men will have no reason to come to Carnyxia."

She conceded that it made sense, although she didn't trust a group of religious fanatics to be entirely rational or predictable.

"Well, if that's the case, I have one question—how fast can mammoths run?"

The merchant frowned but when he saw her point, he shook his head again as they proceeded toward the palisade gate out of the camp. Up ahead, three burly men in matching silver-furred cloaks had words with the guards standing watch. Three of the loping claw-knuckled beasts were bound to stout hitching post behind them.

"You don't need to worry about pursuers, trust me," he said softly as they approached the gate. "Numi's as sly as a fox and a Wain Dwarf besides. If she sets her mind to it, there won't be a soul who knows you're traveling with her until you reach Arukham's gates."

"I suppose it makes sense given that you didn't worry about Tarkhind or anyone else from Jehadim pursuing us." The Thulian shrugged but some dark voice of premonition wondered if even the wiles of *Mehk* Numi would be enough.

"Exactly." He broke into a smile. "I'd travel with Numi's clan for friendship's sake alone, but there are several secondary benefits."

Before she could ask if the old dwarf's crotchety and domineering demeanor was one of those benefits, one of the men talking to the guards saw them and pointed them out to his two comrades. All three men moved toward them and the guards scrambled to follow. Each man with a silver-furred cloak had a fine saber at his belt and the scars on their bare flesh to testify to their use.

Ax-Wed lowered her hand to her belt but a quick word from her companion prevented her from drawing the ax.

"These aren't Bone-men," he said quietly as he moved a step in front of her. "Their cloaks mark them as wardens of Carnyxia. If we can't get you out of here quickly, they will be our best hope to keep you safe."

She felt the urge to sneer at the repeated insistence that she needed protection but she checked the haughty instinct as soon as it reared its head.

The Thulian Empire choked to death on its pride. She reminded herself of her father's solemn words as he stood on the central platform of Xhulth's Grand Forum. *I need to stop thinking like I'm on my own now.*

Thus warned without and chided within, she waited as the three approached and stopped before them.

"Are you the one they call Svarah Vjetgo and a Storm-Caller?" asked a man with a drooping mustache and enough missing teeth that his words whistled slightly.

"I have been called both those things," the Thulian said and her sharp gaze watched all three for signs of danger. "But all by people who I don't know and have no business with."

The man looked at those on either side of him and each

shrugged in turn before they muttered something in the Vitzerkan tongue. He frowned like he struggled to make sense of some vexing enigma as he looked at her.

"Please, good wardens," Vahrem said and held his hands out in an open gesture. "What is this about? Much has happened since we arrived and most of it, as foreigners, we do not understand."

The tails of the man's mustache twitched as he looked at the merchant and the furrow between his brows deepened.

"And who are you to her?" he asked with a curt nod at Ax-Wed.

Who indeed? A small voice asked inside her head and she wondered why she couldn't answer the question easily.

"Her friend first," the caravan master said smoothly. "And her employer second. The good lady helps to guard myself, my caravan, and our goods."

The warrior woman couldn't have said why in that moment but for some reason, Vahrem calling her friend felt somehow disappointing. To the man with the whistling speech, it seemed to have the effect of turning his perplexed frown into a definite scowl.

"Fine." He grunted as though the merchant had told him something he most certainly didn't want to hear. "You can come too."

"Where would that be exactly?" she asked and stepped forward to better reveal that she stood half a head taller than all three of the men in the silver cloaks. The whistler's two comrades who still stood on either side of him seemed to take the point with wide eyes and shared looks of concern. The spokesman's mustache twitched again but otherwise, he didn't seem concerned.

"Before the Titan's Totem," he explained. "The tribes are holding a War Council and they need Svarah Vjetgo present."

"War Council?" She balked as she felt a familiar sinking feeling in the pit of her stomach.

CHAPTER ELEVEN

The wind howled out of the west but instead of the sea-warmed breezes so commonly brought, this gale was cold and sharp-toothed.

A dark bank of clouds seethed in its wake and streamers of its heavy mass were stretched by the wind to create the impression of black fingers reaching out. Rumbles of thunder and even darker sounds roiled behind the keening wind, but those who dared to look back beneath the veil saw only seething darkness flecked with bitter ice and rain. It seemed as dire an omen as any seer could have hoped for, and those driven before it soon learned that even the darkest imaginings were ill-suited to match what lay under that looming embankment, as the Sklavi were soon to learn.

They were a small tribe of western Vitzerka, who spent most of their time ranging along the edge of the Girdle and the Steppes and herding their pho—large flightless birds with rather succulent meat. Being neither particularly interested in trade nor having many of the larger beasts to display before other tribes, they'd chosen to not attend the Thunder-Crush. After all, with winter coming early and hard, they needed to give their avians as much time as possible to fatten up as they pecked along the edge of the Girdle.

Unfortunately, things had not gone as planned and some of the tribe's herders were attacked by Bone-men coming out of the Wooden Cord. The tribe had gathered quickly enough to repel the raiders but scouting parties soon made it clear that the fanatics of Perukh were thick within the area. As quickly as could be managed, the pho had been gathered and the tribe had pushed onto the Steppes.

Then the storm had come upon the bitter wind, and the Sklavi had fled from it as long as they could. At last, they'd circled their beasts, hemmed in the trembling pho, and the storm had enveloped them.

It had now been the better part of three days since they had been swallowed by the unnatural phenomenon and still, there was no sign of an end.

Bratzen Ironarm stood at the mouth of his tent and watched as the storm raged, a perpetually furious deity that would not be appeased. One of his hetman had already come to speak to him that morning—if that was what this cold, lightless time could be called—and had brought news that more of the pho had died during the night. The man had left him to a frustrating and fruitless consideration of the problems they faced.

"Almost a third of the flock," he said bluntly without looking over his shoulder to where his wife sat searing pho fillets on skewers. "We may be eating good now but this winter will be a lean time if this storm doesn't let up."

Mirja Swiftfoot shifted the skewers to stones around the fire and rose stiffly to join her husband. She was not as spry as her moniker implied due to a fall from her mount when they'd tried to push through the storm. It was her injury and the crippling of her lopeclaw which had convinced him to halt the Sklavi and try to wait out the storm.

Both bore that burden together as they leaned on each other at the yawning tent door.

"There is nothing we can do now," she said softly after a moment and pressed her forehead against her husband's strong shoulder. "Come. Let's enjoy a good meal while we still can."

The chieftain seemed deaf to his spouse and continued to stare into the cold blackness that had swallowed the world. At first, it had seemed strange and frightening in its unfamiliarity but now, the storm seemed not only alien but hostile.

"It hates us," he muttered.

"What?" Mirja asked and raised her gaze to study her husband's pale features. "Bratzi, what's wrong?"

But as the thought became a certainty, his voice left him.

There was malice in this storm—a will that wished him and his people harm—and with that realization, he fought back the urge to sob. What had they ever done to deserve such darkness? What sin had he committed against the gods that they would blight his people this way? Was there truly a god so vindictive as to swallow a whole tribe from the world?

"Bratzi, please," his wife pressed and her strong fingers squeezed his hand. "Come and eat. You are worn raw and need rest."

The pressure of her warm hands and the urging of her familiar voice began to draw him back. Perhaps she was right. Maybe this foul situation seemed so much worse because he had not slept in days. Yes, it must be that. His shoulders sagged a little and he nodded, although he still didn't have the heart to laugh at his foolishness.

The darkness without and the darker thoughts within had bewitched him. Hadn't he even imagined that he felt a baleful gaze upon him?

"You are right." Bratzin sighed and shook his head as he fought to drag his gaze away from the storm. "I am tired I need to...to..."

The chieftain of the Sklavi tried to convince himself it was his imagination, but eyes watched him from the storm.

At first, a single pair glared at him, twin sickly stars burning in the swirling icy-black, but as he watched with mounting horror, more emerged. Each light appeared with a mate and like the first, they grew in tiny increments as though coming from a great distance. His breath caught in his throat when he realized these malefic gazes must belong to giants. As they drew closer, he noticed that they stood at least twice the height of a man, but that revelation was nothing compared to what came next.

Beneath the lamp-like eyes of giants came a swarm of smaller gazes like the seething progeny of those hateful glares looming above.

His breath came in a wheeze while at his side, Mirja uttered a choked cry and her hold on her husband's hand tightened to a painful clutch. Her nails biting into his flesh awakened him to face the dire reality. Otherwise, he might have stood there mute and rigid until doom came upon him.

"Mirja!" He tore his hand from his wife's clawed grasp and stepped toward the heart of the tent. "Gather the women and children and ride."

Whether by her husband's stern words or some iron in her soul, she shook off the morbid mesmerization of the doom coming from the storm. Her skin pale and hands trembling, she took a lurching step to snatch her cloak up before she turned to the open tent again.

She paused at the door to look at her husband.

"Where shall we go?" she asked, her tone level although her throat was tight with fear.

"North and west," Bratzen said as he secured his war harness and stooped to take up his shield. The muscles of his bare arms rippled and Mirja felt a desperate desire to believe that those arms that had never failed the Sklavi would win one last time.

Her husband straightened and one look at his face told her that was a fool's hope.

"Take Javor with you," the chieftain said, his voice flat and his expression grim. "If you can get clear of the storm, make for Carnyxia and seek my sister's son Emerik. It shall fall to him to avenge us."

Avenge. The word struck her heart like a hammer blow.

Cursing softly, she turned and saw that the tide of gleaming eyes had only grown, while voices of alarm had begun to sound across the camp. Time was running short but she struggled to take that final step that would carry her to whatever fate this ill wind bore her to.

"I've loved you since the day you came to my father for my hand," she whispered and spoke words that should have been for a time other than this, but she could not wait any longer.

"Even before we were betrothed," she said and refused to look back lest it rob her of the strength to speak. "From that day until this, Bratzen Ironarm was mine and I was his."

The chieftain of the Sklavi stood transfixed, a man of few sentiments and fewer words.

"I love you," he said and although that was all he could think to say, it seemed enough.

With a nod, Mirja looked at her husband for the last time and stepped out into the dark.

Bratzen, his eyes glittering with tears he would not let himself shed, took his spear up and with a final steadying breath, moved into the storm.

The ground crunched and hissed underfoot as Dragahn Shield-shiver dismounted from the hulk that had once been Kollung.

The darkness of the storm around him was as little an impediment to him as the flurries that hissed into steam upon contact with his skin. Perukh's will drove this blighting swarm and as the Wind-Spoken of the Striker, it could do him no harm. He beheld the ruin wrought by his forces upon the latest in a string of lesser tribes.

As expected, the brave but impotent warriors had ridden out to buy time for their wives and children to flee but the warlord's forces had swept in and devoured them in moments. He wondered if it would have been as effective if the bold fools had taken their blades to their own throats, for all that it slowed his implacable horde. It certainly had made no difference and as he stood and surveyed the effects of his labors, he was struck by a vision of not only a field of the dead but a very realm of the dead —a corpse world.

His mind spun across the scope of that vision to visit battle-field after battlefield and city after city, all of them still and silent, and even the wind refused to break the stillness of that mausoleum world. In that yawning vacuous abyss, cities, forests, and even mountains would slowly erode and surrender grain by grain to the ruin of all things until at last, the very heart of the world grew still and the darkness between the stars would advance silent and ravenous to drown even the pale light.

Then he heard a scream, a roar of defiance and anger, and the vision melted with mind-wracking speed.

Dragahn felt something steaming at the corners of his eyes that was not the snow, but he barely noticed as he fought to remember where he was and what he had been doing.

"It happened again," he muttered and looked at the black sword that had not left his hand since he'd struck the black disk in the Frozen City. "Why?"

The blade did not answer but he felt its power seething in his veins and the air filled with the smell of burned hair and immo-lating meat.

The warlord frowned and shook his head as though trying to

muster an argument but the scream rose, hoarser and more frantic.

"Revenant," he muttered as his heavy tread set off toward the sound of the screams. "Yes, that was it."

He reached a gathering of his retainers, the charred and silent un-men who turned to regard him with their alien gazes. The lights within those sockets were like foreign stars in an old, uncaring sky. They still bore the vestiges of their old faces and when they spoke, it was with the hollowed voices of those who had followed him into Hoarlin, but Dragahn knew that what had been those men in truth was long gone, swallowed by Perukh's spreading embrace.

"It is their chieftain," said the creature wearing Tadzi's scorched flesh in a flat buzzing voice. "Strong. Last to fall."

Dragahn looked past the former sword-bearer's shriveled countenance to a living man upon the ground. The chieftain sat and clawed at his legs that were pinned beneath the crushing weight of a revivified mammoth's blackened foot. The beast's dull gaze glared at him with blunt, bestial hatred but it held its position and only secured the captive while the brute that looked like Belug sat on its humped shoulders, its seared claws clutching the chains driven into brutish flesh.

"Ready to join," stated the puppeteer of Volu's body. "Welcome another."

He nodded as he paused to look at the field to see the fallen climb to their feet. Some had completed their transformation before they stood, burned to the hue of charcoal, while others were still in the burning process and contrails of ash and smoke rose from their bodies. As the unnatural light came into their withered eyes, the worst of their injuries repaired as flesh and bone ran like wax heated by the infernal energies within them.

Protruding spines bent as desiccated claws groped to pick up discarded weapons. With clacking teeth, they called without words to the wreckage of their mounts. After a moment of burning hair and blistering hide, inhabited beasts rose from the earth and followed their mute masters.

"Only a few," not-Tadzi remarked, a hint of disappointment in the mechanical utterance. "But strong vessel. Will lead others when we catch them."

Dragahn studied the speaker for a moment and nodded before he stepped toward the chieftain. The last sentence had almost sounded complete and convinced him that his suspicions were correct. They were growing more comfortable in their stolen flesh. All of those who'd risen under the storm, man and beast, seemed to have achieved only animation but his retainers, those "welcomed" by the black sword, were different. At first, they'd seemed like the others, silent and driven only to follow and kill, but then they'd begun to speak to him—a terse word or two ground out between their clacking teeth from rasping throats.

Now, the words came more freely and looked toward the future.

"All the better to serve the will of Perukh," he reminded himself as he moved to stand over the fallen chieftain.

The man flailed at him but only managed to beat his bare fist on a leg that might as well have been made of stone.

"Damn you!" he croaked, his throat too raw for anything else. "My people will be avenged and your eyes will be plucked by crows!"

The warlord stared at the prisoner and the way the twisted and pinched flesh of his thighs disappeared under the un-mammoth's cracked foot. Even if the man were set free now, he would never walk again and the only way he could sit a mount was if he was lashed to the creature's back like a child. He knew that while the chieftain raged against the end he feared, what was being given was a gift. In the oblivion of death there would be no pain, no humiliation, and no regret.

"It is freedom I bring," Dragahn said and the words passed his lips as the visions of the dead world danced at the edge of his mind. "Release from the cruel jest into a peace without end."

In response, the chieftain spat at him and the spittle, pink with blood, landed on the black sword. It created a puff of steam but left not even a hint of residue.

"You'll get to watch." The man snarled in impotent fury. "Watch the beak stab into your sku—"

The black sword stabbed through the man's heart and into the ground. With a hiss, the flesh curled away from the blade and he drew the weapon out and held it before his eyes. Despite the glossy sheen of the blade's surface, no reflection was visible there. With syllables that gouged his throat and rasped over his scarred tongue, he spoke the blasphemous words of invitation.

The body shuddered and twitched as it smoked and the flesh split to vent the fury of the possession. The violence of the inhabitation of the body was worse than he remembered from that of his retainers, and he wondered if a spark of the man's life had clung on. It would explain the savage force that gripped the wracked body now. He could hear the pop of joints and the snap of tendons, but he had no worries. The un-man would repair itself enough to remain useful.

With a final heave like a person waking from a nightmare the entity that had been Bratzen Ironarm arched its back and rose into a seated position. The balestar eyes turned to Dragahn and issued a single word with a tortured gasp.

"Carnyxia."

The warlord shook his head to dislodge another dread daydream.

"Carnyxia." He sighed as though struggling to recall what he was supposed to remember about the place.

"Perukh calls," not-Volu grated in his ear and Dragahn roused to the call with the droning urgency of a fly's wings. "Calls you to Svarah Vjetgo."

"The might of the tribes will be there," he muttered, more in observation than objection. "Even with these forces, my victory will not be certain."

"Others taken along the way," the wearer of Tadzi explained. "Perukh will provide."

Dragahn nodded and then realized that he had done that often lately, but it had not always been so. Once, he had been the one to speak and his retainers nodded—or at least he thought so—but as he considered this, he realized that it wasn't all that had changed.

He could not remember when he slept or ate or drank or even when he wanted to. His heavy limbs hung like weights at his side but when he willed them to move, they did so with the same great speed as before. While his steps seemed to drag across the frosted snow, when necessary, they propelled with all the power and swiftness to which he'd become accustomed. It was almost as if his body was separating itself from him—still mindful of his will's authority but without the love of existence to wed them together, it would do him no favors nor share any comforts with him as it once had. Or at least he thought it once had.

It became increasingly difficult to remember things as the horizon of his thoughts became fixed upon the eclipsing future.

At the crunching tread of a mammoth behind him, he turned to regard the animate remains of Kollung that stared down at him, the round eyes lamp-like amidst the thinning pelt and flesh about its face. Habit more than anything else propelled the warlord's sagging limbs and with a final dreadfully weary heave, Dragahn Shieldshiver took his seat and began to point the brute's head east.

"To Carnyxia," he called to an army that gave no answer other than silent, callous acquiescence.

CHAPTER TWELVE

"How long will we be kept here?"

It was the fourth time Vahrem had asked but she had to give him credit for a note of hopefulness each time he said it. *This time... This time, they will answer,* he seemed to say to himself but at this point, Ax-Wed had given up hoping for answers.

But maybe I'm tired and cranky, she admitted. *Maybe persistence will pay off here.*

As if in response to the thought, the silver-pelted warden grunted and shuffled to the other side of the room. The old warrior's silvered whiskers twitched over his thick lips as he made a commendable attempt to watch them both without looking directly at them.

The wardens had claimed they were bringing them to the Titan's Totem, a kind of memorial and holy place for the Vitzerka. Rather than entering a shrine or temple, however, they had promptly been brought to this structure that looked like nothing so much as a log cabin butted into the earth around the arena. Once there, they were told to wait and left with one warden to watch them in the room and another outside.

They'd arrived before late morning and could now see the

reddening of the setting sun through the small windows set in the far wall. With the deepening crimson, she had assumed the War Council, true to the fashion of such pageantry, had no intention to see them soon or had already concluded and now tried to find a way to get rid of them.

Either way, Ax-Wed's thoughts had ceased to consider her presentation to a host of tribal leaders and instead, she'd begun to foment escape plans.

Being familiar with war waged by a variety of different belligerents, she had no interest or inclination to become involved in a bloody religious conflict. Her only desire was to see Vahrem and herself brought safely to their camp and to leave at the first possible opportunity. His plan to travel with the Wain Dwarves seemed more sensible by the minute, although she still felt a strange kick in her stomach when she contemplated leaving him unguarded.

He and Iyshan seemed formidable enough, she reminded herself. *Besides, he managed to survive Tarkhind's assassins, didn't he?*

She decided that would have to do and examined the room where they were held. The door appeared to only have a simple latch, so she assumed it would be an easy matter to overpower the warden in the room quickly enough that the one outside wouldn't know what was going on. She'd then dispose of the outer guard and they'd have to move quickly before anyone realized they were gone.

They'd even been kind enough to let her keep her namesake hanging on her belt.

And what if you can't take that old warhorse out without raising a ruckus? she asked herself. *And are you truly willing to kill a man simply to leave before you know what is going on?*

The uncertainty at the first question and the dark disquiet of the second made her dismiss the plan for the moment and consider her other options, of which there seemed to be none. The room was bare and had one point of egress. A fanciful thought of using her ax to hew the logs had come, but she shuddered to think of abusing her weapon against the heavy logs and knew it would certainly raise a great deal of noise that would not be readily ignored.

She faced the fact that short of an all-out assault on their guards, she had no other plan. Thus far, it had stopped her from making an attempt. Frustrated, she leaned against the far wall and rolled and stretched occasionally to keep herself as limber as she could.

Vahrem had begun to pace the floor and his mouth moved soundlessly as he engaged in some furious inner dialogue. Ax-Wed had never mastered the art of reading lips as her mother had insisted she do but she didn't need what little she had learned to notice that the merchant snarled Emerik's name more than once.

"You think he will get us out of this?" Ax-Wed asked at last and her companion stopped his pacing.

"I am not even sure what 'this' is," the caravan master admitted and from the look on his face, she could tell the statement was made with no small amount of embarrassment and frustration. "I've never heard of a War Council being called, much less beneath the Titan's Totem."

TheThulian scowled and looked askance at the warden in the room as she straightened from her position against the wall.

"I thought the tribes were always fighting," she stated with a thrust of her chin to the tribes outside. "Good mercenary work, you said."

"It is and they are." The merchant folded his arms in front of him as he scuffed the dirt floor with a boot. "But those are raids and skirmishes and the like, rarely organized and typically opportunistic. A War Council suggests that they are discussing military action on a scale I've never heard of from the Vitzerka. At least outside the sagas of days long ago, that is."

She nodded.

It seemed the Bone-men weren't the only ones who seemed to take this whole prophecy matter seriously.

"Several people have called me a Storm-Caller," she commented and looked at their guard, who darted her a glance before he returned to watching her with his peripheral vision. "Is that like the Svarah Vjetgo? Or is it something else?"

The caravan master shook his head and took his turn to settle his gaze on the warden at the door.

"I don't know." He sighed. "I never learned much about the Vitzerka religion or legends. Emerik was my guide to his people since we were young and well…you heard him. He seems to hold all of it in derision."

He chuckled wryly and an uncharacteristically bitter smile crept across his face.

"As long as it was about business and drinking, Emerik was a boon companion in those days," he muttered and seemed to forget that he was in conversation with someone besides himself. "Now, though, it is like all he does is ride the horns."

The warden cleared his throat and shifted from one leg to another but kept his gaze fixedly averted. For a moment, it was quiet in the bare cabin apart from what dull noises murmured from the rest of Carnyxia.

"He also seems an expert at arranging marriages," she said after a time and gave the merchant a steady look. "I have to say that was not something I expected to deal with on top of this."

Vahrem groaned and lowered his face into his palm.

"Shepherd, find me." He groaned into his hand. "They are an utter mess."

Ax-Wed stifled a smirk, certain that she had better ways to describe the couple.

"So who is the disappointed groom?" she asked and tossed her head carelessly. "After meeting my future family, I can only imagine what kind of man they raised."

The merchant had begun to knead his temples and didn't

seem inclined to take the whole mess with the same wry humor that buoyed her for the moment.

"There is no man because Javor is still a boy," he muttered and paused as if doing a quick mental calculation. "Well, if he is a man, he hasn't been one for long although I'll say that the last time I saw him, he was better than either of his parents have become."

"A high standard." The warrior woman chuckled and folded her arms. "And what exactly was your role in arranging my betrothal?"

He raised his head to peer over his hand, a wary look in his eyes. She had seen men afraid, whether of her or something else, and it wasn't fear precisely in his gaze but certainly caution.

"Nothing," he said slowly, his tone akin to what she'd heard him use to calm a skittish horse. "I made no agreement or plan and played no part."

A voice in the back of her head told her that should be enough, but a hard and petty part of her bludgeoned to the fore. A laugh as sharp and cold as the sylver on her belt cut the air and even the warden winced.

"Why do I have a hard time believing that?" she asked. The question trailed the laughter like a jest but one look at Vahrem's face told her he was unconvinced.

The caravan master's hand settled across his chest and in an instant, she saw him assume the defiant stance she'd seen twice before. His lips folded into an angry line that almost vanished within his frowning beard.

"I've never been anything but honest with you since we met," he said in a low, rumbling tone like a storm murmuring beyond the horizon. "If you would dishonor me by calling me false now, I'd ask you to present your proof."

"Proof?" She scoffed but the voice in the back of her head shouted for her to back off. "Are you a magistrate now? Were you supposed to seal the marriage as well as arrange it?"

"All I hear are more accusations and still no proof." He shrugged and rolled his eyes, a gesture that sparked a blaze of irritation in her chest. "If I were a magistrate, I'd send you out of court in scorn."

Her coppery eyes flashed as she bared her teeth in a dangerous smile.

"So I am supposed to believe that you have no idea what this is all about?"

Now, it was his turn to loose a mocking laugh.

"I think the fact that I had to ask Anja why she was being an inhospitable witch stands as evidence that I didn't."

Surreptitiously—but not so much so that she couldn't see it—the merchant looked at the warden as though he expected him to make a note of his tally. The silver-cloaked man had ceased to pretend to not scrutinize the two but now seemed enthralled by the debate.

It might be the most interesting thing he's seen in a while, she thought as she cast the man a withering glare.

"Fine, forget the shrew," she snapped. "Do you honestly expect me to believe that this dear friend of yours simply fabricated this whole lie about you finding someone to marry his son? And if so, why?"

"Emerik is a drunk and a liar, neither of which proves good for business," Vahrem retorted. "To cover for some of his losses, he might have put Anja off with the promise that I'd come with dowry and a bride for his son."

It seemed plausible enough but there was a momentum to this conversation of marriages and dowries that plumbed deeper than she had expected or would have admitted. She couldn't stop and the old irritated wounds welled with blood and bile.

"And what kind of man must you be that Anja could believe you would snatch a woman to marry into that wretched family?" she snarled before she added with a venomous sneer, "Or what kind of man were you because as you are so quick to point out, the Shepherd leads you?"

Something dangerous and terrible flared in his eyes, an anger —no, a wrath the likes of which even she had never seen. Although he hadn't moved an inch, Ax-Wed inched her fingers along her belt toward her weapon. The voice in the back of her mind positively shrieked now and rattled the bars of her mind, but she set her feet, glared at him, and refused to give an inch.

The caravan master noted the subtle changes in her stance but seemed to regard them as utterly inconsequential. With measured movements that showed he knew exactly what it might cost him, he stepped forward and thrust his chin upward to look into her face.

"I am not who I was," he said, each word spoken in a low tone but with the force of a hammer blow. "If you won't believe me after all this time, I have nothing else to offer. But do not mock my Shepherd if you wish us to remain friends."

And why would I wish for that? The snarled reply birthed itself in her mind but mercifully, sense throttled the words before they could escape her throat.

For a moment, they stood with their gazes locked but her mind was elsewhere, wandering dark and fetid rooms of soured memories she'd locked away with will and wine. When she finally emerged from those dark passages, uncertain how much time had passed in the harrowing revelry, she found she was too tired to keep fighting but still too proud to simply apologize.

She told herself it was because surrender was not in a daughter of Thule, but the bleaker truth insisted that she was simply frightened.

"I am not a tool or a token," she all but hissed between clenched teeth. "I will not be used. I will not be sacrificed."

The ferocious light in Vahrem's gaze didn't vanish but it made way for something even more frightening to her—pity. He looked at her and saw something that banked the fires of his anger so he could regard her with care despite the righteous wrath.

And the warrior woman hated him for it.

"I've never seen you as token or tool," he declared with ringing certainty. "Nor have I ever treated you that way, and nor has anyone who is under my command treated you this way."

Ax-Wed growled in her throat and tore her gaze away from him, disgusted by the way she could hear Mother and Father in his voice. Memories of those last days in Xhult bubbled inside her mind until they burst and coated everything in a caustic slime. Everywhere she looked, she felt the pressing, needling weight of manipulative expectations trying to fit a collar around her neck.

"It's all been a lie, hasn't it?" she demanded. "You're trying to use me, to—"

"Enough!" the merchant roared and in a split second, her weapon was in her hand and arcing forward.

The warden exclaimed violently in his own language. The grin of the ax stopped short of Vahrem's throat but unafraid, the caravan master met her gaze.

"You aren't fighting me right now," he said, his swarthy features flushed but his voice steady. "You attacked a friend to strike at someone out of your reach."

Her stomach churned as her heart kicked in her chest, but her grasp on the ax was unwavering. With her eyes blazing like forge-heated copper, the Thulian leaned down until she was almost nose to nose with him.

"Because you are not yourself," he said and his beard pressed against the ax-blade as he spoke. "I know who you are and this is not you."

Before her eyes, his face seemed to shift and writhe. His dark complexion and oiled beard vanished until she looked into a face of even paler copper than her tones with eyes like heated brass.

The corner of his bare mouth trembled with a tik that almost became a sardonic smile.

"T'Lac," she whispered and the blood drained from her flushed cheeks. "No...no..."

No, this is wrong. Her mind reeled and grasped at the fraying strands of memory.

"Ax-Wed," Vahrem's voice called through the face of a dead man. "Stop this."

The voice beseeched her but there was still no fear in it and no tremble of mortal terror.

The curse! something inside her skull wailed and took his words up with vigor. *Stop this now! Before all is lost again, stop!*

Ax-Wed blinked and shook her head. The vision of T'Lac Te'Hagen's smile did not vanish but instead, melted before her until the only thing she saw was the twitching smirk that faded slowly from Vahrem's face. She stared and waited for some new deception or fresh illusion to appear. When a few heartbeats had passed and the roiling memories settled into the sedimentary pool of years, she heaved a sigh of resignation and stepped back.

She froze when she saw blood adorning the grin of her ax.

The warrior woman drew in a sharp breath and felt the heavy weight of regret and shame like a giant's chisel scoring her to the core. Afraid of what she might find but knowing she had to look, she turned her gaze to the thin crimson line that stretched from under the shadow of Vahrem's beard. From there, her gaze shifted to the caravan master's face, which seemed frozen in a curious expression of determined concern.

"I... I..." she began but found nothing to say. "Vahrem...I..."

"Svarah Vjetgo," the warden whispered and it was only then that she realized that he was at her side, his hands out but hovering a few inches from her shoulder. "Her Wind is speaking to you."

She turned as she stepped away from the man.

"No…what?" she began and narrowed her eyes at him. "No, this isn't… It's nothing to do with your god."

"Svarah's love of Vashen stayed her hand," the old warrior intoned as though repeating a children's fable. "When Vashen's crimes were great and the Dragon-Slayer sought to bring justice, although her blade fell, she could do no more than graze his neck."

With a trembling hand, he leveled a finger at Vahrem's bloodied throat, his eyes shining and face beaming.

The Thulian spluttered and looked helplessly at the merchant and for an instant, they were bound once again in their dread wonder at the fanciful religion of the Vitzerka.

"This…this wasn't…that," she insisted and pushed her ax into its belt loop. "You don't understand… It…it…"

Words continued to fail her until even the last two syllables seemed leaden weights on her tongue.

"My name is Vahrem," the merchant said slowly as though the warden was a small child. "And we are not lovers."

A hand shooed the counter-arguments away like nagging insects while the old man's gaze remained fixed on her. One look at the warden's face told her that he was past believing a word anyone said to contradict his newfound conviction.

"Svarah Vjetgo—a true Vjetgo." He sighed and shook his head slowly. "The gods favor me to let me live to see this day."

Ax-Wed wanted to be angry but the traumatic episode had left her too tired and embarrassed for anything as vigorous as anger. She settled for petty annoyance.

"This has nothing to do with your thrice-damned gods." She groaned and stalked toward the far wall. Although Vahrem had attempted to come to her aid already, she could still feel his gaze watching her. She wondered if the scrutiny was anything like what his horses felt before they were sent to auction.

How much has this one cost me already? she wondered in imitation of what she guessed were the man's thoughts. *How much more will it cost me to keep her around?*

"Tell me, blessed one," the warden pressed as he proceeded to follow her but remained a few steps away. "Is this truly it? Will this be the time when you fall to the Perukh Vjetgo and the end of things shall come?"

The Thulian wasn't certain if it was trepidation or anxiety in the old man's voice but either way, the question irked her.

"What does it matter?" she snapped as she slumped against the timber walls. "Whether it is or isn't doesn't seem to make a damn ounce of difference. According to your stories, in the end, Perukh wins and everything dies."

She lowered her head to rest it against the raw timbers and accepted the uncomfortable pressure as the knobs and knots pressed into the skin of her forehead.

"It's all pointless in the end."

An extended silence so complete followed that she turned from her masochistic sulking to make sure she hadn't been left in the room.

Vahrem still regarded her with his measuring stare but the warden, to her shock and embarrassment, was crying. Quiet, heavy tears rolled down his craggy face to disappear into his mustache.

"So it is true then," he said and his voice cracked. "The followers of Perukh had it right all along."

She scowled and even the merchant stirred from his scrutinizing to frown at him.

"Wait, what?" she protested but even as she spoke, she saw something hard and unyielding come into the old man's eyes.

"The War Council must know this," he rasped as he rubbed the evidence of despair from his face. "They need to know what is coming."

Her companion gave her an exasperated look as she stared bemusedly at the warden, who moved hastily to the door.

"No, wait, that's not—" the caravan master began but the man was already out the door and issued sharp instructions to the one outside.

"Serpent's stinging prick." Vahrem snarled savagely as he turned from the gaping door, both hands thrown in the air as he looked heavenward for deliverance.

For an instant, with hands upraised and his throat streaked with blood, he seemed like some avatar of Natzlan, the wild prophet from the ancient stories of Thule, but the thought only reminded her of home and thus the horror of the madness that had gripped her. She turned away from him lest he see the shame in her eyes or worse, she see the just condemnation in his.

"At least we might get out of here," she commented with a shrug and a meaningful look at the vacant corner.

He opened his mouth to say something but stopped and tilted his head to one side. Beyond the room was the sound of men shouting, although whether in argument or hastily given orders it was hard to tell. He nodded after a moment and seemed to agree that things did indeed seem to be in motion, although he graciously neglected to mention that the direction did not sound particularly promising.

Instead, he looked at her. His gaze bored into her until at last, she dragged her attention from the corner and looked at his face.

"Who did you see?" he asked.

Her throat tightened as though her body was constricted to silence her confession before she even determined to give it. Yet, little by little, she forced the breath from her lungs to pass her throat. Her voice was soft, little more than a whisper, and was almost lost when two wardens entered the room and shouted for them to follow them.

"I saw T'Lac." She gasped. "I saw my husband."

CHAPTER THIRTEEN

The Titan's Totem certainly lived up to its name.

Upon a wheeled platform as wide as a house a column of bone, seemingly from a single enormous creature, stretched into the sky above. In an alternating pattern up its length were hung the skulls of beasts revered and valued by the Vitzerka and each of them an impressive representative of its kind. Between these hallowed trophies were iron rings driven into the yellowed surface for anchoring ropes thicker than a man's leg that ran to the platform.

For Ax-Wed, the shame and anxiety of the past few hours were eclipsed by the monument before her and she only managed a low whistle in response. At her side, Vahrem—who had only seen the barbaric icon from a distance—responded with a low grunt of affirmation.

In all her diverse travels, she had seen many strange and terrible things but in all that time, she'd never seen anything like the towering osseous column before her. The original donor must have stood as tall as the Citadel of Jehadim and been the size of a couple of city blocks. Comprehending the size of the creature that contributed its vertebrae to the looming edifice before her was humbling and mesmerizing in equal measure.

That was, of course, until she learned it was a fraud.

It would be much later that she discovered the stacked vertebrae were not from a single spectacular specimen. Rather, it was a collection of land leviathan bones harvested over decades and perhaps even centuries, and the lowest two were carven stone worked and painted to resemble bone. It was revealed that centuries before, the Titan's Totem had grown so massive that actual bone could not support the weight and the lowest segment was replaced by skilled mason work.

Still, for the moment, she stood so awed that one of the gathered chieftains had to ask his question three times before she turned from the Totem and gave him a quizzical look.

"Is this what?" she asked.

Instinctually, she looked at Vahrem but he seemed transfixed by the monument. She considered doing something to draw his attention but before her eyes, his expression slid from wonder to a scowl. He'd worn the dark look since the wardens came to collect them.

And you mentioned T'Lac, she reminded herself. *He's looked like that since you mentioned your husband, although you neglected to say he is dead or how he came to be that way.*

Ax-Wed shook her head to dismiss the intrusive reflection as the chieftain cleared his throat and began again for the fourth time.

"Svarah Vjetgo," the chieftain said, his face red even as he bowed his head dutifully. "Is this indeed the time of The Great Striking?"

Ax-Wed stared at him for a long moment. Like many of those present, he was a tall, well-built man in his middle years. It seemed the chieftains of the Vitzerka tended to fit a certain type.

"I am…unfamiliar with your religion," the Thulian said and

her gaze wandered across the assembly of man gathered under the Totem. "I am not sure that I should speak on things I don't know."

This sparked murmurs and mutters amongst the gathered leaders until another chieftain stepped forward and pointed a finger to the right where a squad of Carnyxian wardens stood ready.

"Yet we hear a report from the wardens to the contrary." This man was markedly younger, shorter, and more rotund than the others in the gathering. "You told one of their senior members that all things are coming to an end like the followers of Perukh have promised would come upon us."

She looked at the wardens and the silver-mustached man and felt a stabbing pang of uncertainty. He still wore the grimly determined look on his lined face of a man doing his utmost to face his death bravely. She had fought through enough battles to know the expression and as such, she couldn't help but feel empathy and a connection with him. While she had no desire to see such a man brought to shame by her careless words, this was already so far out of hand that she knew she had to say something.

Which will make this so much harder, she admitted as she straightened her shoulders and focused on the chieftains.

"I spoke earlier in ignorance," she confessed and refused to let her gaze stray to the line of wardens. "I'd only heard what the Bone-men believe and so thought that it was what all Vitzerka believed."

Several of the murmuring chieftains looked taken aback and the sharp noises that now issued from their ranks suggested that several arguments had been sparked by her response. The leaders of the Vitzerka turned to one another and fingers were wagged and heads shaken vigorously.

Except for the squat chieftain who'd pointed to the wardens.

He looked like nothing so much as a toad watching a juicy worm creep across his path. His watery blue eyes stared and round cheeks bulged with a barely concealed smile while he sat unmoved by the men around him, his gaze fixed on Ax-Wed.

I don't like the look of this one.

The change in the meeting's tone stirred Vahrem from his glowering reverie and he gave her a dark look that seemed to ask what she'd done now. She bore the look without outward response and willed the familiar frost to creep over her heart.

Let him despise me, she thought as she stared at him in return. *This is my road.*

With a shake of his head that cut her deeper than she ever would have admitted, the merchant turned to the bickering gathering and raised his commanding voice.

"Wise chieftains," he said with a call so resounding that not one of the men didn't attend him. "There seems to have been some great misunderstanding and if you would allow me, I would seek to try to set things right."

"And who are you?" demanded an equally imposing voice and Ax-Wed glanced in its direction. It belonged to a chieftain who stood a head taller than any of those in attendance. He pushed to the front and looked down his crooked nose at Vahrem with open disdain.

"We are here to speak to Svarah Vjetgo, not some sunbaked southerner," he stated coldly with a sweeping look at the men around him, several of whom nodded eagerly. "At this rate, Shieldshiver will come upon us while we are still in this damned War Council. We should send Svarah Vjetgo out with all haste."

Many voices erupted at once, some in favor and some opposed, but the looming man who spoke bore all of it with a smug grin at the merchant.

I don't think I much like that one either, she thought and remembered the toad-like chieftain. *And from the look of it, neither does the amphibian.*

"I am Vahrem Kal'Stru," the caravan master said with a bow much deeper than it needed to be. "I am a companion and the employer of the woman you all refer to as Svarah Vjetgo."

More mutters and more than one bemused look darted from Vahrem to Ax-Wed.

"The chosen of Svarah the Dragon-Slayer is a slave?" one voice called from the back of the gathering.

"No, she's his concubine," another shouted in derision. "Clearly."

"Clearly?" Ax-Wed growled in surprise and one hand gestured to the battered armor she wore. "What kind of women do you keep in your tent?"

A series of deep chuckles came in reply and she thought she heard someone trying to give a sheepish, grumbling retort. Despite herself, she felt a small flare of satisfaction that she had turned the tables a little. Trading blows, physical or verbal, was one thing she could at least understand, especially compared to this nonsense about the gods breaking wind to talk to one fanatic or another.

"No, not a slave or concubine," Vahrem added firmly, for which she offered him a grateful nod. "She is a mercenary, hired as a guard for my caravan."

Did he always say mercenary that way? Or has he ever called me that?

She'd certainly never felt that way, even if it was technically true. Even before the debacle beneath Jehadim, she had felt it was somehow different being part of the caravan. It wasn't merely work or a job, it was…more.

A family, she admitted to herself and a lead weight settled into her heart as she realized that she'd most likely ruined any hope of being part of that family again. Her gaze wandered to the cut scabbing on his throat and the world seemed to shrink and darken again.

I curse you. Mother's voice hissed through her memories like a viper's kiss to poison everything it touched. *The Ashen Road...long may you walk it.*

"Whatever price it may require to free her, I will gladly pay it," the huge chieftain declared. "We've already wasted enough time bickering and now, we allow some sandlurker to come and throw dust in our eyes? Take your money so we can send her to fulfill her destiny."

The giant flicked his hand and the wide eyes of the gathering saw a crude purse, little more than a small leather sack, sail through the air. The hide bag struck the ground at Vahrem's feet and vomited coins on impact to turn the stone before the merchant into a glimmering puddle of gold.

The Thulian saw the wealth so freely pitched at his feet and her gaze darted up to study his gaze. She only understood the caravan master's business in part but she guessed there was enough gold there that he could very nearly double his profits.

"Ax-Wed is neither for sale nor is she mine to sell," the merchant said and turned to give a small bow to her, his expression sad but not unkind. "Her business is hers to conduct as she sees fit."

Is that goodbye? she thought with an angry twist in her heart. *Why did that feel so much like goodbye?*

"We have far more important questions to answer," the toad-like chieftain declared loudly enough to be heard over the rising babble. "What proof do we have that this woman is Svarah Vjetgo? Where are the signs to herald her coming? This has all been so unlike our histories and our traditions that it seems strange beyond accounting."

That almost sounds like good sense, she thought. *And coming from a Vitzerkan no less.*

Although the warrior woman recognized that she might have misjudged the two-legged amphibian, one look across the gathered chieftains told her that his words did not find fertile ground.

More than one scowl was directed at him and too few men nodded in agreement.

"Who are you to speak of these things?" shouted a voice closely resembling the one who had called her a concubine. "You are a godless man, Merko, and everyone knows it."

Several shouted affirmations didn't cause him to even blink.

Is he a friend of Emerik? She began to look more closely at the assembly of chieftains. *Where is the lush?*

After a long moment during which she couldn't locate the lanky chieftain amidst the crowd, she almost turned to Vahrem to ask but something stopped her. She decided in an instant that the idea of facing his gaze, sad and pitying or angry and hostile, seemed too much for her at the moment, especially before these less than hospitable strangers.

"I have not rejected all gods, merely most of them," Merko retorted and his tone implied that he had to give this explanation often. "And regardless, I am one of the Vitzerka and have heard the stories since I was a child like the rest of you. That said, when Shieldshiver arrives with his army, it won't matter what I believe."

A few heads nodded at the blunt wisdom.

"All the more reason for us to send her now," the biggest chieftain bellowed. "Send Svarah Vjetgo to slay Perukh Vjetgo as she has done so many times before!"

Several men uttered hearty roars of approval but they were far from a majority.

"It is said dark magics shroud Shieldshiver's forces," someone shouted over the mock warcries. "And that demons walk with him. How can even Svarah Vjetgo face such things?"

This keeps getting better and better, she moaned internally.

"Of course there are armies and demons." Vahrem snorted as he muttered in a low tone and shook his head heavily. "Why wouldn't there be both?"

Tell me about it. Ax-Wed didn't have the nerve to say it aloud for fear of the dark look she might earn.

"When did I ever fear a man to look at me?" The warrior woman growled under her breath as the debate raged among the chieftains.

"Dragahn Shieldshiver is a killer and a fanatic but no wizard," the huge leader declared and when he saw the concerned frowns, he swept a hand toward her. "But even if the stories are true, we have to trust that the gods have equipped Svarah Vjetgo to dispel such sorceries."

More of the council nodded at that statement, but the toad shook his head so hard his cheeks wobbled.

"But Svarah Vjetgo has never come to our people in this way," Merko insisted. "I think it only wise to question if she is the chosen of Svarah, especially if we are to believe that the End of All hangs upon her."

"End of All? So now you worship Perukh, do you, Merko Kitten-Caller?" The giant laughed at the squat man. "I'm not sure I've ever seen a Bone-man without a little of ivory or did you simply lose yours in those jowls?"

Merko gave the big man a long look before his thin lips curled into a sneer.

"And I've never known a chieftain with as loud a mouth and as empty a head, Goran," he snapped. "First, you condemn me for not worshiping your gods and now, you mock me for knowing of them. Is there a point to your bellyaching or are you merely eager to send a woman to fight for you?"

"I have a point or two for you, Cat-Tickler!" Goran roared and moved his hand to draw the long knife at his belt.

To his credit, Merik didn't balk but drew his blade and it appeared in his hands with such speed that he must have been familiar with its use.

Several shouts followed and things became disorderly.

Some of the chieftains were determined to get out of the way of the two while others seemed determined to restrain them. More than a few were simply caught in midst of the thrashing, shoving, and grasping. One or two of the men staggered away clutching cuts in their hand or arm but in the chaos, it was impossible to tell which of the two was responsible. More blades began to flash and at some point, Ax-Wed was certain she saw a spiked cudgel sweep from the morass.

"And these are the men who make decisions as an army approaches," she muttered.

"And don't forget the demons too." Vahrem grunted.

Things seemed very close to the point of degenerating from a scuffle to a murderous brawl when she mastered herself and looked at the merchant. A frown creased his brow and darkened his features but it was sadness that weighed on him, not anger. Whether the sadness was born of what had passed between them, his concern for the people dependent on the squabbling chieftains, or all that and more besides, the pained expression cut her deeply. It seemed that whatever his peculiarities, he was a good man and his life had been only made more perilous by her entrance into it.

And even though he doesn't know, part of him must suspect that this is more than bad luck. Before long, he will know you are cursed and he will learn that you knew and kept your doom entwined with the lives he is responsible for—the lives of his family.

"At this rate," he observed. "They'll kill each other before this Shieldshiver ever reaches Carnyxia."

The warrior woman looked at the chieftains and it seemed he was barely exaggerating. If they hadn't been so tangled, many seemed ready to gut their neighbors.

Long may you walk it, she thought.

"Let's see if a Thulian curse can outlast Vitzerka prophecies." She sighed as she straightened and squared her shoulders.

"What?" the merchant asked and seemed to sense that something had changed while he was distracted.

Ax-Wed stepped forward, raised her arms, and called out in a loud voice.

"I am Svarah Vjetgo, chosen of the Dragon-Slayer!" she cried, her hands outstretched to embrace this new doom.

"What are you doing?" Vahrem demanded at her back but she refused to look at him.

"In the name of the goddess, stop this squabbling! Now!"

The gathered chieftains ceased their efforts to murder each other and in a heartbeat or two, had disengaged. Shame-faced like boys caught bickering over the last honeyed berry, they stood waiting with weapons and bloodied fists dangling at their sides. To a man, there was not one left unmarked by the fight, but none seemed mortally or even seriously wounded.

"You are the sons of the Steppes and masters of beasts," she shouted and the words came with such strength and scorn that some winced. "Yet you squabble like frightened beggars over scraps."

A few shuffled uncomfortably while others raised their chins to argue, Goran and Merik among them, but even they couldn't meet her withering stare.

"An enemy to all your tribes advances on you." She growled and swept her blazing gaze across everyone before her. "Will you gather your warriors and make ready to stand with me as we meet the forces of Shieldshiver together or will you slink away from this glorious moment?"

Whether roused by her speech or simply enticed by the consummation of the violence they'd tasted, the gathered chieftains responded with affirming cries.

"My warriors ride with Svarah Vjetgo!"

"In the morning we ride for glory!"

"The gods are with us!"

The warrior woman felt the rush of the rousing cries, drew her ax, and raised it skyward.

"To war!" she howled and the call was taken up by almost every member of the War Council.

Except for an amphibian-faced chieftain and his hulking counterpart.

CHAPTER FOURTEEN

Dragahn's army was two days' hard ride from Carnyxia when he noticed a break in the swallowing storm that formed the vanguard.

To be more accurate, there was a hole in the storm and he needed to know who was to blame.

They rode upon the enigma on their way to what passed for the Vitzerka capital while following the trail of the Sklavie survivors. The warlord, mounted on the animated remains of Kollung, had been in the depths of another vision of the reality to come when a light cut through the devouring entropic dark.

His first thought was that he watched the next stage in the ultimate death of all that was but when he stared into the light, he realized that he saw shapes within the beam of pale illumination. A slight, stooped figure knelt upon the ground and a tall, gaunt being loomed above with a staff in its hand.

"That's not right," he rumbled and his eyes squinted into the light until tears ran down his cheeks. "There is nothing at the end."

Something else moved within the light and he thought he heard the thrumming pulse of great wings beating the air.

Like the flaps of a tent folding away from a door, the vision rolled back and he realized that it was no vision but rather the waking world. The black winds and razored flurries howled and seethed in every direction except for directly ahead where the two figures stood. As the army of Dragahn Shieldshiver drew closer, he saw a horse on the ground behind the two figures. The once fine animal's fate was plain to see with one leg twisted at an odd angle and its throat opened by a merciful blade. The keepers of the creature, both men, stood on earth darkened by the poor beast's blood.

He drew up to the edge of the light surrounding them and stared in confusion as his new bodyguards rode forward to offer their council. The intelligences that inhabited his retainers had one answer to the mystery although they each expressed it with different vivid instructions.

"Flay both to the quick."

"Feed both to the fire."

"Trample both to dust."

"Hack to pieces. Rend!"

The last came from the Welcomed chieftain and the pale light within its eyes flashed like hungry steel.

"But what is it?" he asked and straightened a little in his saddle. His whole body ached as though he'd ridden for days without rest. With his mind free of the bedeviling visions, he realized with a heavy groan that he felt that way because he had indeed ridden for days without rest.

And why couldn't he remember the last time he'd eaten or drunk anything?

"It is enemy," all four said at once and their voices droned together like a swarm of locusts. "Kill it."

The black sword rose in his heavy hand and responded instinctually to the call. In the next moment, Dragahn looked at the two men and his fatigue-addled mind cleared enough to force a second musing into focus.

"But why are they here?"

In a peculiar first since their Welcoming, all four un-men seemed uncertain. In the most human of gestures he'd ever seen them give, they looked at each other and their cold eyes flashed and gleamed as their bared teeth ground and clacked. He stared at them while his body slowly cataloged the deprivations heaped upon it with fresh pains that he set aside by only monumental exertions of will.

"Why are they here?" he repeated and an angry growl crept in at the edges of his voice as discomfort began to give way to agony. They continued to look at one another and his mind began to clamor and yearn for the visions. As terrifying as they were, there was no pain in that place where he did nothing but bear witness.

The un-men remained silent and none met his gaze.

"Answer me!" the warlord bellowed.

As one, they turned their shining gazes upon him. They stared through him with an intensity that could quench suns. As he bore their scrutiny, he wondered if they indeed had done so in whatever bleak and distant realm they hailed from. An unfamiliar chill began to creep along his spine.

Again, he lapsed into silence and sank into the smothering ills of his tormented mind and body. He might have wondered why he, the warlord and leader of this army, now waited for the word of those who were supposed to serve him, but thoughts in general were a burden at this point. With no other option, he resigned himself to wait with only the meagerest assurance that Perukh would not let him waste away—at least not yet.

After what felt like an eternity, the un-men turned as one and leveled desiccated fingers at the two within the circle of light.

"Do not speak to it," they buzzed like a chorus of flies. "Kill it."

Without a command for its rider, what remained of Kollung sank to its knees with a force that pitched Dragahn so far forward that he almost lost his seat. With bone-weary movements, he righted himself enough to dismount and his landing triggered a hissed crunch from the storm-chilled earth.

"Kollung never would have done that," he muttered and saw the pale lamp of not-Kollung glare at him. He hadn't bonded with his beasts as some of his people did but the huge pachyderm had never looked on his master with such scorn.

"It'll all be over soon."

He shook his head, turned to the light, and staggered forward as his hand clenched around the black sword. The tighter he gripped it, the lighter it seemed and the less tiresome it was to move.

The warlord's back straightened and his gaze sharpened as the hunger of the sword flowed through him. He came to stand at the edge of the light where the storm was perforated.

His gaze settled on the hunched, kneeling figure of a man of slight aspect wrapped in robes that had once been fine and expensive but were now road-worn and ragged. His head was lowered and his face hidden but at a glance, he could tell the stranger was a southron by birth, probably of the Dry Land tribes in the Great Desert. Behind him loomed a very tall and well-built man whose darker complexion marked him as one from the Wayward Hills or possibly even farther south to Scadish.

"What do you want?" the tall man demanded and his dark gaze flashed with a warning light.

"I have come to kill you." He sniffed and a smile crept across his face although he could not have said why. "And I am not supposed to talk to you."

The tall man took his staff—stout and wound around with iron bands—into both his hands and something in the way he moved revealed clearly that he was not a foe to be trifled with. Once, Dragahn might have taken the prospect of a challenge as something to stir his weary heart but with the black sword in his grasp, all he felt was a hunger to see the dark edge part the man's smooth skin and bite into strong flesh.

"It will not be easy," the tall man said and began to step around the kneeling figure. "I will make certain of that."

The warlord took his first step into the light and a peculiar tingle rippled across his skin. It was almost like what he had felt when he'd hunkered with Tadzi beneath a tree shortly before lightning struck. A hum of power in the air as he proceeded grew until it was a crackle and finally, a peal of thunder sounded. With the blast, an impression came into his mind of a great blade, as hot as the furnace and as sharp as razor, arcing down on him.

The black sword rose in time to intercept the unseen blade, but it was a close call and he staggered back with the impact to the very edge of the light. Now more alert and awake than he had been in days, he looked at the two at the center of the hole in the storm. They appeared unmoved except that the man who knelt on the ground stared at him. His face had once been handsome, that much was clear, but ill-use and poor fortunes had worked the features into a gaunt, manic mask. His breath rasped in and out of flaring nostrils and sunken, staring eyes watched him with mad intensity.

"It seems our keepers are at odds." The madman giggled, then winced, his hands halfway raised to cover his ears. "Oh, there's no need to shout."

Dragahn looked at the tall man and at first, thought him a sorcerer of one kind or another—although by his bearing, he seemed more a warrior if he was any judge. Had that been a spell or some type of ward that he had almost fallen prey to?

"How many spells can you conjure before I take your life?" he wondered aloud and reminded himself that he had nothing to fear. He was dead already. It was only a matter of time, after all.

"No, no, no, no, no," the wild-eyed man chanted and pointed over his shoulder to the taller man with the iron staff.

"He is no magician and I am quite mad," he stated matter of factly. "No, no spell, or charm, or incantation, my dearest, damnedest friend."

The warlord squinted at him and struggled to make sense of things until an insistent, buzzing exhortation arose behind him.

"Kill it!" the un-men cried.

Dragahn, like a spur-pricked horse, reared and launched forward, the black sword in his hand raised high. He closed to the same distance as before when suddenly, the knowledge or the sense of an impending blow drove his blade upward to save his life. This time, the strike seemed to fall with an avalanche of force behind it, and a willful force stirred the air around him. He managed to keep his feet but again, it was a close call and when he raised his head, neither man seemed to have moved.

"Yes, he does that." The smaller man chuckled and pointed upward to the open air. "It's rather obnoxious when you are feeling particularly suicidal. It seems even here at the end of the universe he won't allow me a fitting end."

The tall man shook his head but said nothing.

"How is it that you defy me?" Dragahn demanded and leveled the black blade at the tall man, its length smoking. "Are you the champion of Svarah?"

"I'm no man's champion," his adversary responded, the words almost a confession as he looked at the mad-eyed creature at his feet. "I followed my prince here as penance for my failures that brought about the end of his rule."

The smaller man cackled, a jagged, cutting sound, and shook his head from side to side.

"It's not silly, ol' Guuhal," the broken prince declared before he pointed a finger at the open sky overhead. "He's the one you need to worry about."

The warlord, despite some instinct that told him to fear raising his eyes from the addled creature, gazed upward. For some reason, it suddenly did not seem so empty now.

He scowled and shook his head, certain that he witnessed another of his visions, but this was one that saw what was empty filled. In the illuminated air, something hovered and filled the space with an aura of power and vigilance that was as tangible as it was invisible. He could not see anything, but his mind knew something far more significant than empty air occupied the space, but perhaps not physically.

Dragahn suddenly grappled with concepts and realities outside the brute material realm that had occupied his attention since he was a very young man. For a moment, he balked, uncertain in the face of such unfamiliar forces, but the black sword became hot in his hand and he felt a terrible wrath fill his bowed frame.

"I am the Wind-Spoken of Perukh, the chosen of the Striker," he declared coldly. "I go to face—"

"Oh, I know." The fallen prince tittered behind one filthy hand while the other pointed to the presence above. "He told me and that is why we are here."

The warlord's lips peeled back from his teeth as his feet set themselves for another attack.

"Are you trying to stop me?" he demanded through bared teeth as the black sword rose before him.

The little broken man cackled and rocked as he clutched his stomach. Behind him, the expression on Guuhal's face was the picture of pained forbearance.

"Hehehe. No, I'm not here to stop you." The prince giggled and tears streamed from the corners of his mirth-pinched eyes. "I am here to watch, to see you kill that meddling bitch. Do it for Perukh but also, do it for me!"

A rustle of great wings stirred beyond the edge of hearing followed by a sound—no, sounds—at the edge of what his mind called hearing. All at once, the lowing of oxen, the snarling of lions, the scream of eagles, and the songs of men were woven into a melody he felt in his chest while his ears ached to hear it more clearly.

"She could fail!" the madman shrieked, tore at the sod, and

threw the chaff toward the hovering presence. "Things are not set! You don't know. You don't!"

Dragahn scowled and when he heard a sound behind him, turned to see his un-men retinue skitter toward him. With the graceless speed of hunting spiders, they advanced on him with their voices buzzing.

"Come away."

"We must go."

"No time, none."

"Leave, leave, leave!"

The strength of the black sword left him and he suddenly felt not only his old, accumulated achings but fresh pain where the recent blow had almost forced his arm out of the socket. His huge shoulders slumped and he longed to sit astride Kollung and let the visions take him again.

With surprising gentleness in their cold, skeletal fingers, the un-men led him to the animated hulk of what had been his mammoth. With a little coaxing, he mounted his steed again and his mouth gaped open as his eyes tracked the death of stars and the splintering of heavenly spheres. Visions of oblivion wrapped him as his ponderous mount set off again, drawn to Carnyxia.

Behind him, the un-men did not immediately mount their revivified beasts. For a moment, they stood in silent conference with one another before they turned and approached the circle of light. They came to the very edge of the luminous puncture in the shrouding storm and their eyes shined like unhallowed stars in a dead sky.

Guuhal's skin crawled and he looked away from the ruined creations before him. The mad prince stared beseechingly at the four but saw nothing but cold, hateful wills in their gazes. The little man bowed his head and his shoulders shook as great tears began to drip from his lashes and nose.

"I thought if anyone could drive him off, you could," the madman sobbed and gestured to the army shuffling after

Dragahn. "That your power combined with so many of your kind would be enough to set me free."

The un-men looked at each other, their expressions almost quizzical. Then, they laughed, a braying, harsh sound as though their throats were unfamiliar with such use.

"Fine then, laugh." The prince pouted and began to turn away but paused as a grotesquely stretched smile pulled at the edges of his face. "But I know how it ends—all of it."

The laughter died away as unliving bodies were twisted to strain and stare at the very edge of the hole in the storm. This was why they had come.

"Our plans are many."

"Flexible and convoluted."

"Failure in one ascends the others."

"We are unstoppable!"

The presence above seethed with righteous indignation that set the air to trembling, and the un-men retreated a half-step as the light pulsed like a heartbeat.

"Watchers know no such things!" they cried together as their claws flexed and teeth clacked. "You seek to deceive and to dissuade. We will not be duped."

As one, they turned and began to walk away and the very air seemed to curdle with their displeasure.

"You can not know."

"It was not revealed to you."

"We will not be fooled."

"We are unstoppable!"

With tears still wetting the corners of his eyes, the prince rose to his feet and took a step forward. The light shifted slightly around him although Guuhal placed a long-fingered hand on his shoulder.

"Tarkhind, please," the penitent guardian begged, but with a gentle but firm grip, the madman thrust the hand from his shoulder.

The un-men were still walking away but they slowed when Prince Tarkhind's voice rose behind them in a defiant shout.

"Now who is starting to sound mad?" he asked and one hand rose to his mouth. "She took everything from me, but I think you are obsessed with her. First, the tunnels, now the Steppes, and next, the mountains. I wonder how long she will thwart you before you finally realize she has providence to thwart every scheme?"

The retainers gave no answer and proceeded without looking at him, but when they mounted their beasts, they rode well clear of the ring of light where Tarkhind sat and laughed and pointed as they passed.

CHAPTER FIFTEEN

"I'm not sure I understand what in all the hells just happened, but I am damn sure I don't like it!"

Seated in Vahrem's tent, Ax-Wed turned a startled gaze toward him.

It was not only the ferocity in his tone, but it was also the first time she could remember him using such language. It was tame compared to the salty fare bantered about by mercenaries, but the utter lack of such from the caravan master made her cringe internally. She had seen him snap before and be harsh with his tone but such a loss of control of his tongue was unprecedented.

What did you expect?

"I did what I thought was best," she said flatly, careful to make certain that her face betrayed nothing.

But even as she maintained her mask of composure, she felt his gaze boring into her. It was as though he could see what lay beneath and would excavate the entirety of her soul with the force of his eyes alone.

"Best for who?" he demanded and showed no inclination to shift his weighty gaze until the front of the tent flapped open and two squat figures entered. *Mehk* Numi waddled in from the darkened camp with Durra close behind.

"What is going on with the mad beast lovers?" she demanded, threw her arms out in exasperation, and made the bells of her staff jingle. "They talked about war this entire day, which was no hindrance to business as such things go. But now I hear that the Storm-Caller from the arena will lead them, by which they can only mean our Ax-Wed. Someone, please tell me the whole of Carnyxia is simply drunk and stupid."

Vahrem opened his mouth to say something and the warrior woman braced herself for the accusing statements and the pointed finger, but they never came. He closed his mouth so quickly that his teeth clicked together and without a word, he stormed out of the tent.

Both dwarves watched him leave and their faces settled into pale, grim expressions. As one, their jewel-bright eyes turned to her.

Are those accusations I see or only confusion?

With a breath, she squared her shoulders and looked into their faces, one after the other.

"It is true," she said and wished it didn't sound so much like she was apologizing. "The War Council of the Vitzerka recognize me as Svarah Vjetgo and I have called on them to ride out with me to face the army of Dragahn Shieldshiver, Perukh Vjetgo."

The two dwarves stared at her for a long string of heartbeats, then looked at each other.

"I suppose that explains why Master Kal'Stru stormed off." Durra sighed and shook his head as though he'd heard something tragic.

"I can't say I blame him," the dwarf matron muttered and squinted at her.

"What was I supposed to do?" she snapped, unaware until it was too late how much their words had stung her. "They were talking about sending me to the fanatics alone. At least this way, they'll fight the battle with me."

Durra nodded and turned to Numi but stopped as soon as he saw her scowl.

"I'll seek the Speaker for you, Ax-Wed," he said, turned to his aunt, and bowed. "I'm going to go see that everything is ready for us to leave in the morning."

The elder dwarfess dismissed him with a grunt and a wave of her hand and a moment later, he was gone. Numi and Ax-Wed were left staring at each other until, with a sigh of defeat, the Thulian looked away.

How is it that everyone in this caravan seems to stare into my ugly excuse for a soul?

"What happened?" her companion demanded after a few more moments of squirming discomfort.

"What do you mean?" She let her gaze wander the far wall of the tent and tried not to think of how it smelled of Vahrem, of good earth, and finely ground spices.

"I mean what happened that you did this?" the dwarf asked and her scowl deepened. "Vahrem already had a plan for us to sneak you out at the first opportunity. What happened that you thought leading an army to war was a better idea?"

"I already said they were talking about sending me to the Bone-men," she said and tried but failed to not sound defensive.

"Vahrem would never have let that happen," Numi declared with a confidence so unassailable it was infuriating. "The man has laid everything he holds dear on the line for your sake. He would not let some cowards truss you up and send you on a wagon to death cultists."

"Maybe I didn't trust that Vahrem the almighty could save me," she retorted and ground the words between her teeth as she spoke them. "Did that ever occur to you?"

"Did it ever occur to you that at the least, you are lying to me if not to yourself also?" the matriarch challenged and raised one wiry eyebrow. "Now, what happened?"

Ax-Wed caught herself before she made a disgusted noise in the back of her throat that seemed remarkably similar to what Zoria produced.

Is that where she learned it from? she wondered and her chest tightened. *What am I going to tell her?*

As though summoned by the thought, the tent flap opened and her ward shuffled in, half-leading and half-dragging the boy from the arena. Behind them stood the merchant, his face still set in a thunderous scowl.

"Ax-Wed," the girl cried and lurched forward with her young companion in tow. "I'd like you to meet Nenad."

The boy looked up at the mention of his name and glanced around with an expression that would have been appropriate on the face of a whipped dog. His dark gaze rolled across the tent as he looked for threats and every muscle in his spare frame trembled.

"It's nice to meet you, Nenad," the warrior woman said distractedly and attempted to force her mind to orient itself to a place where she could explain what was about to happen. "Zoria, we ne—"

"He doesn't speak much of the Trade Tongue," the girl said and didn't seem to notice that she was interrupting her guardian's faltering attempts at an explanation. "I've learned a little of Vitzerkan to try to help but we are still on one or two words at a time right now."

Ax-Wed tried to speak again but the girl turned to look at Nenad and a huge smile spread across her face.

"But he is very smart—aren't you, Nenad?" she asked gently and one arm slid around the boy's shoulders. "And he's learning that the caravan is full of friendly people. Nenad, do you like your new home?"

The Thulian's gaze shifted to Vahrem at the mention of the

boy being brought into the caravan, but he didn't bat an eyelid and continued to stare at her with his brows gathered into a stormy glower.

"*Stravycin,*" Nenad said to Zoria in a raspy whisper and stabbed with his chin toward Ax-Wed. "*Ona ju stravycina.*"

"What is he saying?" she asked, shaken out of her thoughts by his reaction to her.

"Straveekin…" The girl thought for a second before her eyes brightened. "Scary! No, Ax-Wed's not…"

She paused and studied her guardian before she turned to the boy again.

"Okay, maybe she is a little scary," she admitted. "But she's good. She takes care of me and now, she'll take care of you."

Ax-Wed's breath caught at that and off to the side, Numi made a soft noise in the back of her throat.

How am I supposed to tell them? How do I explain that I have to go away?

Zoria looked at her and gave a not so subtle nod to the frightened boy under her arm.

And how do I get the boy to stop looking at me like I might eat him?

She swallowed and tried to ignore the hard looks from Numi and Vahrem as she knelt to be at the boy's level. For a moment, she studied his face, the pieces of bone driven through his flesh, and the scars that spoke of long, thin slashes across his face and hands. As she stared, Nenad returned the intense gaze and little by little, the fear in his features melted and was replaced by a curious light. After a few heartbeats, curiosity had almost overcome the fear and his fingers, now cleaned and groomed, stretched slowly toward her face.

The warrior woman held very still as she would when a wary animal sniffed to see if it was safe in her company.

At first, she thought the boy's fingers were reaching for her blue-streaked hair, which seemed the most striking thing about her, but that was not where the pads of his fingers came to rest.

To her surprise, Nenad placed his hand on her face and began to glide his fingers along the seamed valleys of the scars etched in the left side.

Ax-Wed began to try to think of some apologetic statement or at least an explanation for the old wound, but she saw Nenad's other hand run across his scars. Something like a smile spread on a face that seemed unfamiliar with the motion.

"*Prylicna.*" He grunted and with faltering pronunciation added, "Pretty."

"Thank you," she said softly. "You are quite handsome too."

She wasn't certain that he could understand her but the foreign smile widened.

"I knew you two would get along," Zoria said and beamed. "Now, Vahrem said there was something you needed to talk to us about. Does it have to do with all the ruckus in Carnyxia?"

The Thulian extracted herself gently from Nenad's touch and looked over the girl's shoulder to meet Vahrem's gaze. Some of the heat had left his expression, but there was no denying the accusation that still hovered behind his eyes.

"I...I don't know what to say," she whispered and hated the pleading in her tone as she looked at the caravan master for help.

A hard bark of laughter left his lips but a watery shine to his eyes spoke to how little humor he found in the situation.

"And you think I do?" he retorted and held her gaze over the youngsters' heads. "How exactly did you think this would work?"

Ax-Wed stood suddenly and noticed both Nedan and Zoria wince, but a rush of anger burned in her chest and she had to vent it or it would chew through her.

"What exactly was I supposed to do?" she demanded and raised one hand to level an accusing finger toward the arena. "The chieftains were at each other's throats and would soon have been at ours. I did the only thing I could think of to get them to stop."

Vahrem ran a hand over his face and tugged his beard as his head began to shake.

"They are Vitzerka. Being at each other's throats is second nature to them." He groaned. "But now, they are all united behind you and they think you will lead them into battle against an army of demons."

Zoria stiffened and her wide eyes darted a panicked gaze from Ax-Wed to Vahrem.

"What is going on?" she asked.

"Come along, dears," Numi murmured softly as she shuffled forward to herd the youngsters out of the tent. "You don't need to be here for this."

"No," the merchant said sharply but his voice softened. "Numi, please. They do need to be here for this."

The old dwarf gave him a look that said she very much doubted it, but she kept her thoughts to herself. That miraculous event was proof enough to Ax-Wed of how grave the situation was.

"What do you want from me, Vahrem?" she asked and folded her arms.

"First, I want you to acknowledge that what you did was a choice," he said with a hint of a growl in his voice, but as he spoke, he mastered it to keep his tone even. "Then I want you to acknowledge who your choice affects."

She felt Zoria and Nenad's eyes burn her but she refused to look.

"What was I supposed to do?" she demanded for the second time. "Let them stab each other until they finally decided to turn those knives on me? No, I took the initiative in the moment to keep everyone safe."

"Everyone except you," he countered. "They were far from being decided on anything, and they think you are some kind of chosen one. They won't kill you."

Everything the caravan master said was true and she knew it.

"Fine, it wasn't the only option but it seemed the easiest one for everyone," she conceded.

"Easiest for you," he said with a nod that was anything but agreeable.

"You're not making sense," she responded and her jaw clenched in frustration. "How can it be safe for everyone but me yet easiest for me?"

His snort made her hand clench into a fist.

"Everyone here knows you aren't afraid of battles or death," the merchant said with confidence that set her teeth on edge. "But I only had to spend five minutes with you to know you are looking for ways to keep your distance from others. You hide your face, won't speak of the past, and now, you are running off to a battle that is not yours simply to escape being vulnerable."

A surge of frost rushed over Ax-Wed's heart and she met Vahrem's scowl with an icy stare.

"You are—were—my employer so you only need to know if I did my job," she said flatly. "My duty discharged, I ask nothing of you and you can ask nothing else of me."

He shook his head slowly and a pained light began to grow in his eye.

"I was afraid you would try that line on me." The caravan master sighed. "Which is why I wanted Zoria and Nenad here."

Would he honestly try to use them against me?

"This has nothing to do with them," Ax-Wed insisted and fought to still the tremor that seemed to radiate from her chest.

Zoria's arm was still around Nenad and both looked at the adults with fear and confusion on their faces.

"It has everything to do with them." He snarled with a ferocity that made everyone in the tent recoil. "They are your responsibility—your children, saved by your hand."

Ax-Wed's mind reeled at the implication but as she feared, her heart and soul cried out in shrill agreement. She could tell herself otherwise but Zoria and yes, even Nenad, were hers, adopted in her heart before she ever consciously realized it. The rational part of her mind hated herself for making such attachments and hated Vahrem more for making the connection inescapable.

"Will you take them with you as you ride to war?" the caravan master asked as if he sensed her thoughts. "No? Then who will take care of them?"

"I... I..." she began but could not finish and her jaws snapped shut.

"You trusted that the caravan would take care of them," he said for her and traded his growl for a heavy sigh. "But that is not an expectation you would put on an employer. Such expectations only exist within a family, so please don't pretend this is a business contract to be discharged. It hasn't been that way since the first night you broke bread with us."

Again, she despised the truth but she couldn't deny it any more than she could explain exactly how it had happened. She'd become part of a family, even with no intention for it to happen and despite day after day of denial.

"Do we have to leave the caravan?" Zoria cried suddenly and her voice sounded so young and frightened as she sheltered Nedan in her arms.

Vahrem turned, sank to one knee before the children, and set a broad hand gently on her arm.

"Not if I have anything to say about it," he said softly with a hint of steel in his voice. "Zoria, who I saved along with Ax-Wed, you are as much my daughter as she is your mother. You are one of us and will always be."

The Thulian, having endured tantrums and sneers aplenty from the girl, expected her to mock the simple, emotional declaration but to her shock, Zoria's lip quivered and with a sob, she threw her arms around his thick neck.

"Thank you," she cried and pressed her face against his chest. "I don't want to go."

The merchant drew a single hitching breath and gathered Nenad closer with one thick arm to embrace both children.

"By the Shepherd's good grace, you are ours and we are yours," he declared.

Zoria continued to press her face against the merchant's broad chest and even Nenad, at first confused, seemed to settle gratefully against the strong shoulder.

Numi sniffed and Ax-Wed felt something that might have been tears gathering at the corners of her eyes. Only long years of practice and painful lessons kept them at bay but she could not lie to herself that they were not there.

You're a fool, and curse or no, you've spoiled what hope you had, she berated herself. *But maybe a good man like Vahrem could save the little ones.*

Twice, she tried to speak and each time, her words died before they reached her tongue. With a painful clearing of her throat, she managed to master herself enough to speak but it was barely above a whisper.

"Numi, will you please take our children to rest," she said softly. "I'll be along shortly to talk to them."

The old dwarf nodded and didn't bother to hide the tears dancing along the many lines of her face. With a tender touch and soft voice, she drew them from Vahrem's arms and led them out of the tent.

The merchant rose stiffly and one knee popped resentfully. He wiped his damp eyes with the heel of his hand as though trying to grind the tender evidence away.

"Thank you for taking them," Ax-Wed said and did not trust herself to say more in that moment.

"Of course," the caravan master responded, his tone almost wounded. "And we can take you too…if you are willing."

Ax-Wed drew a sharp breath and for a long moment, could do nothing but stare at him.

"It's too late," she said. "If I try to leave now, the tribes will hunt us and they will probably kill all of us."

He shook his head.

"The tribes have been given an objective and for a little while, they will be busy with that," he said. "That gives us enough time to get away before they ride out. It will be close but with Numi and her people's ways, we can put enough distance between us and them that they'll have to deal with Dragahn before they can think of finding us."

"But what about him and his army of demons?" she asked. "Will we leave them to face that alone?"

The caravan master seemed to consider the question for a moment before he replied.

"Are you truly Svarah Vjetgo?" he asked and looked her in the eye.

"No. You know that," she answered.

"Then there is nothing you can do for them that they cannot do for themselves," he declared with a shrug. "Vitzerka will fight Vitzerka. They have done so from the first days of their people, but I will not lose one of mine to their bloodlust."

One of mine, she repeated to herself. *Why does that sound so good?*

"What about your trading arrangements and your partnership with Emerik?"

He laughed and this time, it didn't hurt her to hear it.

"I'm not sure there is any great loss there." He chuckled. "We'll find new paths. I've thought a triangular route from Aruhkahm, Narlish, and Bykarlious was worth investigating. Now I have enough of a reason to take a look."

Ax-Wed's heart pounded in her chest and a flutter stirred in her stomach but it wasn't entirely unpleasant.

"You are saying you still want me here?" she asked and swallowed hard. "After everything?"

To punctuate the point, she gestured to the cut upon the merchant's throat.

In answer, Vahrem took her hand in his. His skin was rough but warm and his fingers strong but gentle.

"You are ours and we are yours," he repeated as he stepped closer. "It wasn't only for the little ones."

She looked into his dark eyes and felt something stir within the ashes of her heart. A call rose within her, strong, primal, and needful, something she'd fought so hard to drive into oblivion with the frost that coated her heart.

But this close to Vahrem, she realized she hadn't killed that part of herself, only left it very, very hungry.

Her body was unfamiliar with the positioning from long disuse but willing all the same, and she began to press against him. Even through her armor, she felt the solid, unflagging muscle there and the sudden thrilling desire to crush against and be crushed by such strength.

As if of their own volition, her lips moved to meet his but the tent door snapped open and a raspy voice broke the stillness.

"Master!" Iyshan called barely beneath a shout. "We've got trouble. It's Emerik!"

A mere inch from the first taste of the cup long denied both of them, Vahrem and Ax-Wed held their breaths.

"Son of a bitch," he growled as he took an ungainly step away from her.

The manservant stood frozen at the tent door, his expression caught between embarrassment and urgency.

"I'm sorry, Vahrem, I-I—"

"No, it's not your fault," the caravan master said and moved to the tent door. "I'll see what my friend needs now."

"You'd best tread carefully and bring her," the manservant said with a nod to Ax-Wed. "He's come with his beast-riders and they are armed."

CHAPTER SIXTEEN

"Vahlin, my old friend. It seems you've not kept your promises to me," the chieftain of the Lecall declared in a loud, dramatic tone. "What kind of world do we live in when friends can not trust friends?"

Emerik sat atop Jakash, his prize mammoth, and looked loftily down his nose at the merchant. No less than six other mammoth riders stood at his left and five more on his right. Behind the bulk of the wooly beasts, more of his men were mounted on the backs of other hairy beasts bristling with horns, antlers, or claws. With only Jakash, he might have trampled their camp so the addition of the others was a display beyond superfluous. He was making a very clear point.

I'd love to rip him off that saddle. Ax-Wed seethed internally. *Piece by piece, preferably.*

"I'm not sure I know what you are talking about," Vahrem said and regarded the scene without the slightest display of discomfort or concern. "Perhaps you could be more specific and come down off that mammoth while you are at it. I've no interest in shouting up at you all night."

The chieftain ran a thumb along the welt still visible across his cheek and gave them an ugly smile as he nudged Jakash forward.

"No, I think not," he said with a mocking kind of graciousness before he turned to look at Ax-Wed. "Daughter, your husband has returned to his people and yet you were not there to welcome him home. How sad you make your family."

Her skin crawled at the way he smiled at her but she fought her natural inclination to draw her ax and start swinging. Even if she could close the distance to the chieftain before one of his lancers put a javelin or three through her, there was the fact that he was seated on several tons of mammoth that could crush her with one toss of its head.

Instead, she looked at him and let a cold sneer twist one corner of her mouth.

"I am no daughter of yours," she said and her teeth flashed at the mention of the word. "And the only husband I've ever had has been dead longer than your whelp has been alive."

Even the mammoths seemed to draw back in shock at the declaration.

"His bones are still in Morah's Rookery in the city of Xhulth if you wish to check," she continued and the sneer turned into a fierce smile. "You'll find they still bear the notches of my ax."

Emerik, for all his bluster and arrogance, was speechless.

Ax-Wed caught the stunned glance from Vahrem but out of the corner of her eye, she wasn't certain if it was merely surprise or if disgust soured the look. She couldn't deny that she hoped for the former.

"You were saying, Emerik?" he asked, the first to find his voice.

"Your sordid past before becoming Svarah Vjetgo is of little consequence," the chieftain said with such force that she could believe he'd manage to convince himself. "What matters now is that you, chosen of the Dragon-Slayer, return to your husband's tent. He has survived an encounter with our foe and is eager to see you."

Her hand strayed to her belt despite herself.

"Why are you doing this, Emerik?" Vahrem demanded and an edge of fire crept into his voice. "Is this a foolish grab at power or is there spite mixed in after the way I treated you this morning?"

Emerik's lips pressed together into a hard, thin line and it was a moment before he spoke. The mammoths shuffled and shifted beneath their riders and their trunks tugged idly at the dead grass beneath them.

"Your greatest crime this morning was taking my son's wife away from her family," the chieftain said and sounded for all the world like he believed the lie. "You took her from our midst and for the sake of our friendship, I allowed it. Now, my son has returned and it is time for her to come back."

The merchant's hands balled into fists and he snarled as he stepped forward.

"You lying, arrogant, faithless son of the Serpent!" he bellowed. "The enemy of your people is headed this way and you decide this is the time to press a false claim for your advancement."

"False?" Emerik cried and rose in his stirrups as though struck by the audacity of the accusation. "Why, my good wife would swear to the fact that Svarah Vjetgo is the bride of our good son. Enough of this. My daughter must come with me—now."

To demonstrate his earnestness, the chieftain urged Jakash forward so the caravan sentinels at the camp edge had to retreat a few steps to stay clear of the sweeping tusks. The point was clear. He was running out of patience.

Undaunted, the caravan master set his feet and would not be moved.

"And a pretty pair of vipers you both are!" he yelled. "She goes only where she wishes and I know she does not wish to go with you!"

Ax-Wed saw several of the beast-riders tighten their hold on the reins and chains of their mounts, and a few even made their creatures shuffle forward a step or two. She watched their eyes and saw them choose their routes through the camp, then noted how several planned to charge into tents where families of the caravan sheltered even now.

"Don't be a fool, Vahlin," Emerik said, any trace of humor gone from his voice. "You know there is nothing more to be gained in denying me."

Vahrem seemed ready to tell his erstwhile friend exactly what he thought of the declaration, but Ax-Wed's hand settled on his shoulder and his defiant shout faded somewhere deep in his chest.

"Vahrem," she said softly. "You said his son was a good man, yes?"

He turned to look at her with incredulity and fear entangled behind his eyes.

"You can't be seriously thinking about this," the merchant whispered hoarsely.

"I don't know any man you would call good who would force a woman into this kind of sham," she said quickly. "If I go with him now, maybe I can convince his son to put an end to this."

The caravan master searched her face as he shook his head.

"Diplomacy is hardly your strong suit," he said, the observation unabashed. "And I knew the lad years ago. Who knows what he is like now?"

She nodded toward the waiting line of behemoths arrayed against them.

"It is a better chance than we have against those beasts," she said and tightened her grasp on his shoulder. "And even if I fail, there may be other chances to escape. If they charge, we gain nothing and could lose much."

The merchant considered her points as he stared at Emerik, who watched them with growing impatience.

"No," Vahrem said firmly. "I won't lose you again—"

"If Zoria and Nenad are our children, you must let me do this. The man I know would not demand that I cling so fiercely to my freedom that I would endanger my children."

His face held a fearsome scowl but his heavy shoulders slumped and his head lowered.

"We should have left last night," he muttered and she could see from his face that he cursed himself internally. "We would have been far from this mess."

Ax-Wed lowered her head forward to rest it against his.

"But then we might never have kissed," she whispered in his ear.

He looked up, his features contorted in bemusement.

"Unless I missed something back there, we never—"

Her lips moved to meet his but she was denied by two strong arms.

"No," he said quietly, his voice leaden. "Not like this."

"But—"

"No, please." Vahrem sighed, the last word pleading. "Not like this. I won't have our first kiss be a kiss goodbye."

Something twisted so hard in her chest that she didn't know if she wanted to scream or sob.

"But then we might never get a chance," she said and tried not to grit her teeth as she forced the words out.

"I trust the Shepherd," he said and the words carried a resilient confidence that she desperately wished to seize but knew she couldn't.

"Let's hope you're right," she muttered as she extracted herself from the strong hands she wished would hold her tightly.

She moved past him, her head held high and shoulders square.

"Fine, take me to your son," she called to the chieftain. "Svarah Vjetgo will see this one who claims her and judge him accordingly."

The return to the Lecall encampment was a surreal experience.

Her lips still tingled where they'd almost met Vahrem's and Ax-Wed fought to keep her wits about her as she moved amongst the Vitzerka preparing for war. She'd been in enough military camps and mustering fields to be quite familiar with the common practices of such places, but the beast-riders of the Norling Steppes seemed determined to prove themselves unique in their preparations.

Everywhere she looked, men girded beasts for battle and affixed leather-scaled harness and rigging or daubed sigils with foul-smelling paste onto the hides of the creatures. Several of the riders also appeared to mark themselves with the same symbols as their mounts, except these were made not with paste but fire and iron. Heating their weapons in the crackling fires until the edge of sword, spear, or ax glowed, they would brand the jagged symbols onto their arms, chests, and bellies. The smell of beast and burned flesh was strong in the air.

"Are you admiring the strength of your new family?" Emerik asked from Jakash's humped shoulders. After she first left Vahrem, the chieftain had offered to let "his daughter" ride on the mammoth with him but she'd ignored the suggestion and walked on.

The Thulian cast a withering look at the man but said nothing.

I'm wondering how many of these poor fools will soon die under the command of a fool, she thought and fought the urge to once again draw her ax and let the chips fall where they may.

They reached Emerik's gathering of tents atop the low rise and found an unexpected guest waiting for them.

Goran, the enormous chieftain from the War Council, stood before the tent alongside Anja.

"Emerik of the Lecall," the big man called to Emerik, who had begun to dismount. "I'm glad to see you."

"Goran of the Croali," he replied and seemed as surprised as Ax-Wed to see the man. "What can I do for you at this late time?"

"Nothing." Goran boomed a laugh as forced as his smile. "I was merely here to congratulate you and your wife on the marriage of your son."

Emerik handed Jakash's lead to one of his retainers and stepped toward the larger chieftain. He seemed to be thinking of what to say and in that time, darted a suspicious glance at Ax-Wed, who stared in return with a blank expression.

There's some kind of game going on here. I'm not sure even Emerik knows who he is playing against.

With that thought, her attention shifted to Anja, who stood at the tent door, her face a flawless mask of matronly attentiveness.

"We are glad to have her back now that our son is with us again," Emerik said and took the proffered hand that engulfed his.

"Indeed," Goran replied and drew him into an uncomfortable embrace. "It is never a sure thing to take a bride amongst those not of our people, but it seems you were most fortunate. Who would have thought your son's foreign bride was Svarah Vjetgo?"

"Yes, most fortunate," Emerik replied and with an awkward squirm, slipped out from the big man's hold. "But it is late and I must see my son and his bride reunited. I will see you tomorrow when we are making battle plans."

With indecent haste, he strode to his wife's side and Ax-Wed, fighting the urge to laugh, followed in his wake.

"Yes, I'm sure," Goran said with a lingering look at her before he flashed another disingenuous smile. "I wish nothing but good fortune to the happy couple. Good night."

With that, the hulking chieftain turned and headed down the slope toward the gate.

"What was he doing here?" Emerik snapped at his wife as

soon as Goran was out of sight.

Anja's eyes shone with defiance in the firelight but she spoke with a demure lilt.

"Why, dear husband, he was concerned for you." She smiled into his accusing glare. "He noticed you were not at the War Council to support him so he came to make certain you were not ill. I explained you were seeing to our son who had arrived after escaping the enemy ambush."

His face flushed and when next he spoke, it was through gritted teeth.

"And what else did you tell him when he saw I was not here?"

"Only the happy news of our son's betrothal to Svarah Vjet-go," she said and shook her head slightly as though overwhelmed by the happy news. "I'm certain that more will come to congratulate us and even offer gifts as the word spreads."

An avaricious sheen flared in Emerik's eyes and his gaze darted about with verminous eagerness.

"Did Goran happen to bring anything?" he asked before he added quickly. "As a gift to our esteemed son, of course."

The woman's facade flickered and for an instant, Ax-Wed could see how deeply the woman loathed her husband.

"No, I'm afraid not," she said icily before the mask was restored and she beamed at him again. "But I'm certain one shall come soon. It is customary after all."

Emerik, so distracted in his disappointment, did not seem to notice the fluctuation in his wife's tenor and instead, turned toward the tent.

"Well, let's get this over with," he ordered sulkily and gestured to Ax-Wed. "It's time to meet your husband."

She tried to brace herself for what lay ahead as he swept into the tent ahead of her but before she could follow, Anja put a hand on her arm. It was not forceful, only the lightest touch, but she froze and stared first at the hand, then its owner in surprise.

"My dear daughter," Anja said in the same tone she had used

with her husband. "I hope you understand that everything I said and did before is much the same as anything I've ever done. I am only looking out for my family."

The woman speaks honeyed smoke. It smells sweet but it'll blind and choke you all the same.

"I think I understand," Ax-Wed said and looked at the hand still on her arm.

"I sincerely hope so," the chieftain's wife said softly as she removed her hand. "It will make everything else going forward that much easier."

The Thulian raised her gaze to the scheming woman's face and saw something lurking behind the mask. Having seen it, there was no way she could not see what wriggled and writhed behind the woman's eyes.

Is that sadness? But for who? Herself? Her son? Surely not Emerik or I?

"Go now," Anja said gently, pained resignation on her face. "Go see my so—eh, I apologize. I mean your husband."

She nodded and did her best to shake the churning sensation she felt when she recalled what lay behind Anja's mask.

Something is going on and whatever it is doesn't bode well for me.

For not the first time since leaving Vahrem's side, she entertained the idea of making a run for it. But for the sake of the caravan and Zoria and Nenud especially, she drew a steadying breath and strode through into the tent.

"Svarah Vjetgo, here is your husband, Javor of the Lecall," Emerik said as she stepped within.

Her "husband" rose from his seat at the center of the tent and it seemed Javor of the Lecall was more of a man than Vahrem had remembered, or at least he looked it. In many ways, he was like his father—tall, long-limbed, and fair-skinned, but he was so much more.

Where his sire was lanky and thin-haired, he was robust with a thick sweep of hair across his forehead and back, although the sides were shorn. Well-muscled—but not with the thick slabs akin to what Vahrem possessed—and with a warm, open face, the chieftain's son would have been a pleasing sight if not for the circumstances.

"My son, this is Svarah Vjetgo, your wife."

As Javor moved stiffly toward her, Ax-Wed saw that despite his obvious vigor and youthful physique, the young man was weary and sore. She recalled the comments made by his father about encountering the enemy. He seemed uninjured but hours spent bent upon the saddle of a surging beast could hobble even an experienced rider. She looked into his gray-green eyes, sparkling in the brazier-lit tent, and saw that despite his fatigue, he had enough energy to look at her with undisguised anxiety.

Battle-worn and terrified to meet a bride he probably knew nothing about.

Even before he'd said a word, she pitied the youth, although it was hard to keep hold of the feeling when she saw Emerik grinning like a jackal behind his son.

"D-do you have a name you go by besides Svarah Vjetgo?" Javor asked as he stood eye to eye with her, although it was clearly a struggle for him to hold her gaze. "I mean no disrespect, but Svarah Vjetgo seems very formal."

"I don't imagine you'll like my name that much better," she replied. "I am called Ax-Wed."

He frowned.

"Ax…Wed?" he asked and as his gaze slid to the weapon at her belt. "As in married to that?"

"It's merely a name son," Emerik interjected hastily. "Now, how about you two both head back there and—"

The Thulian turned a cold glare on him and even Javor looked horrified.

"Father, please," he said sharply and looked at her with real embarrassment. "I'm sorry. my father is…"

"Eager," she supplied dryly and folded her arms.

"Yes." He sounded relieved. "That is a delicate way to put it."

"I'm afraid what I say next won't be, though," she continued in a hard voice that demanded attention. "I was taken from my friends, under threat to their lives, by your father. I was not promised to you nor did I consent to this."

He froze for a moment, then looked from her to his father and seemed utterly terrified.

"You abducted Svarah Vjetgo?" he cried. "Are you mad?"

Emerik gaped for a moment before he glared venomously at her.

"I'm not sure what you expected." The warrior woman laughed. "I'm not some frail, retiring creature—or did the armor and the scene in the arena not paint a clear enough picture?"

Anja stepped into the tent, her hands tucked primly behind her back.

"Did you know about this?" Javor demanded of his mother, his expression horrified.

The woman laughed shrilly as she shook her head vigorously.

"I knew what he planned to do only moments before he left," she said. "But being your father, he didn't bother to ask me what I thought of the plan."

The chieftain snarled in frustration.

"Why am I the only one with vision here?" he howled as he rounded on his wife and son. "They may need Svarah Vjetgo, but she called them all to war and every one of the fools pledged to fight Dragahn and his army of fanatics."

Javor nodded and a haunted look stole over his face. Ax-Wed recognized a soul reliving dark memories it hadn't yet come to grips with. Again, she felt her pity for him grow even as her hatred for his father was stoked to new heights.

She knew the scheme the conniving wretch had concocted.

"And we'll need every single warrior," the young man whispered. "Perukh Vjetgo's army was the largest I've ever seen, and they were... There was something..."

He lapsed into silence with a shiver that left the interior of the tent feeling several degrees cooler.

"Yes, they will need every warrior," Emerik agreed and fought to win back the irate momentum he'd possessed earlier. "And that is why, as one of the largest and most powerful tribes, they won't bat an eyelid when we press our claim that Svarah Vjetgo is our son's bride. They know that at a word, we can bring over a hundred bull mammoths, war trained and blooded, to the field, and that is only a quarter of the strength we have. As fearsome as she may seem, you can't tell me one of those fools would trade our strength for some religious token."

"And if they do?" his son demanded. "If they do contest it, what will you do?"

The chieftain felt the hard stares of his wife and son on him and his superior indignation crumbled. He began to cringe and held his hands up as though pleading some minor point.

"I was not there to pledge our tribe to this god-addled battle," he said stiffly as though trying to brace himself for the response. "I am not obligated to—"

Javor suddenly lunged at his father and knocked him flat with a violent shove.

"He's coming to kill us all, you idiot!" the young man screamed, his voice shrill and cracking. "What part of that don't you understand?"

Emerik stared at his son in alarm and as he did so, the fire of Javor's fury seemed to flicker and fade. The young man stared at his hands and then at his father and horror crept across his face when he realized what he'd done.

"F-F-Father." He groaned and his face filled with dread. "Father, I'm sorry. P—"

The chieftain rose to his feet like a snake rearing to strike.

"You dare!" He snarled in fury.

Before Javor could say another word, his father's hand landed a blow on the side of his face. Javor staggered, off-balance as he tried to absorb the blow flat-footed, but Emerik gave him no chance. Another blow followed and then another, and the young man fell and covered his head with his arms.

"Emerik, stop!" Anja cried. "You'll kill him."

Ax-Wed—more than a little surprised by the explosion of violence—surveyed the scene in silence. While the older man's behavior was despicable, his wife's evaluation was exaggerated. The reality was that even though Javor cringed under his father's hand, Emerik's blows had done no real damage besides a split lip and the cowering. As he continued the attack on his son, it should have been a simple matter for the far stronger and heavier young man to overpower him.

Yet Javor merely curled at his father's feet and winced silently under the blows.

"You ungrateful…thankless…wretch!" The chieftain panted and his narrow chest heaved as he straightened for a moment to catch his breath. "Do you know…know what I've had to do for you? And I practically hand you a crown and this is how you thank me!"

One booted foot thumped into the young man's side followed by another.

"Emerik, please!" his wife shrieked and stepped forward.

If this continues, I might have to save that boy. Ax-Wed took half a step forward and then lurched back at the last second as a cudgel swept past her head.

Anja, having concealed the length of hardwood, set upon her husband with wild swings. Emerik uttered a cry of pain as he was battered to his knees, and the Thulian danced back to avoid the flailing weapon.

Screaming like a wildcat set alight, the slight woman struck the bent form of her husband seemingly at random. From the relative safety of her vantage point, the warrior woman guessed that had Anja been a little stronger or had better aim, Emerick would have been dead. As it was, though, a few blows skidded off his shoulder to knock against his skull and the chieftain was pummeled into unconsciousness on the fur-covered floor of his tent.

The woman gasped for air, the wood held in both hands, and spittle flecked the corners of her mouth as her violence-tousled hair hung over her face. Blue eyes rimmed in red swung her gaze toward Ax-Wed, who gave her an approving nod.

"Well d—" The compliment was swallowed by Anja's furious scream as she rushed toward her with her cudgel held high.

She caught the swing as it began to descend and arrested the woman's momentum with a hard jolt. The chieftain's wife almost lost her grasp on the weapon but somehow, her thin fingers kept their hold and she began the vain struggle for the club.

"That is enough," the Thulian said firmly but the virago continued to throw herself against her despite her lack of success.

"This is your fault!" she ranted and snapped her teeth like a feral animal. "All your fault!"

Anger and disgust surged in Ax-Wed at the woman's frenzied antics and with a sharp twist, she tore the bludgeon away and threw it behind her. Bereft of her weapon, the chieftain's wife leapt forward with her fingers curled into raking claws and aimed at her target's face. Ax-Wed caught the smaller woman by her wrists and pinned them together as a barrier between them.

"I said enough!" she shouted but her attacker began to alternate between kicking her armored legs and lunging forward with snapping teeth.

The warrior woman's temper finally broke and she yanked the pinned hands wide and slammed her forehead into Anja's face. She felt the gristly mash and pop of the woman's nose being crushed by the unyielding dome of her forehead before the chieftain's wife went limp. Still held by the wrists, the woman dangled like a snipped-string marionette before being allowed to flop onto the floor next to her husband. The chieftain's wife was stunned but not unconscious and blood trickled from her crushed nose and split lips, a brilliant scarlet contrast to her pale skin.

"Don't…don't let…let her…" The felled woman groaned and gasped as she struggled to force herself onto her hands and knees. One hand groped blindly for her adversary's leg and the Thulian drew back and fought the urge to lash out with a swift boot to the side of the woman's head.

"I think I'd do the world a favor if I simply put you both out of your misery." She growled belligerently, her blood up and her teeth bared. Her fingers itched to draw her ax and be done with them both, but she remembered Emerik ranting about his hundreds of mammoths and his terrified recollection of Dragahn's army.

Where is Javor?

She turned to look where the young man had cowered and found the answer in a heavy blow across the side of her head. The club hammered her skull and her world became painfully bright and syrupy. She wobbled on her feet, unable to distinguish anything except his frightened, tearful face before her legs betrayed her. Her knees buckled and she sank onto the furs, wobbled a mite more, and surrendered herself face-first to the soft embrace of the pelts.

The warrior woman's head ached abominably and the world refused to keep a definite shape or quality, but she was alert enough to hear Javor sobbing and sniffing as he lifted his mother from the floor.

"What are we going to do?" He moaned as the two clung to each other at the edge of Ax-Wed's floor-bound peripheral vision.

Anja groaned, sniffed, and uttered a louder cry when the sniff no doubt tortured her pulped nose.

"It's all right." She hissed through teeth gritted against the pain. "I can manage this. It will be all right."

"What are we going to do?" Javor repeated and his gaze turned toward Ax-Wed. "Did I kill Svarah Vjetgo?"

Anja patted her distraught son while his arms helped keep her upright. She still struggled to bring herself back from the resounding headbutt she'd been dealt. After a few moments, she shook her head, winced, and drew her son's attention to her with a firm hand and a clear voice.

"No, she's not dead but the bitch won't be down for long," she said and turned a venomous glare on the fallen Thulian. "I placed some cord at the tent door. Fetch it quickly and bind her."

Javor drew back from his mother and held her at arm's length.

"W-what? Why?" he asked, his voice close to cracking. "Do you think she'll attack you again?"

A boy defending his mother, Ax-Wed managed to think amidst the soupy nature of her bludgeoned mind. *I should have seen it coming.*

"Probably, but more than that, Goran will be waiting outside our camp to take her," Anja said and tried to push him toward the door. "Quickly, before she recovers and kills me. Go now!"

He released his mother, who tottered for a moment before she stabilized, and he shuffled to the tent entrance. After mere seconds and before the flap had time to settle, he returned bearing the rope. In that time, Anja had gingerly retrieved the splintering club and held it in her thin hands.

"Why is Goran taking her?" the young man asked, the spool of rope hanging in his hands. "None of this makes any sense!"

"Javor!" Anja hissed sharply as she moved to stand beside Ax-Wed with the bludgeon held firmly, ready to strike. "Stop whining and tie her up."

Her son made a frustrated noise in the back of his throat— almost like something Zoria might do—and hurried toward her. Ax-Wed moaned in protest when her body was shifted by strong but unsteady hands. Once or twice, she fought to resist them but her limbs wouldn't work properly and every time she strained, things grew blurry and cripplingly painful. In the end, she simply endured her senses swimming in a murky pool where time was flexible and did her best to disconnect from the looming pain in her skull.

When next she came to, the two conspirators had been talking for some time and she was bound and being dragged outside.

"Don't let him push you around," Anja told her son as the cold night air revived the Thulian a little. "He'll probably ask where your father is but tell him he was injured in the effort to subdue her."

Ax-Wed tried to groan as her senses awakened to the pounding ache in her head, but the sound was muffled by the gag they'd stuffed and bound into her mouth. Neither of her captors seemed to notice it.

"What will Father do when he wakes up?" Javor asked nervously between grunts as he hauled his captive toward a waiting mammoth. The warrior woman wondered fuzzily how he would haul her onto the back of the beast before he pulled her over what must have been a stone in the path and she had to fight to stifle a cry of pain. The gag helped but not enough that Anja's sharp ears didn't notice.

"I think she's coming to," the woman warned.

The faintest whisper of steel leaving a sheath was followed a second later by a knife that filled the captive's vision.

"You can go to Goran with two eyes or one," the woman stated softly in her ear. "You decide."

The Thulian's mind was still somewhat hazy but the knife seemed very clear in her perception. She glared at the menacing point but said nothing. After a heartbeat or two, the weapon vanished and Javor pulled her toward the waiting beast again.

"Lift, Gruba, lift," he said, and she could feel the heavy, shuffling plod of the woolly pachyderm very close to her.

Even though she knew the plan was to deliver her to Goran,

being bound and prone next to such huge, crushing feet filled her with a particularly ticklish kind of dread. She didn't want Anja's knife to make a reappearance but it was a monumental struggle to not squirm away from the mammoth's steps.

This fear was allayed and replaced with new terror as something like a thick-bodied snake wound around her waist and drew her into the air. She cried out, both in surprise and because the change in elevation made her sag painfully, but the gag muffled most of the sound. When the initial shock faded, she realized the mammoth had taken her in its trunk and now deposited her—with considerable care—across its thick neck.

She settled with the side of her face pressed against the pungent, woolly hide, and the next thing she knew, more rope was being employed to secure her.

"Remember the story and make sure Goran does too," Anja urged her son as he worked. "Out of her love for you, she rode ahead to face Dragahn alone like Svarah did for Vashen at the Battle of Splintered Stars."

Ax-Wed could hear the young man right himself in the saddle after he'd checked that the web of rope holding her in place was secure.

"I understand," he said and sounded something like the man she'd met on first entering the tent.

He's hardening himself, she thought. *If only he'd had the spine when his father laid into him.*

"This is for the best, Javor," Anja said and a touch of tenderness softened her voice. "It is not how I would have wanted things to go but once we get to the other side of this Vjetgo business, you will see."

He hauled on the mammoth's chains and kicked his heels to set it into motion.

"We are Vitzerka, Mother." He sighed and sounded weary and defeated. "There is no end to the Wind-Spoken business."

CHAPTER SEVENTEEN

Dragahn looked through the vision of crumbling worlds and chilled stars, and saw the fires of Carnyxia's watchtowers before him, gleaming on the horizon beyond his enshrouding storm.

"It is not long now," he muttered to the head of the wise woman still lashed to Kollung's saddle.

The spirits of Perukh, those hostile intelligences, had occupied every corpse around him and it seemed the old woman's preserved head was no exception. Even the honored heads, some little more than skulls, that hung from Kollung's trophy had been occupied, although all they did was gnash and clack their teeth in endless impotent fury.

But the head of the wise woman, still filled with some semblance of sorcerous breath, spoke to him—or he at least believed it did. The dividing line between the contents of his mind and the real world had become frighteningly thin.

"Indeed," it responded in a thin, hissing voice. "Soon, you will meet Svarah Vjetgo."

He nodded as the un-mammoth that had been Kollung bore him forward with heavy, unfaltering steps.

"What will she be like?" he wondered. "Will she be a warrior? A witch? Something else?"

"How do you know it will be a woman?" the head whispered sibilantly.

"The little man," he said and leaned forward, but his gaze remained fixed on the distant glowing lights. "The broken one watched over by the—"

"Don't speak of it," the head pleaded and whined like wind through a rocky crag. "It pains me to hear of it. I understand."

The warlord frowned.

"But if she is a woman," the head began after a moment, "she should be easy prey for you, yes?"

"I suppose," he agreed. "I've never known a woman who could fight as well as a man."

"And you've never met a man who could fight as well as you," it wheedled. "So your victory is assured."

He began to nod until a soft, susurrating sound rose from it and drew his attention to the shriveled face. The eyes, already desiccated by the preservation process, had crumbled into ash when the spirit took residency, but the same cold light flickered in the depths of the hollow sockets.

"Yet, for all his travels, Dragahn Shieldshiver has seen little of the world beyond the Steppes." The old woman's head cackled and witchlight flashed in its eyes. "And there are wonders and terrors in the wide world you've yet to imagine. What if she is one of them, eh?"

"You have seen this?" He grunted and one corner of his mouth tilted into a disbelieving sneer. "I can not imagine a woman who could best me in battle."

Again, the coarse, sawing laugh rasped against the edges of his nerves.

"There are lands, nations, worlds, and infinities beyond what you can imagine, little puppet," it hissed and its waxen features twisted into something like a grin. "And yet you seek to bring them—all of them—to an end? To drag this age into an unmaking darkness without end although you've yet to even understand a fraction of it?"

"Life is a cruel jest," Dragahn intoned and the words of his faith fell easily from his lips. "By ending life, we seek to free ourselves and others from the bondage of such a mocking existence. In oblivion is liberation."

Images flashed through his mind as he recalled the litany of indignities he was made to bear that had convinced him of this truth long before. From the death of his father to the cruel, violating hand of his mother, he traced the bitter moments through a lifetime of swelling pain and agony. Each time the humiliations and horrors sought to mound atop his soul, he'd felt his spirit shrug to reject the absurdity of an ugly, pointless life. When at last he encountered the words of Perukh whispering on the wind, it had been like waking from a dream. He knew the truth and in knowing, he was powerful and unstoppable.

The warlord basked for a moment in the dire certainty he felt at the declaration and the liberating conviction of his destiny.

"I am Perukh Vjetgo, Wind-Spoken of the Striker," he said, his voice soft but firm. "It is my duty to usher in the End."

The smile on the severed head had not wavered.

"As has believed every fallen champion before you," it whispered in reply and the intimacy of the sound reached through his fatigue to make his skin crawl.

Dragahn frowned again, uncertain what to think of the statement. His thoughts were disordered often enough, but something that seemed so impossible was even more daunting. He knew who he was and had known it since he was a very young man in the very northeast corner of the Steppes. There where the cold hills gave way to the White Marsh and the Ice Wastes beyond, he'd grown and killed until the Perukh's call came to him on the wind.

He'd told his half-brother Tadzi and from there, they'd ridden to the nearest Bone-men camp and in a night of blood and revelry, claimed leadership. Their quest began and they gathered an army of the faithful unlike anything the Steppes had ever known while they waited for the time when Svarah Vjetgo would come. Through him, the End would finally be brought to obliterate the world.

In all that time, he'd never questioned his destiny, not consciously. He was different than those who came before. He'd been told where to seek the black sword and how to work the will of Perukh to Welcome the spirits into the fallen.

Yet now, the very evidence of his unshakable destiny questioned him.

Had he missed something?

"Don't talk to it," buzzed the sharp drone of an un-man at his side.

Startled, he looked up. While he'd been lost in his thoughts, the body of Tadzi had urged its mount alongside his. It watched him now with cold scrutiny that made him uneasy.

"What?" he asked and his brows settled into a scowl.

"Don't talk to the Curse," it said and pointed a blackened finger at the grinning head on his saddle. "Liar, blasphemer, and faithless."

The string of accusations cut through the fog in his mind, although he was careful to keep it hidden.

"That way destiny," the un-man said and gestured with a spear in its gnarled hand toward Carnyxia. "That way Svarah Vjetgo."

"They know," the head insisted, barely audible over the howling storm. "They know you are not the key but only the one who can bring them to the key."

"Enough!" not-Tadzi snarled and thrust the weapon into the whispering head.

The sharp iron, driven by a strength beyond what the man ever possessed in life, bit deep until the skull cracked. The faintest cry was torn away quickly on the wind and the lights within the empty sockets blinked out.

Dragahn jerked in surprise and the un-man tugged its spear free and left the slack head to stare silently at him.

"Almost there," the being wearing Tadzi said as the warlord's gaze rose to look on in mute shock. "Remember visions and seek destiny."

It pointed again with the offending spear toward Carnyxia.

"There," it said with utter authority before its mount carried it to another part of the army.

Something stirred within the leader, jagged and fractious and just below conscious thought, but the harder he tried to press it down, the deeper it cut him. Eventually, angry and weary beyond anything he'd ever known, he let the thoughts burst through the skein of his mind for examination.

His allies were not what he'd always thought they were.

According to the teachings of the Cult of Perukh, those spirits that were said to fill the corpse with power—whether a single bone ornament to empower a Bone-man or the animated bodies of his retainers—were said to be the spirits of those who followed Perukh. This was even evidenced in legends where the Welcomed rose and claimed to be the souls of those who served the Striker in ancient times. But now, after so much time among them, he began to question this.

These malign intelligences, whether in the wise woman's head or the bodies of his retainers, did not seem like the souls of fallen champions of the Perukhian cult. The way they looked at him with their cold, gleaming eyes made him wonder if they were even the spirits of men at all. The longer he spent with them, the more he felt that the perspective from which they watched him was more akin to the red-mouthed horrors they'd encountered in the Frozen City.

"Little puppet," the head had called him. Was that truly what he was?

The black sword in his hand pricked at his fingers and palm and his grasp on it tightened.

"Maybe," he muttered as hollow but welcome strength filled his flagging body and convictions. He merely wanted it to be over and for there to be an end.

"I've come too far to turn back now," he said to the vacant face with its darkened sockets. "One way or another, this will be over soon."

He lifted the black sword high, took up his war horn, and blew a resounding note.

The horde of un-creatures quickened to the call and bent their heads toward the gleam on the horizon.

A day, maybe two, and Carnyxia would be theirs.

Then, at last, the joke would end.

CHAPTER EIGHTEEN

"I hope you understand that this is nothing personal," Goran called over his shoulder as Ax-Wed watched Carnyxia fade from view.

She was glad he'd taken the gag off once they were a little way from the city, but she was not entirely sure she appreciated that he felt it had earned him a right to her conversation. Still, it helped to pass the time and it seemed to prevent him from noticing that she was close to sawing through a section of rope with a notched edge of her armor.

In the end, she decided to humor him.

"Of course not." She grunted as she craned her neck upward to keep from talking into a face full of mammoth pelt. "You're delivering me to a religious fanatic so he can dance me to death. It's nothing personal at all."

Goran responded with a hearty blast of laughter and stretched back to pat her rump affectionately. She lowered her face to the mammoth fur so the chieftain wouldn't hear her furious snarl.

I'm keeping track, she promised. *You are merely adding to the number of pieces you'll be in when I feed you to the crows. Right now, I'm at three, you handsy bastard.*

"I have to say I'm almost sad it had to be this way," the chieftain said. "I feel like you and I could have gotten along quite well had things been different."

"I'm not sure." She scowled and imagined tears running out of his eyes as she force-fed him his hands. "This whole situation speaks to a difference in values."

As she spoke, she shifted as surreptitiously as she could to rake the metal edge over the rope again. She felt another strand give way and something shifted in her bonds.

I'm getting close.

"It's merely practical," Goran explained and turned halfway around in his saddle. She froze in place. "Either Dragahn kills you and the world doesn't end and his forces crumble because they realize the prophecy is all kak, or you kill Dragahn and his forces scatter because their apocalyptic battle isn't happening today."

"And what if Perukh does show up to destroy the world?" Ax-Wed retorted as she strained to lift herself without letting the ropes show the damage she'd done to them.

"I'll take my chances." The man laughed and returned to facing forward but again, not without another appreciative slap on her backside before he gave it a lingering squeeze. "I've never known our gods to be of much use for anything but stories."

Four—no, that counts for five.

"Weren't you the one who called that frog-faced chieftain godless?" she asked and focused on the incongruity to keep the growl out of her voice.

"What—Merko?" the big man rumbled before he shook his head sadly. "No, that little fool is another kind of deluded."

"It's only you and Emerik then?" she asked through gritted teeth as she flexed and the jagged lame dug at another fibrous cord. "Birds of a feather."

"What?" he asked distractedly over his shoulder.

She assumed the idiom wasn't a common one amongst the Vitzerka.

"You and he think alike," she explained while she worked the edge over the strand repeatedly. "You both think little of gods and prophecies."

I'm almost there.

"I suppose you could say that." Goran seemed to genuinely consider the point. "It's not that I particularly like the man, you understand, but we do seem to be of a more practical mindset."

Keep talking.

As if responding to the mental urging, the Croali chieftain cleared his throat and seemed determined to clarify his position.

"To be honest, there isn't much about the man to like. For one thing, he can't handle his mead, you see, and then there's how things are all upside down in his tent."

"How so?" the warrior woman asked with a grunt as she felt another strand part. Things were shifting markedly in the ropes that bound her now. Surely only one more strand would be sufficient.

"Well, you see, he has things turned around between his wife and his son." Goran waxed philosophic. "He lets that wife of his treat him like a whipped thrall and vents his anger on the boy, whereas what he should be doing is…"

The last fibers lashing her to the saddle parted before she could hear the end of his ruminating and she began to slide off the back of the mammoth. She had almost slipped past the point of no return when she lurched forward enough to sink her teeth into her studded belt, which was strung across the back of the saddle. Her teeth grated painfully against one of the metal disks set in it but when she slid free, the belt that held her ax and dagger came with her.

The chieftain continued to talk while the Thulian, as soft and agile as she could be, tried to land on her feet. She managed it and even hopped clear of the mammoth's tread, but had to throw her head back and pitch the belt over her shoulder to avoid being brained by her ax handle. It was during this maneuver that she discovered her efforts had freed her from what held her to the beast but not the bindings around her arms and legs.

She gyrated wildly in an attempt to stay on her feet but it was hopeless. After two desperate hops toward her cast-off belt, she fell hard on the cold ground.

It can't ever be easy. She wriggled and twisted to see if Goran had heard her ill-fated escape.

To her surprise and relief, the boisterous brute still blabbered atop his meandering mammoth. Stretched ahead of them was the blacker than night line on the horizon that marked the coming of Dragahn. Watching him heading toward the Perukhian fanatics, Ax-Wed allowed a wicked smile to creep onto her face.

Wouldn't it be delicious if he reached Dragahn before he realized I was gone? It was a thought she allowed herself a long moment to savor. *It's almost as good as killing him myself.*

Still, she knew she couldn't count on that and even if she could, she doubted Shieldshiver's force would slow their advance toward Carnyxia. With that in mind, she decided it was best to free herself and return to the caravan. She wasn't even sure she could get close enough to the makeshift city to be picked up by a patrol before the enemy horde descended on her but she had to try.

Her belt and subsequently, her ax and dagger, had been flung several paces away and would have been an effort to reach. That and the fact that her hands were bound so closely to her body made her decide that drawing either would have been difficult and even dangerous.

With a profane word or two in a few different languages, Ax-Wed writhed and squirmed until she was able to position the rough edge of her gauntlets against the ropes that bound her legs together from thigh to ankle. Many a grunt and curse followed as she began to saw her way to freedom. Thankfully, with her no longer lashed to a heaving, shifting beast, it was easier than before and for the first time, she was thankful that her battered armor had so many nicks, burrs, and rough edges.

A minute or two later, the damage to the ropes around her legs was enough that she could shuffle and kick free of the bindings. She was also pleased to discover that her strained efforts had worked her arms a little looser and she thought that with a few more contortions, she could use her dagger to free them.

Ax-Wed struggled to her feet and had barely reached her belted weapons when a shrill whistle cut through the air.

Her heart leapt into her throat when two figures rode toward her on the loping creatures with massive foreclaws. Their eyes reflected the moonlight as they bounded forward with their almost simian gait and they seemed like something out of an absurd nightmare. The fact that men wielding torches stood braced upon their rolling backs only seemed to complete the mad image.

Of course he didn't come alone, she berated herself mentally. *Far enough to avoid attention but close enough to offer aid.*

The Thulian swung her gaze to her captor and confirmed that Goran had brought his beast around. The mammoth surged toward where she crouched as though it intended to spit her on its tusks.

Swearing and suddenly realizing she was drenched in sweat, she fumbled at the dagger hilt jutting at an angle from the grass.

You won't get another chance, a voice inside her head screamed. *Move your ass!*

Somehow, her fingers found purchase and with an awkward yank, she freed the keen blade. In the effort, she lost her footing again but it helped her to contort her body to position the blade effectively.

The Steppes grass partially hid her captors from her view but she didn't give them more than a glance as she drew the blade across the ropes in short, sharp strokes. Twice, she managed to slip the needle-sharp point between a seam in her armor and dig into her flesh. A thin trickle of blood began to ooze and smear across her arm but she ignored it as she felt the fibers parting.

She didn't dare lose focus but she could hear the snorting of beasts between the rhythmic thumps of their tread. They were almost on top of her.

Her sinews flexed as the blade raked upward and Ax-Wed parted the cords with strength and steel. She shrugged and twisted to throw the ropes off. As she spun to her knees, she felt a presence looming over her and caught the barest impression of long, blunt claws sweeping toward her before she threw herself flat.

Where she'd knelt an instant earlier, a furrow almost a foot deep was opened as the loping creature lurched after her with its other forelimb swinging wide.

She ducked under the swing and rushed inside the beast's reach. With one palm pressed to the pommel and the other hand grasped tightly around her weapons, she roared as she threw her body weight behind the dagger point. Steel punched through hide and dug through muscle to gouge into the creature's throat and turn a belligerent bray into a choked gargle. She twisted forward and to one side as it reared and drew the wound wider as the blade came free.

Beast and rider cried out and toppled back but she was already moving, knowing the other was almost upon her. Her feet pounded the hard earth as she rushed to the belt in the grass, tore her namesake free, and turned to face another attacker with a growl.

"Come and die!" she bellowed, her voice like a lioness at bay.

The beast rider hauled on the reins and his mount kicked up chunks of turf and grass as it skittered to a halt. The rider threw his torch to one side, drew a saber, and snarled a challenge in his own tongue. With a snap of the reins and a cluck of his tongue, he directed the beast to circle and heavy claws gouged the earth with each shuffling step.

"I won't waste any time." Ax-Wed growled before she launched into an attack and Thulian sylver flashed in the torchlight. "Morah is waiting!"

She lashed out and the beast batted with its forelimb in an attempt to check the swing but the grinning edge parted thick claws like rotten wood. It hooted in dismay and lurched back as its rider leaned forward to deliver an overhand stroke.

The warrior woman adjusted her hands with fluid grace and deflected the blow with the stout haft before she transitioned seamlessly to thrust with the horn of the ax-blade. The rider shrieked in protest as the point bit into his chest, not deep enough for a mortal blow but sufficient for him to back his mount away and swear bitterly at the blood that ran freely from his breast.

"Stop!" Goran howled somewhere behind her. "Stop!"

Ax-Wed paid him no mind as she danced to her adversary's wounded side, ready to deliver a killing strike to either man or beast when they offered her a fair target.

Unfortunately, she shuffled directly into the path of a sailing javelin.

The iron head lacked the weight and velocity to drive deep enough to give her more than a tickling scratch with its point, but the force of the impact winded and unbalanced her. The rider before her seized the opportunity and urged his mount forward with a snap of the reins. She tried to twist away from the blunt sweep of the claws but even a grazing impact from the blunt, boney sickles of the creature's forepaw tumbled her into the grass.

She sucked air in and tried to get her bearings. When she raised her head, unexpected heat on her face told her she'd fallen next to the dropped torch.

Goran bellowed in the Vitzerkan tongue now as he thundered up on his mammoth.

The Thulian extended one shaking hand to the torch, her entire body still trembling from the impact.

The chieftain snarled and spat instructions as her fingers closed around the shaft of the torch. She tried to force one steadying breath into her body after another and realized that more beast-riders had ridden out of the dark. Among them was another mammoth rider whose platform-mounted lancer had probably been the one to throw the javelin.

I've faced worse odds, she told herself, although the exact nature of the calculation eluded her at the moment. Right then, breathing seemed far more important than tabulating all her previous perils.

"You are impressive," Goran declared, a little breathless from his tirade. "But it's over. We want you to give Dragahn a good showing, now don't we?"

Ax-Wed didn't respond and merely tightened her hold on the torch in one hand and the ax in the other.

"A little out of breath, are we?" he asked and leaned forward in his saddle before he glared at the other mammoth rider. "Laza, if your man seriously damaged her, I'll hand you both to the Bone-men as a gift."

The man flinched and her lips curled into a sneer.

Such brave men, handing me over to a fate they wouldn't face themselves.

"Svarah Vjetgo," Goran called in a sing-song voice as though trying to wake her gently from sleep. "It's time to get up now. We have business to attend to."

She lay motionless, her only movement her even breathing.

"Stejan," he snapped. "Get her up."

The rider whose chest she had gouged uttered a complaint in Vitzercan, only for his chieftain to respond with a growl that needed no translation.

Stejan muttered bitterly under his breath, nudged his mount forward, and leaned back as he did so.

Only a little closer.

The long-limbed creature shuffled forward until she could smell its musty pelt and feel the gusts of its breath on the side of her face. It smelled of churned earth and mushrooms.

"Quickly," Goran rumbled.

Stejan leaned lower over his mount's neck to prod her with the tip of his saber and she bolted to her knees. With her ax in one hand and the torch in the other, she rammed the burning brand into the beast's face and swept the ax in an eviscerating arc through the reeling rider. He fell, his saber forgotten as he clutched his hewn side while his mount honked shrilly and went wild.

Ax-Wed backpedaled and ducked the creature's sweeping limbs and thick, thrashing tail as it wailed in pained fury. Cinders still sizzled in its eyes and nostrils and it trampled its gutted rider in seconds before it lurched to one side to grind its head into a nearby tree in an attempt to quench the tiny coals. In the process, it had almost raked the other riders and each man fought to control his beast.

The Thulian seized the opportunity and rushed at Goran's mammoth with the torch, screaming like a flayed panther. Flame and sparks flashed before the creature's face and the dull eyes widened with terror as the beast trumpeted a scream. She jabbed at the behemoth with the burning brand and pushed as close as she could to the sweeping tusks and furling trunk.

Someone hurled another javelin at her, but their aim was off and the shaft rattled across the mammoth's tusks with a sudden din before it cut across the front of the beast's trunk. This, combined with the torch prodding its face again, proved too much for the giant creature and it ignored Goran's shouted commands, reared, and bellowed in terror. The chieftain upon its back held on for dear life before the beast landed heavily on all fours and charged.

She hurled the torch at the raging pachyderm's face as she dove aside and barely dodged the tusks that raked the air above and behind her. The mammoth continued past her and still tried to shake the embers of the torch from its face. It bore down on Stejan's wounded beast and ripped its flank with one tusk before its massive feet descended to snap thick bones like kindling.

The warrior woman rolled clear of the mess and was about to bolt when Laza and his mammoth loomed. On open ground, she couldn't outrun the huge creature and without a torch, she had nothing to ward it off or distract it.

Dive under the tusks and trunk, she told herself and knew it was madness before the thought finished. *Maybe you can hack at its belly or something.*

Ax-Wed braced herself for the spring when two tawny streaks raced out of the dark and struck the mammoth's sides like twin snarling comets. The pachyderm squealed in shock and pain as the attackers resolved into two stocky felines that raked with their hind claws as they scrambled up the side of the shrieking mammoth. They seemed focused on the rider and lancer although their ascent left the beast's side in bloody tatters.

Laza and his lancer read the situation in an instant and both tried to leap clear of their mount. The lancer dropped the javelins he held in either hand and managed to vault from his platform ahead of a snaring paw, but he landed poorly and one leg folded under him at an awkward angle. One of the felid killers clambered onto the platform, bounded after its quarry, and reached him in an instant. Teeth longer than Ax-Wed's hand from palm to tip flashed in the moonlight and the man's pained scream was cut short forever.

Laza was less fortunate and one foot caught in the stirrup of his saddle as he tried to leap clear. His mammoth began to twist and buck and he swung from his saddle, one leg kicking wildly while the other bound him to the beast. As he hung there, the other feline still clinging to his mount's flank began to rake and bat at the unfortunate rider. By the time he fell with a shriek, his arms, chest, and face had been slashed to ribbons by the cat's raking claws.

The predator sprang free of the pain-maddened mammoth as it trampled the man into the bloodied grass before it fled into the dark.

All this had taken mere seconds, yet she gaped as the night suddenly came alive with more beast-riders while somewhere behind her, a patch of Steppes grass had caught fire. Like moths drawn to the flame, hulking creatures, mammoths, lopeclaws, and more besides, hurtled past where she stood to drive into the remainder of Goran's scattered forces. In the midst of the chaos, a sharp, trilling pipe sounded and the two felines stopped nibbling slivers off Laza and his lancer and hastened to resume the hunt elsewhere.

The warrior woman's head whipped in every direction as she tried to understand what was happening but she almost missed a shape that loomed out of the flashing shadows. She saw the attacker an instant before he rushed in with a roar like a wounded bull.

She intercepted a crushing swing from a cruelly spiked mace but had to give ground to avoid the wild return swing. Behind the flailing bludgeon, Goran's face, bruised and ragged from a hard fall, snarled at her and spittle landed in his beard.

"Stupid whore!" he roared and swung his mace repeatedly like a smith trying to right a stubborn horseshoe. "Stupid, stupid, stupid bitch!"

With each swing, she gave ground and struggled to keep her footing so she could launch an attack when the moment was right. His primary tactic seemed to be to swing hard and swing often but she wouldn't take any chances. He was big enough and probably strong enough that even a Thulian warrior woman would be foolish to not engage him carefully. A glance to either side confirmed that she had no immediate threats from other quarters so a desperate offense wasn't required.

This assurance allowed her to offset his blows when she couldn't shuffle clear and she only had to block one ringing attack with a deflecting sweep of her ax. Soon, Goran's face flushed a deeper shade of red and the time between swings began to lengthen. The mace moved slower and before long, even his frothing curses became shorter.

"You…y-you…s-s-s—"

"Stupid whore?" she suggested and provoked a winded scream as the chieftain lunged at her with an arcing overhand swing.

The Thulian sidestepped the blow and it cratered the earth where she'd stood before her grinning ax swept down. The sylver smile severed both of the chieftain's hands at the wrists.

He staggered back and stared in disbelief, first at his bloodied stumps and then at his severed mitts that still clutched the haft of his mace.

"One, two," she counted with a dark chuckle and stepped to the side.

One hard swing reversed into another and she hewed his legs out from under him. The dying man fell with a pitiful wail.

"Three." She kicked one leg aside and then the other. "Four."

The chieftain lay on his back and his lifeblood rushed out of him to steam on the cold earth as she came to stand over him.

"Five," she said in a chilling whisper and arced her blade into his wobbling throat.

Ax-Wed tugged the weapon up from the grip of the earth it had bitten into and Goran's head rolled to one side.

"A six-course meal for the crows," she muttered with grim satisfaction.

She hefted her ax to her shoulder, turned, and stood face to face with the two feline killers she'd seen earlier. Their tawny coats now matted and smeared with their gory work, they were still instantly recognizable by the fangs that extended past their chins even when their mouths were closed. Muscular shoulders rolled as they padded forward, quieter than anything so big had a right to be. The firelight gleamed in their eyes and a primeval tremor woke in the pit of her stomach.

The Thulian unlimbered her ax and told her knees to stop shaking, a vain attempt to defy some primitive imperative.

As she readied herself for a fight she wasn't sure she could win, sharp piping cut through the air.

Both felines flattened their ears but without further hesitation, they turned and padded away.

She stood motionless to catch her breath and tried to make sense of the events that had unfolded so quickly. When she looked up to see what had become of the rival beast-riders fighting amidst the patches of burning grass, she saw a stout figure riding toward her on a fine horse.

A fine horse she recognized.

"I'm sorry about my pets," the leading man called as one of Varhem's fine mares trotted forward.

On the fair beast's back was Merko, the chieftain Goran had called Kitten-Caller before the Titan's Totem during the War Council.

"I don't think they would have attacked you but better safe than sorry," he said with a thin-lipped smile. "Are you well?"

She stared at him for a moment, then nodded.

"Good," he said and assumed the toad with a fat worm expression. "It seems we have a fair amount to talk about."

CHAPTER NINETEEN

The sun rose over Carnyxia but a second nightfall loomed on the horizon.

Ax-Wed, weary, battered, and hungry, sat in the stands at the top of the amphitheater and alternated between watching the coming storm and looking at the arena floor where Merko and the other chieftains gathered for an impromptu council.

Well, it's not a council so much as a trial, she reminded herself as she looked at the center of the gathering.

Surrounded by the gathering of chieftains was Emerik of the Lecall, his wife Anja, and mounted on a triptych stand, the head of Goran of the Croali.

The acoustics of the Carnyxian amphitheater were such that even though Merko's voice was not quite a shout, she could hear him finish his testimony. He'd insisted that he deliver it in the Trade Tongue so she could understand what was said. At this point, in all honesty, he could have said she was rescued by a horde of furry-eared frogs riding winged jackals and she wouldn't have batted an eyelid. She was tired, overwhelmed, and certain that the only rest she was likely to get in the next few days would come when she joined Goran as crow fodder.

"I arrived as Ax-Wed—the one who is not Svarah Vjetgo—was exacting vengeance upon Goran," the chieftain declared as he leveled a sausage-thick finger at the head on display. "As for the retainers Goran had brought with him, none laid down their arms so they were unfortunately slain."

The corner of her mouth tilted up at the last statement.

I wonder if them laying down arms would have made a difference to Merko's pets? She vividly recalled the felids' eyes reflecting the burning Steppes as blood dripped from their fangs. *Somehow, I think not.*

The chieftains below, having not been there to witness such a chilling sight, merely nodded in agreement.

So far, they seemed to have taken the declaration that she was not Svarah Vjetgo fairly well too. Merko had continually repeated that fact—"my people are stubborn like that," he'd explained—but thus far, no one had raised a blade or even their voice to challenge the squat chieftain.

Involuntarily, her gaze was drawn to look out over the lip of the amphitheater as the line of unnatural dark encroached ever closer.

With that less than a day away, I'd be looking for someone to tell me the world wasn't ending too.

General mutters and some words in Vitzerkan were exchanged before one of the elder chieftains spoke.

"We recognize the truth of your witness, Merko of the Krivik," the gray-headed leader said in a hoarse, thickly accented voice. "For his crimes, the line of Goran will be cut off and the Croali tribe made thralls. All they own is declared spoil to be divided between Ax-Wed the Storm-Caller and Krivik who have beaten them in battle."

And with a word, an entire tribe is dissolved. Dozens and maybe even hundreds of families will be swept away just like that.

She shook her head at the ruthless nature of the beast-riders and waited to see if Merko would do as they had agreed.

"Thank you, Zubin of the Morehv," the chieftain replied. "But the victory belongs to Ax-Wed and it is her wish that the Croali not be enthralled and all they own be left to them. She only insists that any right to blood feud be renounced against her and my people and that they swear to peace among us as long as we and our children still live and abide by that peace."

This stipulation seemed to cause more controversy than anything else he had spoken thus far, and he had told her as much. On the ride to Carnyxia in the predawn light, they'd had a chance to talk at length and he had said that her proposition for the Croali would be as disconcerting to the tribal leaders as the declaration that she was not the Wind-Spoken, and perhaps more contested.

"The Croali are a strong tribe and seeing them broken would remove a rival for many of them," the chieftain of the Krivik had explained on the road. "Also, many of them know you would have little use for so many slaves and so would think to acquire them from you at a good price once the Thunder-Crush is over."

The gathering of tribal leaders did little to hide their displeasure and more than one chieftain threw an irritated look to where she sat but in the end, it came to nothing.

"Very well, but what of the Lecall?" Zubin asked frostily. He seemed to have taken up the role of spokesman. "Does the Storm-Caller know how she would like them to be dealt with?"

"I don't see why there is any talk of punishment at all," Emerik cried stridently and spoke for the first time since he was marched to the center of the arena by the wardens. "The crimes committed were by Goran, who intimidated my wife and used my so—"

The snarl of Vitzerkan curses and rebukes that rose to meet him was like the waves of an angry sea. He and Anja both cringed from the tide of angry faces that pressed in around them and shrank against each other. Their eyes wide and shining with terror, they looked around the encroaching ring and found few, if any, sympathetic faces.

"You violated the peace of the Thunder-Crush festival," Merko said and seemed to be more interested in reminding the gathering than the accused. "You engaged in bride-stealing by threat of violence and your crimes were compounded when your wife and son engaged in slave trading during the festival, both of which are forbidden."

"No money changed hands," Anja said in a tight, shrill voice and cut off her husband's stammered attempt at a defense. "How can we be accused of slave trading if no money changed hands?"

From where she sat, Ax-Wed couldn't see the accuser's face but she knew the pleased amphibian look was on his face again.

"Then it was murder you sought when you gave Ax-Wed to be delivered by Goran," the chieftain said with obvious satisfaction. "In which case, both you and your son should be executed as cowards and conspirators."

The woman wailed and collapsed with her hands over her face. She pawed at Emerik's leg as she yammered something in Vitzerkan. The chieftains seemed as unmoved by the display as her husband, who ignored his wife's distress and looked at Merko.

"I-I intended no murder," he shouted over the woman's bleating. "In fact, I was attacked by my wife and son as they enacted their plan."

Not caring that the sound might carry below, the warrior woman indulged a hearty laugh.

The man spared her a scowl but only for an instant before he returned to searching the faces of his judges.

"There is still the matter of bride-stealing during Thunder-Crush," Zubin of the Morehv declared and folded his white-haired arms over his burly chest. "That is no small charge."

An affirming murmur rippled through the gathering. None of them much liked the idea of their wives and daughters being fair game for an opportunistic "suitor," although she imagined that had more to do with the festival than anything else.

"Th-that was merely a misunderstanding," Emerik stuttered and cast a nervous glance to where she sat. "Perhaps my mastery of the Trade Tongue failed me, or maybe…maybe they were tired and couldn't understand what I was talking about. You see, it was nothing more than miscommunication."

"Liar!"

The shout mirrored the warrior woman's seething thoughts but it had come from a familiar, thundering voice. She turned in her seat, along with the entire company of chieftains, as Vahrem strode into the arena. He marched toward the ring of leaders with his head down and shoulders forward as though ready to charge into their midst, and he hadn't come alone.

Javor of the Lecall was at the caravan master's side and his long legs enabled him to keep pace easily with the shorter man.

"You speak the Trade Tongue better than anyone here." Vahrem's withering declaration resounded over the empty stands. "You are a liar, a traitor, and unworthy of the people you claim to lead!"

The chieftains began to sputter and growl at one another and several pointed to the newcomers, but whether in amazement or repudiation, Ax-Wed couldn't tell.

"This is a meeting of chieftains, Southron," Zubin said, his tone even but cold. "Unless you have something to bring us besides a loud interruption, you do nothing to help the case against the chieftain of the Lecall."

The merchant turned to the elder chief and she felt a thrill of terror, sure that he was about to shout the man down in his fury.

"Careful, my heart," she whispered, only dimly aware of having used the endearment.

But Vahrem Kal'Stru stirred to wrath or not was still a merchant and could read those before him in a heartbeat. He stood before them, drew a steadying breath, and used an open hand to direct their attention to the young Vitzerkan beside him.

"I've come at the request of one of the chieftains to present further testimony," he stated, his tone crisp and level. "And to present to you the new chieftain of the Lecall."

If his entrance had caused a stir, his latest declaration came dangerously close to triggering a brawl comparable to the one that had broken out when they stood under the Titan's Totem. Red-faced and yammering in their native tongue, the chieftains shouted at Vahrem, Javor, Emerik, and each other. The warrior woman pushed to her feet, uncertain what—if anything—she should do and finally chose to walk quickly to the lowest level of the amphitheater seating.

The doom gazing will have to wait.

It took a few minutes of bellows from both Zubin and Merko to get everyone to quiet enough for anything discernable to be understood. By the time she reached the timber platform over the arena floor, the ruckus had settled into an argument in Vitzerkan between the present members of the Lecall family, with occasional commentary from Merko and Zubin thrown in.

Vahrem watched everything with his arms folded over his broad chest and nodded occasionally when Merko and Javor spoke and generally frowned and made irritated expressions any time Emerik and Anja said anything.

Ax-Wed stood on the platform while the exchange continued. She was about to shout for someone to translate when the merchant interrupted, although he still seemed ignorant of her presence.

"Face it, Emerik. Under the enduring laws of your people, you've broken trust and exposed the tribe to shame. You can surrender the leadership of the Lecall and avoid further disgrace and punishment for those you lead or you can run the risk of having your whole tribe enthralled."

Anja seemed to finally come to some realization, turned from glaring at Vahrem, and began to address her husband in a low, angry voice. He blanched at first but when he saw the smirking faces of the chieftains around him, his countenance turned scarlet. With sudden viciousness, his hand lashed out and struck his wife across her swollen lips. She staggered back a step and collapsed to her knees.

A moment of stunned silence was broken by a tormented roar and several cries of surprise as Javor charged into the midst of the chieftains.

He rushed past and in some cases, bowled those in his way over until the strapping young man drove through the crowd like the prow of a swift ship before he pounded into his father. Emerik barely had time to squawk in surprise before his son seized him around the throat and threw him onto the hard stone floor.

The older man landed badly and his head met the ground with a dense thump. He gazed around with unfocused, bleary eyes as Javor descended on him. Everyone stood clear of the young man as he battered his father repeatedly with foot and fist while a wordless scream ripped from his throat. The chieftain attempted to fight back and kicked out as he tried to guard his head but soon, all he could do was cower and wait for the storm to subside.

For a moment, the Thulian thought the young man might beat his father to death but little by little, the fury burned out and finally, he straightened. His chest heaved and limbs trembled as he glared at his father and with a look of revulsion, turned away from the shivering, sniffling wreck of a man before him to see his mother. Steadying his hand with obvious effort, Javor helped her to her feet but when she tried to embrace him, he held her at arm's length. Gently but firmly, he positioned her beside his father before he turned to the chieftains and met each eye as he spoke with a voice that shook only a little.

"I am Chieftain of the Lecall and I will make right our

wrongs," he said. "For the crimes of my father, our warriors shall be the vanguard sent against Dragahn Shieldshiver. Every warrior of our tribe shall be the first to ride against the common enemy of our people."

Ax-Wed was no keen student of human interactions but the grim nods and approving murmurs of the crowd told her that no one was likely to gainsay the young man. Emerik continued to lay upon the stone with his downcast face in the cold stew of tears, snot, and blood. Anja looked horrified and ready to faint, but she remained silent and looked only furtively from her broken husband to her ascendant son.

Again, silence prevailed as it seemed the chieftains were unsure of how to continue after such unusual occurrences. Finally, Merko cleared his throat and seemed ready to address the crowd when, from outside the arena, a howling wind preempted him. Frigid and keening, the gale rushed over the top of the amphitheater and pounded those on the arena floor with a biting blast. Men shivered and drew their cloaks closer, and even Ax-Wed folded her arms when she felt the stinging cold seep through her armor.

The wind had not traveled alone, however, and on its heels came the sound of a single apocalyptic horn.

With faces whitened to the shade of milk, the chieftains looked at each other and again, Merko tried to speak but was interrupted by a wheezing laugh. As one, the gathering followed the sound to its source and recoiled in horror.

The severed head of Goran of the Croali, its eyes gleaming with unhallowed light, spasmed and twitched in an imitation of laughter as the creaking cackle continued.

"I was sent ahead by my masters to tell you the End has come for you," it croaked in a brittle, buzzing voice. "Take the field or fly, fight or flee, it matters not."

Every man shrank from the prophesying head but couldn't tear their gazes from the sight of it. Men of many wars cowered, their weapons forgotten at their belts as they ran trembling hands over their faces.

But among them, a tall shape moved unnoticed before the malevolent gaze of Goran's animated remains.

"The storm will grow amidst the slaughter to come, a cloud to swallow the world." The head continued to rant and the voice rose to the tune of screeching locusts. "Everything green and good will choke and die as—"

An ax swept down and split Goran's skull in two before it cleaved through the stand beneath. The wreckage of the broken skull and its contents landed wetly amongst the remnants of the hewn staves. With that sound, the spell that seemed cast over the gathering broke and the men, still frightfully pale, raised their eyes and saw Ax-Wed standing defiant in their midst.

"Well, you heard him. There's no more time for talk," she declared and met each blanched face with forge-hot eyes. "Stir yourselves and prepare for battle!"

On the horizon was nothing but darkness and death, yet Carnyxia seethed with fire and life. The vast menagerie of beasts, in battle harness and daubed for war, set out from the city within less than two hours from when Ax-Wed had issued the command. At the head of the column of mammoths bearing the banners and painted hides of the Lecall coming from the city was Javor. The young chieftain, his long lance in hand, sat on Jakash, lord and father to the hundred-strong column behind him.

At his side was a platform drawn by four lopeclaws, upon which had been placed one of the great braziers that typically sat atop the watchtowers of Carnyxia. Even as they headed into the dark, cold winds that whipped about them, men were busy heaping fuel for the fire into the basin to feed the blaze already within. A wagon drawn by a team of stout Steppes ponies pulled alongside the platform and men threw bundles of wood to waiting arms.

Ax-Wed watched, her weapon resting on her shoulder, while Vahrem called to her from the head of the wagon.

"I have four teams working to keep the light burning," the merchant shouted over the rumbling platform and the wailing wind. "But if you see we need more fuel, I've told the drivers to keep an eye out for you."

She nodded but knew one way or another that they wouldn't need regular refueling. There was time for little maneuvering on either side in this battle so it would simply be a matter of a sudden crushing clash. Dragahn's forces would carve through the vanguard and bear down upon the mustering tribes, or they would somehow wound the beast of an army enough to delay the advance so the rest of the tribes could sweep through.

The blazing fire behind her was more about men's hearts than tactics.

Despite this, as she looked at the storm about to envelop them, she couldn't find it in herself to be worried about them.

"Are you sure Numi got clear of all this?" she shouted, her gaze still fixed on the swirling blackness. She remembered Javor's muttered words about the eyes of demons being seen in the storm but so far, there was nothing but a churning void before her.

Why does that make it worse? she asked herself before coming to the answer. *Because what good is an ax and a little fire against the Abyss?*

"They're safe," Vahrem said and it sounded like a promise. "We'll see them in Aruhkham if not before."

The warrior woman swallowed her grim denials and settled for a slow nod as she forced herself to turn and look at him.

"I wish you could be here," she said and gestured to the platform under her boots. "Standing with me."

"No, you don't." He laughed, a wild and joyous sound to beat back the dark gale if only for a moment. "I'm a poor soldier and no great warrior like you. I'll keep running supplies out, whether fuel for the fire or javelins for the riders, and bring back the wounded. That will stop you from having to save me, I hope."

She forced a smile but wasn't sure he was being honest with her or himself on any of those points.

"Be careful then," she called when she saw that the wagon he drove was almost empty.

"I would tell you the same," he responded, still smiling. "But I'd rather tell you to give Shieldshiver a hard knock from me."

"I'm not Svarah Vjecto," she shouted as the men at the back of the wagon whistled to signal they were ready to return for more supplies.

"I don't think that matters much to him," Vahrem said as he began to turn the team of ponies away. "But you can give a hard knock as Ax-Wed of Kal'Stru caravan."

The Thulian raised her ax in salute as he cracked his whip over equine ears.

Her gaze followed the wagon as it swung wide and headed to Carnyxia.

"Whatever gods truly rule this forsaken land, keep him safe," she whispered and paused when she considered what he might have said to her prayer. After a moment, she shook her head and bowed it as she had seen done dozens of times in the caravan and, feeling utterly foolish all the while, raised her voice over the howling winds.

"Shepherd," she called and winced at how awkward the word felt on her tongue and in her ear. "If you can hear the words of a damned soul like me, please look after Vahrem. I've not known many of your followers but he seems one of the best."

As she looked out from under her brows, the first lights emerged from the darkness, each pair bright and unwholesome.

"And if it is not too much trouble," she added as one hand

groped for her repaired helm, "let me see him and my...my children one more time."

There was no sign whether the Shepherd heard or not, but the storm was upon her and even with the blazing brazier at her back, she shivered at the touch of jagged flurries. Yet, as they passed under the sky-devouring clouds, the light shined in defiance of the darkness and several of the men on the platform raised a bold shout as they threw more fuel on the fire.

Javor blew several short blasts on his war horn and the column of beast-riders behind him quickened their pace. In a moment, the platform was flanked on either side by a line of thundering mammoths. The luminous platform was the anchor that bound the two wings together as they pounded toward the enemy.

After a moment and despite the storm, the beast-riders took up song with something as steady and relentless as the tread of their beasts. Ax-Wed felt an old familiar stirring in her breast.

At the edge of the brazier's straining light, they saw the ranks of the enemy.

She barely had time to make out the fearfully wretched appearance of the demons arrayed to meet them before Javor raised the horn and sounded the charge.

CHAPTER TWENTY

"Awaken!"

Dragahn registered the intrusive voice in his ear but he tried to block it out. He was beholding the death of celestial wonders he had no name for and would brook no interruption.

"I may not know what they are called," he muttered, his throat dry and his tongue clinging roughly behind his teeth, "but at least I can know how they end."

"Awaken!"

The voice came with such power that the blow to his senses was almost physical and with a cry, he lurched away from the impact. He began to slide from his saddle as he crashed into the waking world, but a life lived mounted and the vigor of the black sword kept him on his steed's humped shoulders.

It took him a moment to steady himself as the un-mammoth that had once been Kollung quickened its pace to match the rushing brutes around it. His mind sluggish after the rude awakening, the Wind-Spoken of Perukh still knew the feel of a charging mount beneath his legs and his laboring heart quickened.

The warlord looked around with eyes so bloodshot that they

seemed like nothing but layers of pink and crimson swirling into the black pupil. The un-men were on their hulking beasts as they rushed toward a line of beast-riders formed around something that seemed to blaze like an infant sun to mock the storm's dark clutches.

"The enemy is at hand," he shouted and stifled a small sense of surprise. It seemed like only moments before that he had spoken to the broken little prince. He knew there was something the pitiful royal had asked him to do but he couldn't quite remember what it was.

The world became indistinct again and blurred at the edges so it would bleed into an expanse of stars where he could watch another heavenly holocaust occur. Before he could slide into that place, a painful rush of energy rose from the black sword in his hand and his whole arm clenched to the point of bursting.

On either side of him, the un-men chorused their directions.

"This is your hour!"

"Bear the key!"

"With it break your enemies!"

"Kill! Kill! Kill!"

The words seemed to probe inside him, looking for the certainty and the unassailable will to gird for a final push. He was as surprised as they were to find that in the intervening time, it had shrunk within him to a small, hard knot of embittered resolve.

All the ravages of his neglected body and the words of the mocking spirit within the head of the wise woman had gnawed at him, silent as maggots worrying at entombed flesh. The grandeur of his apocalyptic convictions, the majesty of his omnicidal ideals, and even the transgressive thrill of his masochism were all devoured. What he had left was this mean kernel like the pit at the center of some rotten fruit, an injured sense of entitlement that existence had dealt unfairly with him and so, like a child having lost a game, he would sweep the board clean.

It was petty, small, and not at all what he'd understood of the mythology of himself, Dragahn Shieldshiver, Perukh Vjecto, but in this moment, it would have to do. He was so close to the end after all.

"If you are the key," he whispered to the black sword in his hand, "let us unlock the End together."

Something stirred in the absolute darkness of the blade and the warlord felt a vast monocular intellect bend toward him. A presence that had been there and watched everything die in his visions, unmoving yet inescapable, brushed against him, and the warlord's withered flesh revived. This last gift would send him sailing into the tides of the Abyss.

Dragahn raised the black sword and howled.

"End! End it all!"

The wreck of Kollung raised its pitted skull and added a booming roar to its rider's. The atonal bellow was taken up by the bodies of beasts across the whole of his ruined army.

"Ah, savor the sweet tune of oblivion," he crowed as he directed his mount toward the sun at the heart of the enemy line.

He'd seen the death of stars in his visions but now, he must douse the lights in the waking world.

The enemy, however, seemed to have different ideas.

Too late to adjust his charge, the warlord realized that the enemy leader was not content with a simple bludgeoning charge. With a skill that was a testimony to both mammoth and rider, the enemy line swept forward in interlacing trajectories that swept the path clear before them in a widening course that drove outward from the center.

His mount seemed ready to swipe past an onrushing foe to crash into the sun—which resolved itself into a blazing fire upon a beast-drawn platform—only to suffer a crushing impact on its flank.

He snarled and fought to keep his mount as tusks thrust through the peeling hide to sunder bones and rip at moldering organs. The tusks' owner, a young bull full of impetuous vigor, threw itself against its foe, determined to upend and trample the larger beast through sheer momentum and ferocity. From its back, the rider urged his mount forward while the lancer hurled javelins at Dragahn, although none drew close enough to hit him.

Kollung's hulking body shivered as its broad feet fought for purchase on the frost-flecked grass but eventually, its huge, jagged nails bit into the earth and the animated beast could bring its unnatural strength to bear. Sinews clenched and strained beyond what any mortal creature could endure and his mount pressed back until the broken spurs of its ribs jabbed at the eyes of its attacker.

Unprepared for such an unnatural assault, the mammoth lurched away but not before the warlord twisted in his saddle to slash at the rider. The warrior shied away from the sweeping stroke, one arm upraised, but it was not enough to escape the edge that cut through his arm like cloth to gouge a furrow across his chest.

The man screamed, first in pain but then in horror as his body began to betray him and the infectious ruin of the black sword worked through his flesh. His remaining hand clawed at his body as he felt the preparations for the intrusive presence that hovered hungrily beyond the veil.

"Welcome it." Dragahn laughed into the shriveling visage. "It is a gift!"

A javelin streaked over the shoulder of the dying rider but the black sword flicked up as though it weighed no more than a willow wand. The broken shaft spun into the storm but its target rose in the stirrups to grin wildly at the cringing lancer.

"I have a gift for you too!" He laughed and lunged with his sword outstretched.

The man shuffled back but not fast enough to avoid the tip of utter dark that gouged his thigh and tore down around the joint of his knee. He fell on his platform and one hand clutched the fouling wound, while the other fought desperately to hold him on the wooden boards strapped to the rocking back of a mammoth.

"Embrace it!" the dark warlord said and swept a hand toward the rider. "See what awaits if you surrender and let them set you free."

The rider's body, its eyes now shining with the malign will of a new occupant, uttered a coughing laugh and expelled ash and bile. With the hand left to it, the fresh un-man drew the war-pick at his belt to hammer the head of the mammoth it rode. The poor beast screamed in surprise and pain as the hard iron battered its skull, driven by the hand of the one it had once trusted for life itself.

The stricken mammoth staggered and finally freed Kollung's body of the impaling tusks as it swung its head from side to side. Before his attention was drawn away, the warlord saw both rider and lancer raining blows upon the beast. It would take a moment but he trusted that the vicious strength of the fresh un-men would win out and before long, the slain mammoth would rise to join his horde.

Before he could savor it further, the damaged bulk of Kollung was rocked by impacts as two mammoths powered in from either side.

Even as the mount he rode began to buckle, the hordes on foot pelted out of the darkness until the Steppes seemed to glitter like the night sky with their hungry eyes.

"Every gift begets another," he declared as he stood in the saddle and began to lay about him. The black sword bit through hide, flesh, and bone to spread doom to man and beast alike.

CHAPTER TWENTY-ONE

At first, it seemed that things were going well.

Like the self-annihilating cultists they were, Dragahn's forces surged forward in an unruly rush and the mammoth riders seemed to have little to no formation to their movements. At a sweep from Javor's lance and a sharp blast of the horn, the Lecall beast-riders executed what they called the Sunder, a complex maneuver designed to fracture an unruly charge like the one they faced.

The warriors, experts at their craft, drove deep into the very heart of the enemy and with a ferocious yet disciplined rush, they splintered the enemy line like kindling. The ragged, sickly-looking mammoths of Perukh's followers were thrown back and some buckled entirely under the attack. The men on the platform cheered and beat their chests while Ax-Wed studied the field revealed by the blazing fire.

Unfortunately, the broken ones would not lay down and die.

An unnatural light in the eyes of the crumbling behemoths flashed with a terrible vengeance as they fought on with an endurance and strength no living creature could muster. Bellies split by eviscerating tusks did not slow them as they trampled their own black guts, and crushed rib cages were only used to rake and slash at their attackers.

Even when the beasts fell in the dirt, their skulls crushed beneath the tread of a mammoth, the riders leapt upon their enemies with graceless speed and strength. With bones twisted to breaking and muscles as taut as a drawn bowstring, the beings that could not be mortal men threw themselves from their doomed creatures and cleared the height of a mammoth with a single leap.

Sometimes, the Lecall riders caught them with an upraised spear or a sweeping blade but many times, the beast-riders were too shocked to strike in time. When this happened, the monstrous enemies in the shapes of men fell upon them like wolves on sheep to tear them apart. Some were hacked by weapons wielded with reckless strength and others were savaged by gouging fingers and tearing teeth. Even the mammoths were not immune to the violence as once rider and lancer had been thrown to the earth, they set upon the beasts and hammered skulls, stabbed eyes, and sliced throats.

Javor rallied the mammoth riders who had trampled their targets and escaped unscathed, but it was far fewer than Ax-Wed had expected at the outset of the conflict. Of the hundred who had been part of the initial charge, less than eighty galloped after their chieftain. Before her eyes, even some of those were bogged down and overrun by the smaller beasts that trailed after the mammoths, lopeclaws, and spikesnouts that struck at the mammoth's flanks when they could and let themselves be crushed and tangled underfoot when they could not.

A flight of lopeclaw riders of the Lecall issued forth to offer support, but the broken bodies of mammoths, either Dragahn's or the Lecall's, created treacherous islands on the field that broke their formation. As their riders moved forward on their bounding mounts between the intervening piles of meat and bone, the frenzied Perukhians launched an attack on them. The attempted support maneuver devolved into a separate bloody melee, while Javor tried to turn his dwindling mammoths for another assault.

The darkness beyond the racing mammoths sprang to life with hundreds of gleaming eyes. Unmounted creatures loped along at first with as long a stride as they could manage and what looked like men taken from a furnace and filled with hellish vigor began to rush across grass.

"Shepherd have mercy!"

The cry drew Ax-Wed's eyes from the scene and she saw that another of Vahrem's teams had drawn up. The volunteers from the caravan were to deliver fuel and see if any wounded could be taken from the field but currently, they along with the Vitzerkans on the platform stood and gazed in horror at the unfolding battle.

"Get that fuel unloaded fast!" she shouted.

One of the Vitzerkans threw a bundle of wood down and reached for the reins to the team that drew the brazier platform.

"Are you mad?" he screamed. "We need to get out of here!"

Before he could snag the reins, she caught him by the neck of his garment and threw him back.

"Get that fuel off that wagon." She growled a warning. "Now!"

Something in her tone or perhaps the fire-catching grin of her ax made the men hasten to obey. She turned to the wagon driver and called his attention with a sharp shout.

"Listen! Tell Merko he'd better get things in order fast," she shouted. "And tell him not to send another wagon without an escort."

The man nodded dumbly and turned to help the others offload the fuel.

Ax-Wed looked at the seething line of advancing horrors and estimated their rate of advance across the field. Legs rose and fell like the pumps in a water mill during a flood and Ax-Wed could tell at a glance that there was no way they could bring the cumbersome platform around before they were overrun.

And even if you could, those monsters could run you down with ease.

Despite this, she stooped and took up the leather reins of the nervous lopeclaws. While she was hardly the right one to do this, the others were busy doing what she'd ordered. She wrapped the reins around her fist once to get a feel for the thick straps. Although she was a competent rider, she only ever fought from horseback out of dire necessity, but this was different than either of those scenarios. Driving these creatures that were certainly not horses was not the same as riding, but she was certainly in a dire circumstance. She tried to envision what it looked like when she'd seen the Vitzerkans snap and haul on the reins.

A whistle pierced her thoughts and signaled that the wagon team was heading off, and she tightened her grasp.

"Hang on!" she shouted over her shoulder and raised her hand to give the reins a hearty snap like she'd seen others do earlier.

"Heng on to vaht?" The reply was spoken in a thick Vitzerkan accent but the reins popped and with a startled bray, the lopeclaws surged. The platform lurched forward with a tremendous groan and for one terrifying second, the warrior woman thought the brazier might break free of its hammered mountings.

She half-turned to look over her shoulder but remembered the needle she was trying to thread and decided it was better to not see if immolation was in her future. Behind her, the Vitzerkans screamed although some sounded more exhilarated than fearful—or perhaps equal parts of both, but that might have been wishful thinking on her part.

With her gaze fixed ahead and her grasp tight on the reins, the Thulian dragged the lopeclaw team onto a course that would take them between two fallen mammoths from Dragahn's forces. Beyond the crumpled remains, the hundreds of gleaming eyes bounded toward her. Some of the man-fleshed aberrations had given up on bipedal movement and with spines unnaturally bent, raced forward on all fours.

"Get two bundles lit!" she shouted over her shoulder.

"Vaht?"

"Get two of the fuel bundles lit," she called even as she fought to keep the beasts on course. "I need them burning and ready to throw. Get some of the oil ready too."

Ax-Wed didn't have time to ask whether she was understood or not as they rumbled toward the shattered hulks.

"Here goes nothing," she muttered, released the reins, and set to work with her ax. First, she parted the leather riggings and ropes easily enough, but then she had to work on the crossbar. Her weapon was of spectacular workmanship but it was not designed for hewing and splitting wood. Each stroke bit deep into the timber but it was a labor to tug it free as the wood pinched and flexed around the narrow profile of the blade.

"Vaht are you doing!" someone screamed behind her but the platform hit a patch of roughened earth and shuddered.

The hacked crossbar flexed up for a second to expose the thinnest portion where she'd been hewing. Seizing the opportunity, she drove down with all her strength. The Thulian sylver bit deep although it didn't quite shear through. But as the platform pitched downward on the uneven ground, the crossbar flexed down and it proved too much for the tortured timber.

With a resounding crack, the team of lopeclaws broke free and raced between the mammoth corpses with a chorus of wild hoots. Behind them, the brazier, carried by momentum, rolled on until it came to a shuddering halt a little beyond the enormous bodies.

As the wheels slowed to a stop, the warrior woman was already in motion and thankful to see that despite their incredulity, the men had lit two bundles of fuel at one end and set aside two measures of oil. She had the barest moment to wonder if it was because they still thought of her as Svarah Vjetgo before she shoved her ax into her belt to free both her hands.

"Douse the other and get it burning!" she shouted as she hefted an oil jar and with a grunt, pitched it onto the mammoth's body.

The sound of the clay vessel shattering was music to her ears, matched only by the rush of air-hungry flames a moment later when she threw the burning fuel in after the oil. Had they been freshly dead creatures, it was unlikely to work as the juices of their bodies would quench the fire. Instead, the flesh kindled beneath the lapping flames.

Ax-Wed had guessed rightly that such fluids had been wrung out of these corpses by both natural decomposition and the possessing spirits that had taken them. Old, half-remembered trivia of her eldritch studies had bubbled from her time in her father's study. She remembered the scolding she'd earned for bringing a candle too close to one of his specimens and kindling the flesh of a severed head whose jaws worked and strained toward it as though still hungry. The beating she'd received from her mother had ensured that the lesson was not forgotten, but perhaps it had not been the lesson she was intended to recall.

Now, though, she stood on the platform and felt the hot stink of burning fur and flesh wash over her as a smile spread behind her mailed veil. A moment later, the other mammoth corpse was aflame and she stood at the head of a trinity of blazing bonfires.

When she turned her gaze to the advancing enemy, she saw that the ranks of creatures had faltered and their rush slowed to a crawl. The light of the fires, now a full and glorious bulwark against the storm's darkness, revealed the hell-scorched frames and the sockets that shined with a light that had nothing to do with the honest light of the fire.

Demons indeed.

"Don't bother with their flesh but try to crack the skull open if you can," she said without looking over her shoulder as the men drew their weapons. "It releases the foul spirit within. Even cutting off the head won't stop the body."

Their mouths pressed into grim lines but to a man, they nodded.

"If not that, then throw them into the flames. They hate real fire."

Her ax was in her hand now and she spared the men who formed up behind her a glance.

Their pale faces were bleached almost to transparency in the glare of the blaze around them and each man seemed like a ghost taking up arms on some long-forgotten battlefield. Not one of them cowered or flinched away, however, but came to stand beside her at the forefront of the platform.

"They will come here to try to snuff us out," she warned, a growl in her tone as though the very temerity of the idea insulted her. "We will hold."

"Until the tribes come?" a young Vitzerkan asked, his hand steady but eyes wide.

"We will hold." She met the warrior's strained stare.

"We will hold." The Vitzerkan nodded and turned his face to the fearful enemy. "We will hold."

One by one, the warriors around her turned and recited the declaration until it became a chant.

"We will hold."

"We will hold!"

"We will hold!"

The swarm of un-men replied in their droning screech, a sound of chaos and unmaking that was an assault of pure noise. Yet for all its cacophonic fury, the chant of the fire-keepers would not be silenced. Even as they descended like ravening locusts, the cry of the warriors cut through screaming fiends and howling winds.

"We will hold!"

Vahrem watched the Vitzerkan move out and prayed for supernatural swiftness to be theirs.

"Shepherd, give them wings," he whispered as he snatched up another bundle of wooden staves.

He looked at the storm as the rest of the tribes began to deploy across the area before Carnyxia. Two sweeping arms of beast-riders stretched to the northeast and the southwest respectively. Like the horns of an aurochs, they would advance together and seek to pierce the forces of Dragahn from either side. The light of Ax-Wed's bonfire would serve as the guiding star which drew the points of the pincer horns together.

She and the vanguard merely had to hold on long enough to do so.

The merchant threw his burden into the back of the wagon and then went to see if the fresh ponies were secure. Had he continued to watch, he might have seen the light burning in the darkness suddenly gain two sisters, but his attention was drawn elsewhere when a scream rent the air behind him and he spun quickly, his heart in his throat.

Smoke rose from the encampments at the southern edge of Carnyxia. A moment later, the source of the screams was revealed when a woman ran out from the tents. With one hand, she dragged a small boy of no more than five or six while in her other, she struggled to carry the limp form of a little girl a few years older.

"Get this wagon moving!" he roared over his shoulder as he moved toward her as more fleeing figures emerged from between the tents.

"*Kostolych!*," she cried hoarsely and then, as though she noticed his swarthy features, she added, "Bone-men!"

His stomach twisted but he forced his lungs full of air to raise his voice in a commanding bellow that all the caravan men could hear.

"Anyone not with the last wagon, with me!" he bellowed. "Arm yourselves and unhitch as many mounts as you can. We move out in a minute."

The men around him stared for a moment but as one, they received the order and set to work. Several of them already had their weapons at hand, but those who were without quickly snatched up whatever was available and shoved hammer, hatchet, and knife into their belts.

"Iyshan!" the caravan master shouted as he selected a pony and began to secure a saddle. "Iyshan, to me!"

The manservant appeared out of the crowd of surging men, one hand on his saber and the other already leading the largest Steppes pony his master had ever seen.

"I ride with you, master," he declared.

"No," he said and ignored the wounded look on the man's face as he tightened the straps in his hand. "I need you to ride out and make sure the wardens are headed that way."

Iyshan looked ready to argue but the merchant turned, clapped a hand on his shoulder, and squeezed.

"You are the only one I know who will get there fast enough and can make them listen," Vahrem said in a tone that would brook no further discussion. "Deliver the message and ride back to my rescue."

The other man's taut chest swelled with a shivering breath but he nodded. His master punched his shoulder with a meaty fist.

"And be quick about it," he said with a smirk before they parted to mount their steeds.

The pony beneath Vahrem uttered a disgruntled huff as the stout man settled his weight on the beast's back, but that was the only complaint and when he urged it into motion, the creature responded readily. The caravan master looked around and saw that many of his men had joined him in mounting ponies and the rest seemed to be in the process. Despite the screams of more fleeing victims, he waited until every man was mounted before he raised his voice.

"We'll sweep around the outside of the camps," he shouted and pointed with one hand while the other steadied his mount. "Hopefully, we'll come upon their flank. Stay together and don't get bogged down. If you are separated, try to fight clear to the outside and watch for us from there."

He looked into the faces of men who were family to him—fathers, sons, uncles, cousins, and nephews. They weren't soldiers but to a man, he knew they would not ride away when women, children, and the infirm were left to the hands of cruel and callous men. Not when they could try to do something.

"Ride out!" Vahrem cried and put heels to his mount. "And Shepherd keep us all!"

CHAPTER TWENTY-TWO

She had to kick another corpse off her ax and the acrid smoke of burning bodies threatened to choke her.

"Tighten up!" Ax-Wed shouted when she felt space at her elbow but she couldn't spare the time to look as her gaze charted the course of another leaper.

At some point, the piled bodies of the broken un-men before the brazier platform had been set alight so those remaining were slow to rush in. Their bloodlust couldn't be stalled for long, however, and twisted flesh under cruel control soon launched stolen bodies into great sailing bounds to come down swinging and clawing at everyone within reach. Some were caught on spear or sword and the rest were hacked down or thrown into the blaze.

The warrior woman timed her strike as the leaper descended and with mocking ease, the grinning edge sliced through wasted arms before it split the skull like a rotten melon. A second leaper she hadn't noticed thudded beside her and managed to clang a blow off the dome of her helm. She accepted the blow and let it turn her. The creature uttered a rasped laugh as it made to pursue but she had already used the momentum of the turn to propel her into a scything strike. The un-man's clumsy attack slid noisily off her pauldron as Thulian sylver sheared through skin, bone, and brain.

Her shoulder ached from the impact as she brought her ax back to guard. The entities that possessed the bodies of these men and women were strong, fast, and cruel, but they had no skill and little interest in defending themselves. If given an opportunity, they would overwhelm their target in a tireless flurry of attacks but if even a halfway competent warrior remained composed, they could be dispatched quickly.

Still, one misstep was all it took for the fiends to pile in and smash, stab, and hack.

With a grunt, she kicked the limp remains off the platform and into the blaze below and searched for more targets. For a spare second, there seemed to be none although the gleaming eyes flashed through the smoke that rose above the fire that ringed their position. Squinting through the flames, she realized how thickly they were packed to the point where they practically seethed over each other.

They're massing for another push.

"Tighten up!" Ax-Wed snarled and turned to assess the situation, confused as to why she was still exposed on either side. With a start, she realized it was because there was no one to tighten up.

The line of warriors around her had been systematically reduced to barely more than a half-dozen weary souls spread across the front of the platform. Their faces streaked with soot and blood, both fresh and fouled, they held their weapons in sagging grasps as they kicked their vanquished foes into the flames. Here and there, a few bent to split the skulls of their comrades who'd fallen, having learned quickly that even the freshly slain could find their shells filled with the unclean wills that teemed within the storm around them. This grim duty done, those bodies were pushed behind them to keep the platform clear.

The warrior woman's gaze settled on the body of the young warrior she'd spoken to at the start of the fight, his fair features riven by a friendly blow to the forehead. Sightless eyes that would never know the foul gleam of the un-men stared at her as though asking if his duty was done.

Stop pondering the dead, she told herself and dragged her gaze upward. She discovered that the brazier's flame had sunk so low that the red tongues barely licked above the basin.

Not daring to look over her shoulder yet, she shuffled forward and with arms burning from exertion, hauled up the last few bundles of fuel they had.

How long has it been since fuel came? Minutes? Hours? Longer? And where are Javor and his riders?

The thought swam through her weary mind, scudded and paddled about, but found little to land on. With a grunt, she pitched two bundles into the brazier and it flared with eager flames to gleam on her helm before she shuffled to deposit the last bundles in the smoldering carcasses that had become impromptu firepits.

"We will hold," a warrior said with a heavy nod as she shuffled past him with the lashed staves of wood.

"We will hold," she echoed, although she knew one look over her shoulder would tell her that they wouldn't hold much longer. The fact that no more leapers had pounced during the lull confirmed that they were indeed preparing for another surge forward.

This time, there was no way they could stop them.

They would smother the flames with the foremost bodies before they swept over the platform. With so few to stand against them, she and the remaining warriors would be surrounded and borne down, and they would be torn to pieces. The Thulian accepted the fact that as she was the most heavily armed, it was most likely that she would survive the longest. This would give her time to watch between the blows and rending fingers as the brazier was upended and the light extinguished.

It seemed Mother's curse ended today.

Long may you walk it.

"I suppose long is a relative term." She sighed, squared her shoulders, and prepared herself for the end. "It was longer than I thought but not longer than I hoped or feared."

The warrior woman heaved a sigh and allowed herself to look over her shoulder but toward Carnyxia. The storm had swallowed the sight of the city but deep in her heart, she felt a yearning to see a wagon ride out of the dark and one bearded caravan master crack the air with his whip.

But there was only darkness, thick and seething with malice. Remembering the transported face of the Bone-men that night after the Thunder-Crush, she wondered if that was the merciful oblivion they had imagined. Somehow, she doubted it.

With darkness behind and dying flames ahead, Ax-Wed turned to face the enemy and her ax rose to the ready. Across the platform, the remaining warriors did the same.

"We will hold," she called, her voice raw but strong.

"We will hold," they answered, their voices worn but unbowed.

Beyond the flames, the un-men screeched and buzzed with mocking laughter as they began to press forward.

She set her feet to make sure that her first few strokes were rooted and strong. As a sworn sister of the Grim Handmaiden, she would not meet death any other way.

The first of the un-men, driven by the press of those behind, met the flames with shrieks like the squeals of tortured animals but they were soon drowned out as more unwilling bodies piled on top of them. Here and there, the flames leapt up, hungry for fresh fuel, but she knew those could not endure the smothering wave.

A sharp horn blast lanced through the air and she tilted her head to one side as her doom-fixed mind struggled to understand its purpose. In answer, the ground trembled with earthbound thunder and a chorus of pachyderm trumpets rose along with the voices of men.

From the edge of the flagging light, Javor of the Lecall atop the mighty Jakash led the last of his beast-riders into a sweeping charge. Iron-banded tusks swept twisted bodies into the air like chaff before a thresher, while those underfoot were crushed to a pulp. Some among the enemy had the awareness to leap at the riders but were spitted on spear points or hewn down by flashing blades. The gathering press of un-men only made them easier prey as the mammoths' bulk crushed mounded bodies like grapes in a winepress.

Ax-Wed and her remaining warriors cheered the young chieftain and his bold charge.

Javor brandished his gory spear in salute as Jakash plowed through the enemy, then took his horn up and blasted a short series of braying notes. Like a flock of gargantuan birds wheeling in the wind, the charging mammoths rounded the field for another charge.

The remaining host of malefic bodies swiveled their gleaming eyes from the chieftain's riders to the brazier and appeared to be caught between their hatred of the light and the real threat of the mammoths. They were still clacking their teeth at one another and spinning irresolutely as though debating the tactics of the moment when Javor and his beast-riders bore down on them again.

Bodies catapulted away in pieces and the tread of the great pachyderms left twitching wreckage with every step. Nothing seemed able to stand before the Lecall.

Until the trap was sprung.

Standing atop the head of his heaving, rushing mammoth corpse, Dragahn Shieldshiver launched himself at the young chieftain. At his side rode four hell-eyed retainers on their monstrous mounts and threescore more shambling beasts followed closely. Ax-Wed could see at a glance that the greatly reduced forces of the Lecall, now barely a score of riders, were about to be overrun in short order and there was nothing she could do besides shout a desperate warning.

Jakash, the wily and mighty mammoth king that he was, sensed the danger at hand and wheeled with amazing speed for one so massive, his tusks forward to meet the charge. All around him, his kindred followed suit, although a few that weren't so nimble or practiced staggered and one fell when its thick leg twisted under the strain of the sudden turn.

Had this been a charge of mortal beasts, the bristling wall of tusks and spears might have dissuaded even such a numerous charge. But these desecrated frames were driven by infernal wills that cared nothing for their broken vessels, so the charge crashed upon the Lecall with reckless, self-destructive fury.

The Thulian watched as Dragahn, his black sword clasped in both hands, leapt upward, propelled by a toss of his unholy mount. He sailed over Jakash's sweeping tusks that impaled the mount and he gave a fell and lonesome howl before he drove down on the regal mammoth's head. The black sword bit deep and Jakash, champion of the Thunder-Crush and mightiest of his august line, shuddered as his great legs began to buckle.

From the heaving shoulders, Javor made to thrust at the slayer of this mighty beast, but in a flash of blood and bone, Dragahn tore his blade free and swept it up into a parry that took the head off the young man's spear. The chieftain of the Lecall, his men and their mounts dying around him as more of the enemy piled upon them, fumbled for the saber at his belt. The warlord raised his sword for the felling stroke but even in death, Jakash seemed determined to serve his rider.

The great mammoth listed to one side, and the dark warlord's stroke went wide and missed its target by inches. Before either could recover to make another attack, Jakash's dying might finally succumbed and the beast fell and flung both adversaries to the earth. The two champions were now separated by broken, hulking frames for the moment.

Ax-Wed saw Javor struggle to rise and hoped the young man might succeed and lead what was left of his men toward the fire. Then she saw him collapse and noticed the way one leg stretched behind him at a sickening angle. One hand clutched his saber and the other clawed the ground as he crawled and hopped across the grass, his injured leg trailing behind him.

While she could not see Dragahn amidst the chaos, she knew the warlord was unlikely to let his prize evade him for long.

She shifted her gaze to the un-men still milling about in the wreckage of their kind and the broken, ravaged wasteland between herself and the young man who needed her help. She had to get to him if only to keep Dragahn occupied with them for a little longer.

Her mind racing, she turned and saw the brazier and an idea seized her in a wild rush.

"Help me!" she cried as she rushed to the hammered staples that held the brazier in place and didn't stop for even a second to make sure the others followed.

Reversing her grip, she drove the beak-like bill of her ax into the joint of the heavy iron staple. Sparks flew and metal warped.

"Help me!" she cried again but didn't look up as she drove a second strike home and then another.

A gap appeared and she almost cried out with relief before she thrust the bill of her ax under the gap. She leveraged her armored body against the staple and at first, the mounting came up with painful slowness, but little by little, it rose. With a grunt of exertion, the staple finally popped off.

The Thulian gathered herself and when she felt the strain in every muscle in her back, she wondered how she could do this three more times.

She heard sounds like a smithy gone mad and raised her head. The weary warriors left on the platform had heeded her cries and set to work on the other three. Hammering, hacking, and prying, their bodies slicked with sweat and smeared with soot, that bold half-dozen saw the other mountings undone. Exhausted but with determined eyes set in glistening faces, they turned to her and saw she'd already set her shoulder against the stand. To a man, they flocked to her, heedless of the blistering heat emanating from the metal frame.

The growing sting of the hot metal seeped through her armor but she used the pain to galvanize her. Around her, the hands and shoulders of the warriors, some momentarily protected by armor and others not, pushed with her. A mingled roar of agony and determination rose from them as the smell of seared hair and burning skin rose.

Finally, with a ponderous groan, the brazier began to tip and with a glacial certainty, it pitched forward.

Blazing fuel—far more than she had expected—poured across the earth before the platform. The un-men in the field, those on two legs and those crushed by mammoth tread, all kindled beneath the flaming avalanche. Some ran about with their grinding, droning screams while others collapsed as they clawed at their stolen carcasses, but none were left untouched by the burning wave.

Fast on the heels of the scorching tide, kicking up cinders with every step, Ax-Wed led the last guardians of the light.

"To your chieftain!" she shouted and her namesake licked at anything around her. "To Javor!"

Vahrem was reminded once again why he was no soldier when he and the men of the caravan accidentally rode into the midst of the Bone-men as they ravaged the camps around Carnyxia. A soldier wouldn't have misread the lay of the land to ride directly into the middle of the enemy forces, but they had foolishly done so and now wheeled their ponies in search of a way out.

Only the fact that the Bone-men seemed even less organized in their attempted slaughter of anything that moved kept his little group of would-be rescuers alive. Still, there were more than enough of the frothing fanatics to keep them fighting for their lives.

His whip snapped and a Bone-man fell back and clutched the hollow of his throat where a raw strip had been torn down to the clavicle. Another of the caravan volunteers battered the injured foe's head with a passing swing of a grain flail as he rushed past, but the company had no time to celebrate.

At their flanks, another pack of Bone-men appeared and screamed and waved their weapons. The ponies, beasts trained for labor, not war, shied away from the fearsome display and soon, it was all their riders could do to keep them from colliding with one another. Tents were flattened as the frightened equines bucked, surged, and lashed out at anything nearby including their fellows.

Vahrem fought to keep his seat, bent low over his mount's neck, and tried desperately to soothe the creature. Being so occupied, he didn't see the flying spear until it took the pony in its bared, rearing breast.

The caravan master cried out as the steed screamed but he had the sense to spring clear.

He landed with a practiced roll but came up as flailing hooves flashed toward his face. He ducked away from another floundering pony and scrambled back as another beast and its rider pitched toward him. For what seemed like an eternity of several seconds, he did nothing but dodge, dive, and scuttle across the ground to escape the collapse of his little cavalry troop.

Once he finally emerged, winded, battered, and scuffed, he had only a second to catch his breath as he stood in shock. He had time to wonder how many of his men were still fit to fight before the first Bone-man bounded forward with a spear leveled at his chest.

The merchant realized his whip had been lost in his fall and he had no time to draw the short stabbing sword he wore at his belt. He twisted and back peddled to stay ahead of the thrusting iron point until his foot slipped on something and he fell back. On instinct, his hand reached out for support and by some happy chance, closed over the extended haft of the spear. The Bone-man growled like a wild animal as he fought to free his weapon but this only served to pull the caravan master closer.

With his feet under him and his other hand closing, Vahrem used his greater weight and strength to twist the spear from the enemy's hand. The Perukhian fanatic reached for a blade at his belt but the merchant used the spear to yank the man off his feet. He spun the weapon in his hand and threw his weight forward, and iron parted flesh and split bone until it struck the sod below.

The foe spitted on his own spear arched his entire body as he looked at him, his mouth stretched in a silent scream. He planted his foot on the dying man's chest, yanked the spear free, and ignored the fingers that grasped feebly at his foot.

He knew he should feel some remorse or sorrow at one of the lost dying without hearing the Shepherd's voice, but when he raised his eyes he saw the burning tents and the bodies of women and children hewn upon the earth. Looking upon the carnage, he felt no remorse, only a growing burden to see it end.

Another Bone-man came into view and coughed as he emerged from a cloud of smoke vomited from a tent.

A terrible wrath filled Vahrem from head to heel and with a scream of fury, he launched forward with the spear held before him. The fanatic barely had time to register that he was under attack before the iron point punched through his belly and out his back. His legs buckled and he fell heavily, his hands wrapped around the bloodied shaft protruding from his stomach.

The caravan master kicked him off the spearhead and squinted through the smoke for another target. He heard a scream, a cry of pain and fear, and something quickened in him alongside the wrath. The urgent desperation drove his feet forward across the burned and bloodied soil.

He burst through a veiling wall of smoke and came upon three of his riders desperately fending off a pack of Bone-men. Two more of their number lay dead upon the ground and a third clutched his chest weakly where a vicious stroke had caved his ribs in. Behind the flagging defenders, an old woman held two small children against her.

The Bone-men stalked forward and uttered cruel, lascivious promises in Vizerkan as they brandished their weapons. They were seven to the three, and their weapons sat comfortably in their bloodied hands but they seemed intent on savoring their kill.

In their revels, they hadn't noticed the caravan master and he seized the initiative. His feet churned the dust and he launched himself at the largest of the fanatics, driving the spear forward as he had before.

The warrior, through instinct or the last traces of the merchant's luck running dry, sensed the attack at the last second and tried to twist away as he slashed with a cleaver-bladed sword. Vahrem tried to adjust his thrust but his weight and momentum made it hard to alter the course. As a result, the fanatic's face was gouged by his spear tip before the sword swing sliced the top third of the spear off.

He tried to bring the haft around for a strike but had to raise the length of wood over his head to catch a hewing stroke. The blade bit deep and stuck in the wood, but before he could try to wrestle it away from the man, a heavy boot caught him in the belly.

His breath exploded from his lungs and he lost his balance and his footing as he staggered back. Desperate to force a deep breath, the merchant dragged himself back with one hand while the other groped for the sword at his belt.

The Bone-man, grinning despite half his cheek flapping open, loomed over him with his sword in hand. With a guttural chuckle, he called to his companions to watch him free another wretch from the Great Jest.

Vahrem's hand landed on something behind him as he pulled the sword free in an arc to stop the descending cleaver. Steel flashed upon steel as the Bone-man sought to batter through his opponent's block. Laughing wildly, the fanatic reared with both hands holding his sword for a hewing stroke. From where he sprawled in the dirt, the merchant couldn't reach his enemy with his short sword.

Instead. he thrust up with the cloven spearhead he'd found inadvertently when he fell.

His adversary gaped in surprise at the broken weapon that seemed to have grown from his ribs and collapsed as the spearhead came free in a welter of his heart's blood.

Still wheezing, the caravan master scrambled to his feet with his short sword in one hand and the broken spear in the other. The other Perukhians pressed in but he gave ground and soon shuffled into line with the three remaining caravan men.

"Fancy seeing you here, Master Kal'Stru." The man at his right chuckled darkly. "What brings you?"

Despite his aching chest and pained lungs, Vahrem forced a smile.

"Can't you see, Amal?" he said with a laugh and immediately winced. "I'm here to rescue you."

"Lucky us." The man smirked and together, they turned to the enemy as more of the bone-pierced maniacs emerged from the burning tents.

CHAPTER TWENTY-THREE

He saw her striding across a field of burning corpses and she was the most striking thing he'd ever seen.

She was tall and powerfully built yet so ferociously feminine at the curve of her hip and the swell of her breast that even her battered armor could not hide it. The metalwork of her helm suggested braids, while the aventail seemed like a bridal veil for a war goddess.

Swift and sure, she strode over the burning ground and appeared untouched by the blazing dead as each step cast cinders up. When one of the spirit-animated wretches dared to stray too close, her ax, bright and gleaming like moonlight upon ice, dispatched any threat with contemptuous ease.

Equal parts lust, adoration, and wonder squirmed between the cracks left in the warlord's shriveled heart.

He'd known that the chosen of Svarah the Dragon-Slayer would have to be a spectacular creature, but he never imagined she would be so...so beautiful.

"And there are wonders and terrors in the wide world you've yet to imagine, and what if she is one of them, eh?"

The voice from the wise woman's head came back to him with cruel, piercing clarity.

"She is," he whispered as the black sword almost dragged him to engage her. "By Perukh, she truly is."

He had hoped for an end and could he conceive of one better than this? To snatch this most glorious being away from the Great Jest or to see himself stolen by her instead?

The warlord still struggled to convince himself he couldn't be beaten, even by one such as her, but if he was to fall, he would do so glad that it was her hand that struck the blow.

"Strike now!" said the chorus at his back as the four Welcomed appeared behind him. Each frame bore signs of the battle's mutilations but still, their eyes shone with a cold, pale light.

"The hour has come," they droned in unison.

Dragahn held the black sword to his eyes and felt the pressure to obey flood into his body. Like tendrils of some deep-sea horror probing a crustaceans shell, the dark will looked for purchase, some venue to seize and control.

But his shrunken spirit, rendered to its lowest and pettiest form, had no such weakness.

He allowed himself a cold smile.

"The hour has come." He laughed. "And that means I need only one voice in my ear and that is Perukh."

The un-men still stared at him when he fell on them with the black sword. As he struck, he felt their wills press through the fell weapon against his mind in an attempt to plunge it into visions of a ruined reality again. The phantasms and sensations vanished as unhallowed edge met scorched flesh and blackened bone.

It was the work of a moment but in a dizzying pattern of sweeping cuts, all four lay in broken and twitching heaps. Four skeletal faces turned burning eyes toward him.

"This changes nothing," they croaked together through stolen air.

"But you won't be here to see it," the warlord said with a rumbling chuckle. "And I'll have some quiet."

His boot stamped repeatedly, a macabre dance of splintering skulls and black ichor.

Finally, once he'd scuffed the remains on the grass, he turned. Svarah Vjetgo had reached the young leader of the mammoth riders with her bedraggled entourage. With one hand, she hauled the crippled warrior up to put his arm over her shoulder while the other held her ax at the ready. Her handful of warriors watched over her, their weapons drawn and eyes searching through darkness and choking smoke.

Dragahn began to jog forward. The black sword, now wholly at his command, filled him with vigor and a lightness of body he'd not known since his youth. The whisper of Perukh in his mind became a roar and he gave vent to its fury through jagged syllables. Blood flowed from his mouth and blue flames leapt along the sable blade.

This was the fire not of material heat and light but the rippling flames of unmaking, Perukh's very entropic essence. He basked in it even as he exulted in his command of it and thought that if he'd known such power could be his, he would have thrown off the presence of his handlers some time before. With such power, he would not bear witness to the death of everything. He would be the death of everything.

"Perukh Vjetgo!" he howled to the black sky with bloodied lips. "I am the Striker of the Heavens!"

His declaration drew the eyes of Svarah Vjetgo and her warriors but the yards between them disappeared in the blink of an eye. In another flutter of eyelids, two of the entourage were dead before they could raise weapons from sagging shoulders. The blue flame lapped over them and before the horrified eyes of their companions, their bodies withered into edifices of ash that scattered at a breath.

Now Dragahn knew why the selfish un-men had trammeled

him and sought yet more stolen frames. They had been parasites, drawn in the wake of his slaughter. Perhaps they had waited in demon-haunted Hoarlin until they could find one they could deceive into setting them loose. With twists of his zeal and besotting visions, they'd bound him and used him.

But he was unleashed to unmake all and by Perukh, it was all he'd ever imagined it would be and more.

"Come, Svarah Vjecto!" he called as the black sword parted another man from his life with a casual slash. "Join me in the Eternal Dance."

To punctuate the point, the black sword licked out again and gifted a fourth man with a touch of blue flame. His body crumbled as another breath of flurries rolled across the scorched grass and the warlord held his hand out to feel the grains pass through his fingers.

The warrior woman turned burning, coppery eyes upon him, even as she called the two remaining warriors to take the wounded chieftain. Shieldshiver dismissed them with a flap of his hand and together, they staggered away and the young chieftain cried out in pained protest.

Unencumbered, the majestic creature took her shining ax in both hands and the two began to circle.

"It seems we have an audience," she observed as gleaming eyes appeared all around them. "Do you think they can wait their turn while I kill you?"

At the edge of the flaming grass, the unhallowed creatures had begun to gather as more of them shuffled out of the depths of the storm, a force whose size Dragahn could not count. How many had they swallowed on their approach? Not only beast-riders and their mounts but every creature, no matter age, gender, or haleness, all formed a host hungry for nothing but destruction. Undirected by the four Welcomed, they were drawn by the power of the black sword.

"They wait on me." Dragahn smiled and brandished the shimmering sword. "Although, with the full power in this, I hardly need them."

Svarah Vjetgo glared at the blade and a troubling recollection passed over her face as she studied the singular weapon.

"You meddle with things you shouldn't," she said, her voice flat and hard. "And now it will get you killed and worse."

"Life is the Great Jest," he repeated. "Will you come and set me free?"

In answer, the ax sang out in a tightly looped series of cuts that made him give ground.

"Oh, that was beautiful." He chortled. "Think what you might have done as one of Perukh's own."

"Ivory clashes with my skin tone." She sniffed and advanced another step with her ax raised.

At a glance, Dragahn could tell this would be a struggle like none he'd known before.

"I've waited for this moment all my life," he said with a sudden soft yearning. "All my life, I've waited for you."

The grin of her ax flashed again and this time, the black sword had to bat aside swings that threatened to take a limb in one swift chop.

"Anticipation is better than consummation." She grunted and kicked aside a smoldering ribcage in a spray of sparks. "Is that why you keep talking?"

Before the warlord could answer she lunged again, working high and low and back again. He parried and warded off all but the last stroke, which made him strain to avoid the smiling blade that kissed the edge of his cheek before he drove her back with a feinted thrust.

"Thank you for this." He sighed with satisfaction as blood ran freely across his cheek.

"You've seen nothing yet," she promised and he could see in her eyes it was no bluff.

"Neither have you," he replied and with a wild laugh, he launched into an attack and the black sword moved like a razored gale in his hands.

CHAPTER TWENTY-FOUR

At first, the Bone-men attacked in ones or twos although whether this was out of stupidity or sheer bloodlust was unclear.

The first few fell quickly enough when they were met by coordinated slashes and thrusts from Vahrem and the men of the caravan. After this, reinforced in greater numbers by those coming from the burning tents, the invaders began to form a constricting ring of blades that pressed them back.

"Is there any chance of escape?" the merchant asked as he shuffled back.

"Not unless you have the Shining One with you." Amal grunted and hooked his thumb toward the blazing web of canvas, rigging, and tent staves at their back. "It's hot enough to cook the Three Princes back there."

The caravan master didn't need to turn to feel the heat of the flames beginning to press at his back. If they shuffled much further, they'd drive the old woman and the children close enough they might catch fire. But everywhere he looked was only death at the hands of the leering fanatics.

One glance at their flame-lit faces told him surrender would only promise a messy end.

"We drive forward," he rumbled and his whole body coiled like a spring. "We try to cut our way out."

"We'll be hacked to pieces!" someone said at his shoulder.

"You can die bloody or die burned and bloody," he snapped. "I know which I'll take."

He looked over his shoulder and caught the old woman's eye.

"Stay close to me," he said and willed her to understand.

Whether she grasped the words or simply his meaning, she nodded and drew the little ones tightly against her.

Vahrem turned to the Bone-men and flashed them his ferocious smile.

"Now!" he bellowed as he sprang forward.

The sheer force of the exclamation combined with his charge seemed to catch the first fanatic off guard, and he fell with the spear point in his throat. He managed to slash another across the face and ram his short sword through the chest of a third before pain like hot iron lanced through his leg and he stumbled.

He raised his sword to deflect an ax stroke and prevented his head from being split but its wielder pivoted to hammer the haft across his face. His pierced leg buckled and his senses swam from the blow as he toppled and flailed in every direction with his weapons. His sword struck something hard and spun from his grasp and a second later, a gash ripped across his forearm and the broken spear end fell beside him.

The caravan master snarled and swung as he tried to make sense of the whirl of threats around him. He began to sit but a foot stamped on his face. Blood exploded from his nose and lips as his head was driven down to bounce against the ground. This happened a second and then a third time, and he knew he should be concerned that he felt each impact less and less. His mind scrambled for purchase on an increasingly fluid sense of the world but the more he tried to make sense of things, the more he merely felt exhausted.

He decided to stop trying to sit and as he settled onto the

ground, he realized that one eye wouldn't open. It didn't bother him as much as it should but he thought that was probably because the one that was still open saw everything in hazy shades of red splotched with black dots. Maybe it would be better if he closed both his eyes and rested.

The shrill scream of a child shocked him back to the world and Vahrem realized he was on his knees. Someone held him by his hair and something sharp pressed against his throat.

A voice overhead said something in Vitzerkan and he knew he should have understood it, but the sounds only seemed like a bestial growling.

As if from a distance, he heard a whimper.

Prying his one eye open, he saw through the blurred edges of black and red that the old woman was on her knees. The whimper was from the little boy huddled under her while the girl beside him stared at everything with huge, terrified eyes. Her mouth hung open as silent tears traced lines through the soot on her face.

The staring child seemed to look at him so he tried to manage a reassuring smile although he couldn't say exactly why.

With a guttural laugh, the Bone-man above him slid the sharp blade at his throat up along his chin and across the side of his face. He felt the skin parting and there was a little pain, but not as much as he expected. The barest trickle of blood began to slide down his face and beard as whatever grasped his hair pulled back.

His bleary eye saw plumes of smoke rising into a black hemmed sky.

Below the darkening heavens, a jagged sword rose for the final stroke.

Ax-Wed knocked away another heart-seeking stab of the wicked blade but like the other five times she'd done so, she felt herself growing slower. Everything had become an effort, from each measured step of her footwork to her hold on her ax.

On the other hand, Dragahn's hulking frame seemed to only move with greater and greater litheness.

The Eternal Dance? It is almost like he is dancing, she thought wearily. *Although a man so large has no right to be so light on his feet.*

The blue flames surrounding the black sword rippled as he spun it in his hand with obvious pleasure. He seemed to want to draw things out a little longer as if he was enjoying himself too much to simply bludgeon through her defenses with all the strength and vigor he had. She almost wished he would try as she had one or two tricks she'd learned that might give her the barest chance to turn the tables, but she doubted she'd be so fortunate. For now, he'd trade blows with her until she was too exhausted to provide good sport. At that point, he'd turn her to ash like the poor souls who'd charged from the platform with her.

Or you miss the next parry or block. Whether you die now or die later, either way, you're dead.

She lifted her ax high in defiance of the thought and lunged forward. Her shoulders burned and each step shuddered through her aching bones, but when she let the ax weave into a series of low strokes, the movements were flawless.

Unbidden, Mother's words came to her mind.

No one knows how deep they can dig until they fight to the death.

Dragahn's fiery blade batted the blows aside and she could feel the momentum shift away from her. Still, Mother's instructions came as though the woman were standing right there.

You haven't reached the end of your strength until the last drop of blood and the final beat of your heart.

Ax-Wed, every fiber of muscle screaming for mercy, poured more of herself into the swings although she couldn't be sure it wasn't killing her to do so.

Now stop whining and prove you want to live!

She pulled a cut to the legs and surprised even herself with the speed of the feint, then swept upward. Thulian sylver met flesh and she cut a long furrow in the warlord's chest before the smiling blade flashed away. Her adversary snarled in pain and rocked back.

Seeing her opportunity, she bore down on her return stroke to hew into his neck.

Scant inches from his skin, one huge hand seized the ax haft and arrested the stroke with jarring force. Ingrained habit and cramping muscles alone maintained her hold on the ax, but she uttered a pained cry as the sudden stop shafted pain up her arms.

"Close," the warlord whispered to her and his other hand held the black sword up. "If it weren't for this, perhaps you might have won."

This close, Ax-Wed saw the light-drinking darkness of the blade and felt a familiar resonance humming within. She couldn't have said how, but she knew from whence that darkness came and knew better than most her connection to it.

Sorcery is our birthright, Mother declared, the words echoing from years long past. *And the Eye of the King is the hallmark of this, each one a sign of the covenant between our people and the Kingdom.*

Unwelcomed and unsought, the sorcerous energies roiled inside her. In answer, the blue flames wavered and surged to new and terrible brilliance.

"What are you doing?" Dragahn asked and followed her gaze to the weapon in his hand.

The warrior woman knew what came next. She felt it building inside her but also knew what it cost—not only the blood and the pain but the corruption in her soul. It had wracked and flowed through her beneath Jehadim as never before, and having almost drowned in the taint, she'd sworn to never endure its touch again.

Now, however, without it, she would never comfort Zoria in

her night terrors again, never give Nenud another reason to smile, and never…never get to know what Vahrem's kiss tasted like.

Mother's voice shrieked in her head as she felt the spell reaching critical mass.

Do you want to see him again or not?

With a scream, she threw her head back and let the blasphemous syllables tear free from her.

She stretched one hand out and the black sword was yanked from Dragahn's suddenly limp hold as the infernal weapon withdrew its power. The warlord stared in mute shock as his legs buckled and the tide of deprivation his body had sustained descended upon him.

"How?" He gasped as he sank to his knees and his arms fell limply at his sides.

"You meddled with things you shouldn't," she reminded him and held the black sword before him. Something pricked the inside of her hand. "And now…"

For a moment, the warlord looked at the entropic flames with angry accusation in his eyes but slowly, the hurt melted into accepting adoration. With obvious effort, he raised his head and bared his throat.

"Life is a Great Jest." He sighed. "Set me free."

"Free?" Ax-Wed demanded, a hard laugh in her throat. "I'm afraid you've been wrong from the start on that one."

Dragahn stared at her in bemusement.

"I welcome oblivion," he said, as though quoting some obvious truth. "In death is annihilation, and in annihilation is an end to the indignity of pain and the false promise of pleasure."

She shook her head slowly as she lowered the point level to the warlord's bloodied chest.

"Wrong again." She sighed this time and held the blue flames a breath away from his skin. "Death is a gateway, and for damned souls like you and me, that gate leads to one place."

He tried to shake his head but the strain was so much that all he could do was loll his head to one side. The glowing eyes of the un-men watched him and each one seemed to twinkle with a mocking smile.

A shiver raced across his drooping frame.

"Where did you think they came from?" Ax-Wed asked.

A struggling sob grew to a wail.

"No, wait—please." He moaned. "I didn't know. I-I didn't understand. I—"

The black sword sank in with hardly an effort and the blue flames began their deadly work.

"Sorry," she whispered. "I don't want to keep your friends waiting."

His body twisted and curled and he opened his mouth to scream, but the entropic fires vaulted down his throat and denied him even that final cry. She drew the weapon out and watched as Dragahn Shieldshiver, Wind-Spoken of Perukh, shrank into an ashen edifice and crumbled in the breath of the storm that had borne him to Carnyxia.

The warlord was gone, but the army—that seemed to not have been his after all—stood all around her. Gleaming eyes stretched into the distance and everyone looked to her as she considered the scope of what lay before her.

An army that would never tire, never falter, and grew with each victory. With such a force, she could conquer the Norling Steppes within a year. And with the black sword, that was only the beginning.

Ax-Wed felt the power course through her body but she understood that what lay within the reshaped Eye of the King was so much more than simple strength of arms. With this, she could carve an empire or perhaps the foundations of one that could rival even that of all her forebears. Mother and Father and all their schemes had spoken of restoring Thule but here and now, she had the power to begin such a mighty work.

How good it would feel to walk into the City of Gates, her head high as every noble house groveled at her feet, not least of all that of the Xhulth. Would they beg, would they weep, or would they try to bargain? Would she wait to execute them once her likeness was raised over the Promenade of Victors, or would that be a pleasure too long denied?

In the distance, a chorus of horns sounded and drew her from her reverie.

She was not on the gleaming streets of the city of her birth but outside Carnyxia with an army of horrors waiting to charge and overrun the armies of men she'd been forced to aid. With one word and one gesture with the black sword, she would be set upon the road to those visions. All she had to do was yield.

You are ours, we are yours.

Ax-Wed shook her head and looked down in horror at the blade in her hand.

"Close," she whispered and scowled at the seething weapon. "But I think I have a better use for all that power."

In the years to come there would be much debate over what had taken place as the marshaled armies of Carnyxia rode to face the horde of Warlord Dragahn Shieldshiver.

The account was most famously and subsequently told by Merko Clawtamer, chieftain of the Krivik, who led the first main column of beast-riders into the gathered storm that came with Perukh's chosen. Other tellings emerged, of course, but he was one of the few of his people who valued the written word in those days and so had his account recorded for posterity.

As such, for many long generations after the event, his account was the one that endured the test of time. Scholars tried to track down various other accounts, of course, half-legible scrawlings on scrolls of questionable provenance or overly analyzed snippets of local folklore, but as has already been told, acolytes of the academia often pursue things that wiser, unlettered men know to leave alone.

But as for Merko and his account, what follows is so peculiar yet simple that it can almost be understood why overly curious minds would probe the gutters of history for something more substantial.

Merko and the marshaled tribes came to the edge of the storm as Javor Tuskleg of the Lecall, still a young man, limped out with the very last of the valiant vanguard. Those brave souls had stalled the bulk of Shieldshiver's forces. True, a contingent of raiders had come up from the south of Carnyxia but those were repelled in short order by the wardens of Carnyxia with minimal casualties, but there can be little doubt that the Lecall's bravery spared the Carnyxian alliance from being set upon before they were prepared.

This is only reinforced by the fact that much honor was heaped upon the Lecall and despite their considerable losses, the tribe would only ascend to greater heights of influence and affluence in the years to come.

Yet all that would have mattered little if not for what had come next in Merko's account.

With Javor and the last of the vanguard on a wagon back to Carnyxia, Merko and his forces moved into the storm, which by all accounts was pitch dark and acted as some kind of sorcerous concealment for Shieldshiver's forces. It was rumored that within the storm, a force of enemies unlike any seen before moved, and the sudden disappearance of several tribes in the western and southern Steppes at that time seems to give credence to this. Yet, as Merko and his column plunged into the storm, there was a flash of light, which the chieftain compares to a vast wave of blue flame rolling out and away into the heart of the darkness.

Once they recovered from the shock of this display, the chieftain claims the army moved deeper into the darkness but to their surprise, met no resistance. Indeed, even as they pressed forward, he and his retinue noted how the storm seemed to be diminishing. By the time the entire column had passed under the shadow of the brooding clouds, the tempest had abated to such an extent that a darkness once as deep as night had thinned to the point that soon, the entire field became visible to the naked eye.

And what stood revealed in that field whereupon the great doom of the Vitzerka was supposed to have come?

A vast field of black ash stretched to the horizon, already being stirred and driven away by a fresh breeze out of the south.

And what of Dragahn Shieldshiver, Wind-Spoken of Perukh?

Only a broken sword, its shards scattered before the blackened field.

Ax-Wed didn't wait for the wagon to stop when she rode into the caravan camp.

With her heart in her throat, she leapt from the vehicle as the driver slowed the ponies to come to a stop.

Her feet landed with a heavy thud and she crumpled to her knees. Fatigue bowed her head to the grass where sweat dripped from her nose to the earth.

Get up! she screamed at herself and with a snarl, she forced herself to unsteady feet.

Everything hurt and her armor, so often like a second skin, felt like a constricting shell. She'd already thrown her helm off in the wagon, desperate for air that didn't smell of blood, iron, and ash.

She was weary beyond all thought but she didn't dare to stop. The Thulian knew the reasons why she had done what she had but now she learned that it might have all been for nothing. She had to see and had to know if it was true.

By the exertion of will alone, she stood, moved one foot after the other, and commanded her knees to not give way. She could collapse once she saw but first, she had to get there.

Thankfully, the tent wasn't far and no one sought to stop her. She dragged her ax behind her with one hand and staggered forward as some wild thought told her she needed it at the ready. Who or what she needed it for she couldn't have said, but it seemed like one of the few things that anchored her to consciousness.

Instinctively, she grasped it as tightly as her trembling hands could and lurched, painful step after painful step, to the tent door.

It was dark within and only a low fire burned in a tight ring of stones.

That's a bad sign, she thought but if asked to explain why she couldn't have.

Her heavy steps sounded like thunderclaps as she stepped under the canvas shelter. Ax-Wed forced herself toward a solid shape stretched out at the back of the tent.

It can't be.

Overwhelmed, her will failed her along with her body. Her legs gave out and she was reduced to crawling the last few feet. With her head hanging low, her world became the lacquered reed mats layered across the tent floor until at last, a single bandaged hand filled her view.

It looks so pale, she thought with a pained gulp as she lowered her face to kiss the bruised fingers.

It's so cold.

She knew what she had to do and had to force herself to finish what she'd come to do, but for a moment, she hesitated. Fighting and failing to hold back the tears, she let them mingle with her sweat to wash the cold, lifeless hand.

Then, little by little and inch by inch, she drew her gaze up and looked into the man's face. This time, a violent sob shook her body.

His face was misshapen from the abuse it had suffered and his countenance colorless from loss of blood, and there were places where his hair and beard had been yanked out at the root. For all the damage, however, she could see it was Vahrem who now lay as cold and lifeless as the hand she'd bathed in her tears.

Another sob tore through her and curled her body in on itself with a deeper pain than steel or sorcery had ever driven through her.

"I wanted to know…" she whispered and her lips trembled. "I wanted to believe that…believe that maybe you would…that we could have…"

Her shaking fingers released the ax and she stretched both hands to hold his cold, pallid face. Despite everything, it still seemed so handsome and so regal to her, and the sight of it drove the ache deeper than her bones.

"To believe you could have loved me," she whispered and bent to kiss dead lips.

The dead man's eye, the one not swallowed in bruised, swollen flesh, jerked open and he stared at her in shock.

Ax-Wed lurched back and her hand groped behind her for her weapon until she realized no unholy light shone forth. She saw the heavy chest rise and fall, weak but steady. For a moment, his blood-drained lips worked but no sound emerged until, with a wincing cough, his throat cleared.

"Were you…" he wheezed in a labored voice, each word a burden. "Were you about to have our first real kiss without me?"

She stared at him with tears still on her cheeks but something like agonized joy in her chest.

"They said you fell fighting the Bone-men," she said and her breath caught in her throat.

"I did," Vahrem replied.

"Th-th-they said you were hurt," she stammered.

He nodded, but that movement drew another wince.

"I am," he answered.

"They said you might be dying." She tried to force the trembling from her voice.

"I might have been." He sighed and seemed ready to nod off at any second. "But Iyshan saved my life twice today."

Ax-Wed stared at him and slid her hands slowly to hold his.

"Twice?"

"First, he rides in like a great bloody hero with the wardens." Vahrem grunted and shifted slightly. "Then he sees I'm bleeding like a stuck pig and brings me here where I've stashed a few healing tinctures bought from a magician in Narlish."

She shook her head slowly as a smile worked across her face.

"Maybe it's Iyshan I should be kissing," she teased. "It seems he did all the work."

"I suppose," Vahrem muttered. "But if you do, there are more than a few women you'll have to answer to when we reach Aruhkham."

That drew a burst of spontaneous laughter from her but she remembered the mark left on her hand by her efforts to reach this moment and quietly drew her left hand from his limp hold.

"So no ladies waiting for you in any ports of call then?" she asked and hoped he wouldn't notice the change.

"The only one I know or care about is in Carnyxia right now," he said and a slow smile spread across his face. "She probably just won a battle or something. Speaking of which, I assume we won?"

Ax-Wed tucked her stained hand behind her leg as she nodded.

"We did," she said and forced a smile.

At what cost?

"Well, that's good." He drew a deep breath and his eyelids began to flutter. "I'm glad to hear it."

"I can tell." She laughed and let her head sink to his chest again.

Vahrem sighed and his chin began to dip, but he came up with another wince and his eye found her again.

"I think…I think if you want, eh…want me to be awake for that first kiss you should move quickly," he muttered. "I'm afraid the tincture was mixed with a sizable sleeping draught."

"I can wait," she told him and savored the gentle pulse of his chest against her cheek. "I'm not going anywhere."

He grunted and cleared his throat again.

"And what if I don't want to wait?"

Ax-Wed looked into his dark eye and saw—a little softer and a little farther off—the same fire and same longing that had woken something in her in this very tent.

"All right," she said, shifted her position, and leaned forward. "If you insist."

Dear Reader,

We've seen the Norling Steppes, felt the horrified thrill of knowing what moves in the dark, and then seen at what a dire cost victory must come. Ax-Wed's suffered much and we've still got one more book to go. I could tell you that there will be no more loss and no more pain… But that would make me a liar and I value you all far too much to waste your trust on such a petty fib.

Oh, things can get much worse…but also much better.

After all, for all the darkness, there's something precious and pure in sealing this latest passage with a kiss. Call me a romantic and I will say guilty as charged, but I just can't let my characters have these sweet moments without a little work.

No, like our world, I'm determined that love be mingled with grief that it may grow the greater as the crafter of Bobbadils and Silmarils so artfully put it.

Please don't do yourself the disservice of not seeing this through, because I do believe I've crafted the fitting end where grief and love can ascend to that realm of the eucatastrophic.

Come see where the Ashen Road leads our dear Thulian, and perhaps find something changed in yourself along the way.

Until that day, though, you have my affection and appreciation, dear reader.

Thank you,

Aaron D. Schneider

08/01/2021

P.S. - I'm going to be an absolute nuisance with these but I hope you'll bear with me if you are bothering to read this. Last time I talked about dissatisfaction, and I thought I'd touch on something which spawns this important reaction—evil.

It is a word that gets bandied about too freely and too easily, and Heaven knows I'm as guilty as anyone of doing it. It's not that any of us haven't experienced it, whether from the mouth of a stranger, at the hand of those who should have loved us, or even in those dark, revealing moments when the mirror of our thoughts shows us how ugly we are. But even with all this, we toss the word around like something cheap and trivial, but it encapsulates why we can't be satisfied with this world and this life.

Evil poisons our world and our souls, and its touch is so inescapable that even in the realms of art—yes, my art—I won't escape it. So rather than pretend it isn't present—not only "out there" but "in here"—I paint it plain as I've seen and felt it. I write stories of traitors and Bone-men, of parts of our world and parts of me, which thrill and chill because for all their pageantry and savagery, they smell of something familiar, something we've all seen. If you haven't, well then, dear reader, I'm afraid you closed your eyes, and I'd not have you live in willful blindness.

Yet, as dark as this all seems and as dark as this all is, I am not without hope and neither should you be. There is a reason why we can smile through tears and look for more than Perukh's answer. If I didn't believe that, I'd be guilty of only deepening the dark and thickening the night with my sad dreams, but because I do believe in hope, I can claim the picture I paint with a dark palette is only so that the light can burn brighter and burn clearer.

If you, dear reader, have read this far, I'd ask one more thing —look for the light in the last book, coming so very soon. Look for it and when you see it, hopefully burning bright and clear, don't turn aside until you've given it a good long look.

If staring into the dark Abyss can make monsters of men, imagine what gazing to the bright Celestial can make of a man…

Regards,
Aaron D. Schneider

AUTHOR NOTES - MICHAEL ANDERLE
AUGUST 17, 2021

Thank you for not only reading this book but this entire series and these author notes as well.

Movies and Timelines

So, I've either read or listened to a few discussions about how movies have a definitive timeline within their framework related to how to tell a story.

For example (and I'm making this up) at six minutes into the movie, you need to have a hook, at twelve minutes you need to have a turn, and twenty-two minutes, there needs to be a switchback situation, etc. etc. In short, a roadmap to the beats of the story.

There are a LOT of similar beats set up for writing fiction stories, as well. I've never been fond of using these beats so I don't.

I wish I did at some level since it would make the stories easier to build.

While we have put out well over a thousand books in the last five years at LMBPN, we have a few that have been shelved. They were stories the Beta / JIT readers canned, and those of us who wrote them would scratch our heads and try to figure out:

1. How did we go so wrong?

2. What can we do to fix this book?

3. Where is the alcohol when we can't figure out a solution to fix the book.

4. Where is the Ibuprofen to counteract the headache from #3.

5. How about just starting a new story?

I'm thankful we haven't shelved more than a handful of stories in the thousand-plus we have published. There are a couple where the lack of sales made me wonder what we missed. Frankly, often the stories are solid, but the marketing is off-target.

I am very thankful you are reading this series. First, because I like Aaron's talent and believe it produces solid stories. The second is I love this world of *Skharr DeathEater*. We have two more series coming out this year.

The first is *The Barbarian Princess* (a character from the *Skharr DeathEater* series) in the same vein as Skharr DeathEater (Sword & Sorcery). The second is *Myth of the Dragon: In the Shadow of Ziammotienth* (Fantasy).

Between now and when these stories all get released (end of 2022 for the sixth book in the Myth of the Dragon series), we will have approximately twenty stories in this genre. Already, *Skharr DeathEater* and *Myth of the Dragon* have been picked up by audio companies.

Loving it!

Our first beta feedback is fantastic for *In the Shadow of Ziammotienth,* which has me excited. This story is about 195,000 words – so LONG!

Anyway, stay safe and sane out there. I look forward to talking to you in the next book!

Ad Aeternitatem,
Michael Anderle

ACKNOWLEDGMENTS

The hardest part of these Acknowledgments is that so many people help to make these works a reality that it seems almost criminal to only choose a small group to thank.

But for this one, I'd like to take time to thank and acknowledge the brothers and sisters (by blood, by law, and by Grace) who've kindly encouraged and supported me through this and so many other projects. I'm hardly a social animal, but you coax me out of my cave when I need it and are also patient and kind enough to leave me in there when I have deadlines. In dozens and dozens of ways, you've sparked my imagination, made me feel loved, and found a way to tolerate my brand of crazy, all of which is an inescapable part of making these books possible.

I love you all dearly, whatever my growling, and wherever you are, know that I hold you close in my heart and prayers.

Sign up for the LMBPN email list to be notified of new releases and special deals!

https://lmbpn.com/email/

For a complete list of books by Michael Anderle, please visit:

www.lmbpn.com/ma-books/

www.ingramcontent.com/pod-product-compliance
Lightning Source LLC
Chambersburg PA
CBHW021244060726
47590CB00005B/1891